Praise for

BETTY ROWLANDS
'A clearly gifted and knowledgeable writer, never less
than engaging and readable'
Financial Times

FINISHING TOUCH
'Gently old fashioned whodunnit, riddled with
lurking anguish'
The Times

OVER THE EDGE
'She has the rare skill that grabs the reader's complete
attention at page one and holds it to the end'
Wilts and Gloucestershire Standard

EXHAUSTIVE ENQUIRIES
'Engaging . . . keeps you happily hooked on the mys-
tery from opening to denouement'
Gloucestershire Echo

MALICE POETIC
'Full of sharp insights with an unexpected twist in the
tail. A satisfying read'
Val McDermid, *Manchester Evening News*

SMILING AT DEATH
'All the best ingredients of English crime . . . a novel of
sharp insights'
Cotswold Life

About the author

In 1988 Betty Rowlands won the Sunday Express/
Veuve Clicquot Crime Short Story of the Year Competition.
Her success continued with the publication of seven acclaimed
Melissa Craig mysteries. She is an active member of the
Crime Writers' Association and regularly gives talks and
readings, runs workshops and serves on panels at crime
writing conventions.
She lives in the heart of the Cotswolds where her Melissa
Craig mysteries are set and has three grown-up children and
four grandchildren.

The Cherry Pickers

Betty Rowlands

NEW ENGLISH LIBRARY
Hodder and Stoughton

To C.C.W.
In Affectionate Memory

Chapter One

By the end of August, summer was becoming tired. One felt it in the shortening days and the lengthening shadows that foretold the approaching September equinox, and the drab, uniform foliage of trees that two months earlier had still retained something of their springtime variety. Already, after several weeks without rain, there were streaks of brown and yellow among the green.

This year, Melissa Craig regarded the onset of autumn with mixed feelings. There was the usual satisfaction from the crops of fruit and vegetables that she grew in the little garden of Hawthorn Cottage, where she had lived in increasing contentment since escaping from London a few years ago. There was relief in the cooler evenings after the long period of exceptionally hot, dry weather. The mist that lay each morning along the floor of the secluded Cotswold valley until burned off by the sun transformed myriads of cobwebs in the hedgerows into coverlets of glistening lace and brought a welcome touch of moisture to the sultry air. There were blackberries to be gathered and made into pies with fruit from her own apple tree. There was the harvest festival to look forward to, when the little Norman church in Upper Benbury would be overflowing with the rich variety of produce that its residents coaxed from the stony but fertile soil. And then would come the end of October when, as usual, her friend and neighbour Iris Ash would pack her bags and her artist's impedimenta and head for the South of France for the winter.

Only this year, things were different. This year, Iris was leaving for good.

Ever since Melissa came to the village, the cottage that adjoined her own had stood empty from November to the end of March. Iris's return signalled not only the welcome prospect of her companionship during the ensuing months, but also the onset of spring. Not that the winter had ever seemed to drag. There was always a new book to be written and research to be done, Christmas to look forward to and drinks parties with friends. And there was Ken Harris: dependable, companionable, loving . . . and as persistent in his efforts to persuade her to marry him as she was to retain her independence.

It was an idyllic existence, but in a few weeks it would change for ever. After more than half a century of spinsterhood, Iris was going to marry Jack Hammond and the two of them planned to make their permanent home in Provence. Elder Cottage was to be sold and Melissa was now faced with one of the toughest decisions of her life.

On this late August afternoon she was lifting onions and laying them in rows in the sunniest corner of her garden while mentally wrestling with the problem, when a voice hailed her from the other side of the fence. Major Dudley Ford had approached unnoticed along the short track that connected the cottages with the steep, narrow lane leading to the village.

'Mrs Craig . . . Melissa,' he called. 'Can you spare a minute?'

Reluctantly, she put down her fork and walked across to where he was standing. He looked agitated, his normally florid face flushed purple, his bushy white moustache quivering and his ancient panama hat askew.

'It's an absolute disgrace!' he spluttered. 'I don't know what the world is coming to – something will have to be done!' He brandished his walking stick so vigorously that Sinbad, his fat King Charles spaniel, backed away from him in alarm.

'Whatever's wrong, Dudley?' Melissa asked in some concern. It was probably something quite trivial, but it was generally feared that his habit of treating every minor upset as a catastrophe, coupled with his high blood pressure, would one day have serious results.

'Thieves and vagabonds, that's what's wrong,' he exclaimed. Suddenly remembering his manners, he raised his hat, revealing a shock of white hair that did not appear to have been recently combed. 'I've been robbed . . . and the police simply aren't interested,' he complained.

'Robbed!' Melissa exclaimed. 'Good gracious, when? Was there much stolen?'

'A chest freezer.' He uttered the words as dramatically as if announcing the loss of the Crown Jewels.

'Oh dear! Was there much food in it?'

'Well, er, no . . . as a matter of fact it was an old one we were getting rid of,' he admitted. 'But that's beside the point,' he added as Melissa's eyebrows went up. 'Robbery is robbery. It's a disgrace!' he repeated, using the hat to fan his overheated countenance. 'What do we pay taxes for if the police don't do their job, that's what I want to know!'

During this tirade Binkie, Iris's half-Persian cat, suddenly appeared on top of a nearby stone wall. Spotting Sinbad, he arched his back and spat; the dog responded with a furious yapping and leapt forward, almost tugging his lead from his master's hand. Recognising that fur might, literally, be about to fly, Melissa said, 'Perhaps you'd like to come in and tell me all about it,' and opened her gate. From previous experience she knew that it would take at least half an hour for her irascible visitor to get whatever was bugging him off his chest.

The Major accepted her invitation with alacrity. She led the way along the short path to the rear of the cottage, saying, 'I apologise for bringing you in through the kitchen, but I keep the front door locked when I'm out in the garden. In any case,' she added, after he had earnestly commended her for being so security conscious, 'it might be as well if we talked in here . . . it's cooler than my sitting-room as it doesn't get much sun.' *And it will keep your dog off my furniture*, she added to herself. Sinbad had the run of the house at home and to sit down in Tanners Cottage meant a subsequent battle to rid one's clothes of dog hairs.

The Major dropped into a chair, placed his hat on the table and propped his stick against the wall. Sinbad waddled round the kitchen, sniffing and panting. Melissa gave him a dish of water, poured cold drinks for herself and her visitor and sat down. 'Now, tell me about this robbery,' she said.

'You know we've been having a new kitchen installed,' the Major began. Melissa gave a wry nod. Everyone in the village knew about the up-market firm of contractors that had been commissioned to make the Fords' kitchen worthy of a feature in *Country Living*, if for no other reason than that both he and his wife had been at pains to give progress reports every time they set foot in the village shop.

'Well, we had the old units to dispose of, and we gave those to a charity.' He paused, as if to give Melissa the opportunity to commend him and his wife for this act of generosity. As she merely nodded and waited he went on. 'And there was this old chest freezer that had been standing empty in the garage for a couple of years, ever since it broke down. It was going to be too expensive to repair, so we replaced it. We thought this was a good opportunity to get it out of the way, but the charity people wouldn't take it.' The peevish tone in which he uttered the last few words suggested that this refusal was tantamount to base ingratitude after the receipt of so much largesse.

'Well,' he resumed, after a further pause during which Melissa still made no comment. 'I saw a notice in the shop the other day, announcing a new service from the Council – a monthly collection of bulky household items. All you have to do is ring 'em up, they tell you what day they'll call, you put your stuff outside your gate and they pick it up. No charge. Simple.' He drank deeply from the glass of lemonade that Melissa had poured for him and she recharged it from a jug.

'Let me guess the rest,' she said. 'You went to the garage to shift the freezer outside and found it had disappeared.'

'Not quite.' The Major drained his glass for the second time, pulled out a handkerchief and blotted his moustache. 'The council people couldn't tell me what time the men'd be along to pick it up, but said it could be quite early, so to be on the safe side I got a couple of the village lads to get it to the gate the evening before.'

'And someone nicked it during the night?'

'No, it was still there at ten o'clock next morning, when Maddy and I left the house to go shopping in Cheltenham. We got back about one, and it was gone. Naturally, we assumed the council men had collected it. But an hour later, one of them knocked on the door asking where it was. Some thieving rogues had taken it while we were out.' During the early part of his narrative the Major had become progressively calmer; now he was showing signs of renewed agitation. 'Stolen it in broad daylight!' He banged a fist on Melissa's kitchen table and Sinbad, who had been dozing at his feet, woke up with a start.

'Of course, there's no doubt who the culprits are,' he went on. 'A load of travelling tinkers have been camping on that disused council dump on the main road. They're always prowling about, looking for something to steal. I got on to the police straight away, of course, and they sent the local Bobby round, but d'you know what he said?' As Melissa shook her head and tried to appear interested, indignation made the next words almost incomprehensible. 'He said someone had been "cherry picking" – scouting around for items people put out for collection and making off with them before the genuine collectors arrive. The fellow seemed to think it was a bit of a joke . . . did you ever hear of such a thing?'

'No, I can't say I have, but it sounds perfectly feasible. And I'm quite sure PC Barker is taking your complaint seriously,' Melissa added soothingly, since he was still bristling with rage at having been the victim of such blatant chicanery. 'When did this happen, by the way?'

'A couple of days or so ago . . . Tuesday, to be exact.'

'And today's Friday. I imagine the trail will have gone a bit cold by now.' *Really, Dudley*, she thought, *only you could expect the police to turn the theft of a piece of household rubbish into a major incident.* 'At least,' she continued aloud, 'you haven't lost anything of value . . . I mean, it was going for scrap, wasn't it?'

The Major glowered. 'That's beside the point,' he snapped. 'Thieving is thieving. I told Barker that I expected him to bring the culprits to justice . . . and I told him where he'd almost certainly find the evidence. He said something about making enquiries, but we all know what that means, don't we?'

'The police are pretty stretched at the moment.' Melissa was beginning to lose patience; time was passing and she wanted to finish lifting the onions before tea. 'And if it was someone from the gipsy encampment who took your freezer, it's almost certainly been broken up for scrap by now, so it would be impossible to identify. Frankly, Dudley, I'd forget about it if I were you.' She gave him what she hoped was a sympathetic smile.

He responded with an indignant snort. 'I can't agree with you there. Why should these crooks be allowed to get away with it?'

'I know it's annoying, but I don't see what you can do about it,' she said. 'I gather from what you've told me that no one even saw the freezer being taken, so you've no idea what these people look like or what kind of vehicle they were using.'

He cleared his throat and avoided her gaze. It dawned on her that there might be more to this visit than a mere desire to enlist her sympathy. Even as the suspicion formed in her mind, his next words confirmed it. 'I don't suppose your friend Mr Harris would be prepared to do a bit of sniffing around?' he said hopefully.

Mclissa suppressed a desire to laugh. Since his retirement from the police after completing thirty years' service, ex-Detective Chief Inspector Harris had been operating as a private investigator. He had been approached with some odd requests before, but to track down a piece of disused kitchen equipment that was destined for the junkyard anyway would surely count among the most bizarre. However, it was plain that the Major was perfectly serious.

'It's not the kind of case he normally handles,' she said diplomatically. 'I could mention it to him, of course . . . see if he's got the time, ask him what sort of fee he would charge and so on.'

At the mention of the word 'fee', the Major appeared to wince. 'Er, yes, well, of course, I take your point,' he mumbled, fingering his moustache. 'I'll quite understand if he's too busy with other cases . . . just thought I'd mention it.' He pushed back his chair and tugged at Sinbad's lead. 'Come on old fellow, mustn't take up any more of the lady's time, must we?' He got to his feet and Melissa politely escorted him out of the cottage and back to the gate.

From the corner of her eye she spotted Iris, who was busy in her own garden, ducking out of sight behind a row of runner beans. Evidently *she* had no intention of being collared by their garrulous neighbour. Two minutes later she was calling to Melissa over the fence separating their back gardens, demanding to know what 'the old buzzard' was on about this time.

'You aren't going to believe this,' said Melissa when she had repeated the saga of the 'cherry pickers' and the missing freezer. 'He actually had the cheek to suggest that Ken might take the case on – as a favour, of course. You should have seen the way he backed off when I mentioned the word "fee".'

'Surprised he didn't suggest starting a "hue and cry",' said Iris. 'He'd like to see people hanged for sheep stealing. Born centuries too late, that's his trouble.'

'You've got a point there. Well, I'd better finish lifting my onions.'

'Pop round for a cuppa when you've done.'

'Thanks, I will.'

The two women were drinking herbal tea in Iris's kitchen when they heard the rattle of the letter-box as the evening paper landed on the floor in the hall. Iris went to fetch it and returned with eyes like saucers. Dumbly, she held out the paper for Melissa to see the black headlines which read:

BODY FOUND IN ABANDONED FREEZER.

Chapter Two

The report was brief but sensational. The gruesome discovery had been made by children the previous evening and much was made of their shock and terror after one of them had opened an abandoned chest freezer with the object of climbing inside in the course of a game of hide-and-seek. Apart from the fact that the victim was a woman, few details had been available at the time of going to press; in the absence of information about her identity, how she had met her death or how her body had reached the spot where it was found, the remaining space was given up to a description of the location – a dry, overgrown ditch skirting a patch of woodland which, despite notices warning of fines for anyone caught dumping rubbish, was more often than not littered with empty drinks cans, old tyres, discarded mattresses and stolen supermarket trolleys.

The two women digested the story in silence. At last, Iris said drily, 'Have to take Dudley seriously now, won't they?'

'Who – the police?' Melissa put the paper down and absent-mindedly refolded it.

'Who else?'

'It could be a coincidence. Langley Woods are fifteen miles from here.'

'So? Whoever nicked that freezer had transport. Could've taken it anywhere.'

'That's true. Still, there must be more than one redundant

freezer in the county. I wonder if the Fords have seen this report. Do they read the *Gazette*?'

'Sure to – have to keep up with local affairs, don't they? Couldn't interfere if they didn't know what's going on.' Iris took the empty mugs to the sink and rinsed them under the tap. Over her shoulder, she asked, 'Seeing Ken this evening?'

'Yes, why?'

'Come for supper. Jack'll be here.'

Melissa hesitated. 'I'm not sure – Ken said something about going out. Is it okay if I let you know in half an hour or so?'

'Sure. Always cook plenty in any case. Jack eats like a horse.'

'He's sticking to his part of the bargain, then?' A condition of the engagement had been that Jack convert to vegetarianism.

'Of course.' Iris dried the mugs and put them away in a cupboard. Her keen grey eyes held a sly twinkle as she added, 'Ten times fitter than he used to be. Pity you and Ken don't do the same. Shift a few pounds in no time.'

'I'm not overweight,' said Melissa, feigning indignation.

'Never said you were, but it wouldn't hurt Ken to lose a bit. Healthy diet and regular yoga'd make a new man of him. You can laugh,' Iris went on, catching Melissa's eye. 'Do you both the world of good. You ask Jack.'

'Maybe I will. Anyway, I'll see if I can catch Ken at the office and let you know about this evening.'

'Fine.' After a brief pause, Iris asked, 'Decided about the cottage yet?'

It was a question Melissa had been asked repeatedly during recent weeks and one that she was beginning to dread. Ever since Iris and Jack had announced their future plans, the fate of Elder Cottage had been the subject of considerable argument between herself and Ken. He was pressing her to agree that they jointly buy it and convert the two dwellings into one, which they would then share. Still fighting a rearguard action against making a commitment, she had mooted buying it herself and letting it as a holiday retreat. He had countered with a threat to oppose any application for change of use, to outbid her for the purchase and live there himself, saying that if she wouldn't marry him, or at least live with him, she would have to put up with him as a next-door neighbour who might – and at this point in their discussions she became uncertain whether he was serious or not – be guilty of anti-social behaviour of the type that regularly resulted in ludicrous court cases, such as obstructing the driveway, mowing the lawn at midnight, holding noisy parties or ruining the outlook with unclipped hedges.

'Well, have you?' Iris demanded, as Melissa remained silent. She wrung out her dish-cloth, dried her hands, hung the tea-towel on a rail and sat down again. Normally undemonstrative, she reached out and touched her friend on the arm.

Melissa stared down at the thin brown hand with its gleaming solitaire and said, 'You used to be so cynical about marriage, Iris. What changed your mind?'

The sharp features softened in a self-conscious smile. 'Good question. Asked it myself a few times.'

'And?'

'There came a moment when I realised Jack wouldn't wait for ever. Couldn't bear the idea of life without him . . . so—' She broke off and began gently turning the ring with tapering, artist's fingers. Then she looked Melissa directly in the eyes and said, 'Ken won't either, you know.'

'Won't what?' said Melissa, although she knew perfectly well what the answer would be.

'Wait for ever.' Iris gave her friend's arm a gentle squeeze before drawing her hand away. 'Neither will I,' she added. 'So get on and think about it.'

'I don't seem to be able to think about anything else. It's interfering with my work . . . I haven't written a line worth reading for days.' Melissa got up and began prowling restlessly round Iris's small but beautifully appointed kitchen. 'I've got this strange notion that I'm waiting for some sort of signal . . . something to help me decide what to do—'

'What, like reading your horoscope?' Iris jeered. She picked up the copy of the *Gazette* that still lay, temporarily forgotten, on the table. 'See what it says for today, if you're too feeble to make up your own mind.'

'Don't be so sarky.' Melissa stood up and headed for the door. 'Thanks for the tea. I'll give you an answer within a week, that's a promise.'

Back indoors, she called Harris Investigations and told Ken about Iris's invitation. His lack of enthusiasm came as no surprise.

'Do we have to?' he grumbled. 'I thought we'd go to the Manoir this evening – we haven't been for ages, and you know how I feel about rabbit food anyway.' So far, he had managed to avoid eating anything but the odd snack from Iris's culinary repertoire and – while admitting that she baked excellent bread and made a tasty mushroom pâté – he clung obstinately to the belief that there was no substitute for a hefty steak or a succulent roast to satisfy the appetite of a red-blooded man.

'Oh Ken, don't be such a stick-in-the-mud. You should give Iris's cooking a try – it really is delicious. Jack loves it.'

'That's because he's so besotted with her that he'd eat his hat to please her.'

'Which proves that his devotion to his beloved is superior to yours.'

'Not true. It's probably just a ploy to get her to agree to marry him.'

'I notice you haven't tried any comparable ploy on me.'

'Certainly not, I prefer the direct approach.' A gravelly chuckle rumbled along the wire as he went on, 'Wait till those two have been married and living in France for six months . . . he'll be sneaking off to the local *auberge* for a *coq au vin* or a *boeuf bourguignon* whenever her back's turned.'

'I wouldn't bet on it. She maintains he's a lot healthier . . . and slimmer,' Melissa added, aiming a sly barb at her lover's tendency to overweight. 'Please say yes, Ken,' she coaxed. 'It's only another couple of months before she leaves . . . we can go to the Manoir any time. If you're still hungry when we get home, I'll cook you some bacon and eggs.'

'I might require a greater inducement than that,' he said, lowering his voice to an erotic whisper that kindled within her a spontaneous, glowing surge of desire. Iris's words flashed into her mind. *He won't wait for ever*, she had warned, and the recollection was swiftly followed by the stark question, *Can I bear the thought of losing him?*

It was an effort to keep her own voice normal as she responded, 'Do I take it that means yes?'

'All right,' he conceded with a sigh. 'See you about six, then.'

She was on the point of hanging up when she thought of something else. 'By the way, have you seen the front-page report in today's *Gazette*?'

'About the body in the freezer? Yes – why?'

'See if you can get any more details out of one of your ex-chums at the nick, will you?'

'What's your interest?'

'Tell you this evening. Bye.'

She had barely put the phone down when it rang. Madeleine Ford was on the line.

'Have you seen the local paper, Melissa?' Her voice, normally strong and autocratic, was a petulant squeak. 'That freezer . . . the one with the body in it . . . the police think it may be the one Dudley reported stolen. He's gone with them to see if he can identify it. Isn't it terrible? What can it mean?'

'I don't know . . . perhaps someone happened to have a body to dispose of and your freezer was just what they were looking for.'

13

'Melissa, I don't think you're taking this seriously.'

'I'm sorry, I didn't mean to sound flippant. Of course it's serious when someone's been murdered, but I don't see why you should be so worried.'

'But don't you see, if that freezer is the one that was taken from outside our house, the papers will get hold of it . . . and there'll be reporters on the doorstep . . . and gossip . . . it isn't very nice to be connected with—' In her agitation, Madeleine's voice hit an even higher frequency before tailing off altogether.

How typical, thought Melissa, that she should consider the effect of the tragedy on her own social standing before the comparatively minor problem of tracking down a killer. She tried to think of something anodyne to say that would not reveal her contempt for such a selfish attitude, but failed. Meanwhile, Madeleine recovered her voice.

'I told Dudley it was pointless dragging the police into it, but he wouldn't listen,' she complained. 'You know what he's like about crime.'

Don't I just, thought Melissa, recalling countless tirades on the subject. Aloud, she said 'There must be more than one clapped-out freezer kicking around on rubbish tips. Maybe it isn't yours at all.'

'But supposing it is, what should we do?'

'Just say you know nothing if the reporters bother you, but I doubt if they'll be particularly interested in where the thing came from. They're more likely to concentrate on the victim.'

'Oh, do you think so.' Melissa was uncertain whether the change in tone indicated relief or disappointment.

'And possible suspects . . . they'll be looking for witnesses who saw the thing being taken. Dudley said it happened when you were out, so they can't expect you to be able to tell them anything more than he has done already.'

'No, of course not.' There was a pause before Madeleine

said, in something like her normal voice, 'Well, thank you for putting my mind at rest, Melissa,' and rang off.

'I can't tell you much about the victim,' said Ken Harris, 'except that it was a young woman – about eighteen or twenty according to the doctor who certified her dead. She was naked, there was no sign of her clothing and she hasn't yet been identified. They're waiting for the result of the post-mortem to establish the cause of death.'

'What about the freezer?' Iris wanted to know. 'Is it the one Dudley Ford was having apoplexy about?'

'There's some doubt about that.' Ken took a deep draught of Iris's elderflower cordial and gave a nod of approval. 'That's pretty good,' he remarked. 'So are these,' he added, helping himself to a handful of home-made cheese balls and popping one into his mouth with evident relish. Melissa shot him a *What did I tell you?* smirk which he studiously ignored.

The four friends were enjoying their apéritifs on the small, secluded patio of Elder Cottage, surrounded by beds of old-fashioned roses, phlox and night-scented stock whose perfume sweetened the cool evening air. Birds twittered in the hedgerows or hopped around in the undergrowth. From somewhere on the other side of the valley, washed golden by the setting sun, came the regular throb of a combine harvester, beating out the message that summer was nearly over. Melissa found herself thinking wistfully that with Iris and Jack gone, such pleasant gatherings would soon be a thing of the past.

Her thoughts were switched back to the present by Jack, who asked, 'What sort of doubt?' as he reached for the bottle to top up their glasses.

'The old boy – Major Ford – said he couldn't be sure if it was the one he'd reported stolen or not,' Ken explained. 'It was the same make and model, but there was damage on it that he didn't recognise. That could have been caused by the thieves stripping out the electrics – I don't know any more details.'

'If it is the same one, Dudley's prints will be on it,' Melissa pointed out. 'I presume he's had them taken for comparison?'

'Naturally. I gather he was a bit put out by that at first. Seemed to think he was being treated as a suspect.' There were chuckles all round at the picture of affronted innocence that the ex-policeman's words conjured up. 'Still, if it does turn out to be the one he reported missing it'll be a very useful lead.' For a few seconds he appeared lost in thought; then he picked up his glass, drained it and said, almost regretfully, 'Not my problem, of course.'

Chapter Three

On Saturday, twenty-four hours after the story first appeared in the *Gazette*, a further report – claiming to be exclusive – speculated that the body in the freezer might be that of a young woman who had been working since early June as a chambermaid in a hotel near Stow-on-the-Wold. When she failed to report for duty on Wednesday morning one of her colleagues, thinking she must have overslept, knocked on her bedroom door. Receiving no reply, she went in and found the room empty and the bed apparently not slept in. Tuesday had been her day off and at first it was assumed that she had spent it with friends and stayed with them overnight, but when by the evening she had still not reappeared, a search of the hotel and its grounds was carried out. No trace of the girl was found and eventually the police were notified that she was missing. The reporter had evidently put two and two together and made five.

Melissa Craig was still reading the report when the telephone rang. 'Bruce Ingram here,' said a familiar voice.

'Well, what a coincidence,' she responded drily. 'I was just reading your latest scoop.'

'You mean about the body in the freezer?'

'What else?'

'How did you know I'd written it – there's no by-line. Of course,' he added, without giving her time to reply, 'you obviously recognised my crisp, punchy style.'

'I recognised your gift for jumping to conclusions – and your

17

uncanny nose for tracking down a story,' Melissa retorted. 'What's your secret – a girlfriend in every village in the county, keeping you supplied with tip-offs?'

'Something like that,' he replied cheerfully. 'Anyway, the Bill haven't released many details so it's obvious the freezer victim hasn't been formally identified yet. I'll bet you ten to one it was that girl, though. The interesting thing is, no one at the hotel seems to know who she really was.'

'What do you mean?'

'She called herself Hilda Rice, but my informant doesn't think that was her real name.'

'Why not?'

'Seems she was very cagey about herself and her past. Never mixed with the others off duty, never spoke about her family or where she came from. The consensus was that she had something to hide.'

'Interesting,' said Melissa, 'but why are you telling me all this?'

'Because I thought you might be able to give me a bit of help in writing the next bit of the saga.'

'And there was I, thinking that out of the goodness of your heart you were offering a struggling crime writer an idea for a good meaty plot,' said Melissa drily. 'All right, Mister Ace Reporter, how can I help you?'

'There's an old war-horse in your village, ex-army, white hair and moustache, face like a squashed beetroot, right?'

'You mean, Major . . .' Just in time, Melissa remembered Madeleine Ford's horror of publicity. 'Yes, I know who you mean. What about him?'

'What did you say his name was?'

'I didn't. Why do you want to know?'

'I was down at the nick yesterday afternoon, trying to winkle some more info from the desk sergeant. He claimed he didn't know any more than what was in the press release, but I've heard that one before. Anyway, I happened to glance out of the window and I saw this old gaffer walking across the yard, accompanied by a detective. I knew I'd seen him before but I couldn't place him at first and I didn't pay much attention. Now I've remembered – I saw him once in Upper Benbury. You whispered in my ear that he was an old busybody.'

'So he is, but why the interest?'

'It didn't occur to me at the time that his being there had anything to do with the murder, but it so happens that the DS with him was the same one I saw this morning talking to the proprietor of the Crossed Keys.'

'The hotel where the murdered girl used to work?'

'Right. I reckon that was more than a coincidence, don't you? Come on, Mel,' he coaxed, as she made no reply. 'You do know something, don't you?'

'What makes you so sure of that?'

'You didn't sound a bit surprised when I told you where I'd seen your neighbour. That suggests you already have a shrewd idea.'

'Quite the little mind-reader, aren't we?' During the conversation, Melissa had been doing some rapid thinking. 'Look Bruce, I know the Major has some information which might – only might – be relevant to the case, because he told me before either of us knew about the murder. If I tell you, will you promise not to go after him . . . or print anything that might identify the village? The last thing we want is a crowd of reporters swarming all over the place.'

'Okay, it's a deal.'

Briefly, Melissa told him about the broken-down freezer that had been spirited away, presumably by people described by the police as 'cherry pickers'.

'As far as I know, it hasn't been established yet whether it's the one the body was found in or not,' she finished.

'Find out for me, there's a love.'

'And then what? There's no point in your tracking the Major

down and pestering him or his wife for information. They've no time for the press.'

'I'm not interested in them, but I think I know who their "cherry pickers" might be. Now, if the freezer that was pinched from outside his house and the one the girl was found in *are* one and the same, I'll have a good idea who the police will be questioning next. And once again, Bloodhound Bruce will be ahead of the pack.'

'I can almost see your nose to the ground and your tail wagging,' Melissa told him. 'And it's an unedifying spectacle,' she added as he gave an appreciative chuckle.

'At the moment I'm sitting up and begging. You will help me, won't you?' This was Bruce at his most persuasive. 'Please,' he wheedled.

'All right, I'll see what I can do,' she said after a moment's further hesitation. 'I'll let you know what I find out – if anything.' She hung up, cutting short his thanks and asking herself for the umpteenth time why she allowed herself to become involved in his periodic bouts of sleuthing.

At six o'clock Ken Harris appeared bearing a box of her favourite chocolates and two tickets for a concert in Cheltenham Town Hall.

'Present from a client,' he explained.

'The chocolates?'

'No, the tickets. The lady bought them several weeks ago as a surprise treat for hubby. That was before she began suspecting him of being up to no good with his secretary and engaged me to keep tabs on him. I got the evidence and she gave me the tickets along with my fee.' He had taken off his jacket and loosened his tie while he was speaking, his demeanour that of a man completely at ease in his surroundings. 'Any chance of a beer, love?'

'Of course – you know where it's kept. Help yourself.'

He took a can from the fridge and a glass from a cupboard and sat down with them at the kitchen table. 'I imagine my client had planned a different sort of surprise for hubby,' he went on with a hoarse chuckle, 'and she won't have waited for his birthday, either.' He glanced at Melissa as he spoke, but received no answering smile. 'Something wrong?'

'Not exactly, but . . . I don't see anything to laugh at in a broken marriage.'

'Neither do I . . . what do you take me for? It represents a hell of a lot of unhappiness for at least two people, usually more.'

'Then why joke about it?'

'For the same reason the police make flip remarks when some poor sod tops himself, or gets mangled in a car accident,' he replied, tugging the ring off the can and pouring the contents into the glass. He held it up to the light to appraise its colour before taking a good pull. 'It's not callousness, it's a defence mechanism,' he explained. 'Helps us to cope with the grimness of it all . . . I thought you understood that, Mel.'

'Of course I do. We've talked about it before.' She was fiddling abstractedly with the ribbon on the chocolate box as she spoke, her face serious. 'It's just that when it comes to personal relationships, it seems different somehow.'

'I know what you're thinking.' He set down the glass and reached for her hand. 'You're thinking it might happen to us, aren't you? Is that why you're so reluctant to commit yourself?'

'There seems to be so much that could come between us. I've got used to doing my own thing, making my own decisions. I shut myself away for hours when I'm writing, I spend time away on research or at conferences, sometimes at short notice . . . and I hop over to New York to see Simon from time to time and I have to feel free to go on doing that—'

'Have I ever suggested preventing you from doing any of these things?'

'No, but when push comes to shove, you might.'

'I promise you I won't. And anyway, what about my job? It

takes me here there and everywhere and I often keep irregular hours. It's been like that ever since we met and it hasn't caused any problems.'

'That's because neither of us has had any claim on the other.'

He was still holding her hand, gently turning between his fingers the plain gold ring that she had worn since before Simon was born. It was the one thing the parents of her student lover, tragically killed in a road accident without ever knowing that she was pregnant, had asked of her when they took her into their home after her own mother and father had rejected her. They had never uttered a word of blame, but were pathetically anxious that no one outside the family should know that their grandson was illegitimate. Ken knew her history; she had concealed nothing from him, nor had he from her.

He was silent for a few moments, then said quietly, 'I don't think of our relationship in terms of claim and counter-claim. I want us to build a life together that satisfies us both. I'd like that life to begin here, in a house made from this cottage where you're obviously so happy and the one next door that has always seemed part of it. This is where we first met . . . it's as if we have our roots here. Don't you feel that?'

'I suppose so.'

'And Iris can't wait indefinitely for a decision about Elder Cottage, can she?'

'No,' she admitted. 'As a matter of fact, we were talking about it yesterday. I promised to give her an answer within a week.'

As if sensing an advantage, he gave her hand a squeeze and drew her closer. 'Will you make me the same promise?' he asked softly.

It was far and away the most serious conversation they had ever had. From the very beginning of their affair she had resisted all his efforts to put the relationship on a permanent footing, taking an impish delight in turning his every effort to pin her down into a light-hearted sparring match. Only once – when still in shock after finding a neighbour dead in particularly gruesome circumstances – had she allowed him to stay in her cottage overnight. Today, somehow, he had slipped past her guard. There was a gleam in his eyes – on the small side for his rather lumpy features but clear and penetrating – that told her he knew it. 'Well?' he persisted as she continued to hesitate.

'Okay,' she said at last, but could not resist adding, 'On one condition.'

'And that is?'

'That you promise not to raise the subject again in the meantime.'

He laughed and released her. 'It's a deal. Now, are we going to this concert or not?'

'Of course. As a matter of fact I tried to get tickets, but it was a sell-out ages ago.'

Some hours later, as they drove back from the concert, Melissa remembered the telephone call from Bruce Ingram and said, 'Ken, have you heard any more about that poor girl who was found in the freezer? Is she the girl missing from the hotel, and is the freezer the one the Fords had stolen?'

'Yes, and yes. I was going to tell you, but it slipped my mind. Matt Waters rang me to say the Major's prints were on the freezer, along with umpteen others. Apparently his wife had handled it as well – naturally – and so had the lads who helped manhandle it to the gate for the council people to collect. An officer was sent to get elims from all of them and the old girl got really uptight when he came knocking on the door. He had quite a job to convince her that she wasn't a suspect.'

'It'd serve her right if she was!' said Melissa with a chuckle. 'She's always so proud of being a "sea-green Incorruptible" and all that. Maybe this'll teach her to be a little less holier-than-thou . . . although I very much doubt it.'

'Matt thought that would amuse you. That's why he told me. He sends his regards, by the way.'

'Thanks.' Matt Waters was a detective sergeant, one of ex-DCI Kenneth Harris's former colleagues with whom he kept in regular contact. Melissa knew him well.

'The next task,' Ken went on as he turned off the main road into the lane leading to Upper Benbury, 'will be to find out who nicked the freezer – which shouldn't be difficult. Then they have to establish how and when the body got into it . . . and of course, to formally identify the dead girl.'

'I gathered from the report in today's *Gazette* that there's some doubt about who she really is.'

'That's right. It may take some time to find out her real name or where she came from. It seems she turned up at the hotel out of the blue looking for a job just when two domestics had walked out and left them short-staffed at the busiest time of the year. She was attractive to look at, seemed clean and respectable and all that, and the proprietor engaged her for a week's trial. She proved satisfactory and he said she could stay until the end of the season. He thought she had probably run away from home, but says she appeared to be over sixteen so he didn't think it was his business to enquire. And he conveniently overlooked the fact that she produced no ID or social security number.'

'Of course not. It meant he could get away with paying her a pittance,' said Melissa scornfully.

'No doubt. And it didn't seem to have bothered him at first that she should have stayed out all night – except for the inconvenience it caused him. "It's the sort of thing these girls do," he kept saying. I think Matt found his attitude a bit hard to take.'

'It happens so often, doesn't it?' she sighed. 'People say, "It's none of my business", or "I don't want to get involved"

– and the next thing, there's a tragedy that could have been avoided.'

They had reached Hawthorn Cottage. He cut the engine and switched off the lights. In the darkness, he put an arm round her. '"It's none of my business" is something I've never heard *you* say,' he teased.

She jerked away, feigning indignation. 'Are you implying that I poke my nose into things that don't concern me?' she demanded.

'Not implying. Stating.' With a hand cupping the back of her head he drew her face towards his. 'You're the interferingest woman I've ever met.'

She opened her mouth to deny it, but he silenced her with his.

Chapter Four

There was no Sunday edition of the *Gazette* and the national press had not found the death of an anonymous woman in a remote Gloucestershire village of sufficient importance to compete for space with yet another European crisis and the contents of a leaked document that threatened to cause serious embarrassment to the government. One or two of the tabloids gave the murder limited coverage, indulging in a few flights of fancy concerning the identity of the victim, but since the disappearance of Hilda Rice had never been publicised outside the county it was considered of minor interest compared with the recent scandalous behaviour of certain members of the cast of a TV soap opera.

But if the case failed to shake the nation it was the number one topic of conversation in Upper Benbury village stores, as Melissa discovered when she called to collect her daily paper on Monday morning. There was a small knot of customers at the counter, all having apparently made their purchases but showing no inclination to leave. When Melissa entered, heads turned in her direction. Mrs Foster, the proprietor, immediately exclaimed, 'Here's Mrs Craig, she'll know!' and she found herself facing a ring of expectant faces.

'Know what?' she asked.

'Whether it was Major Ford's freezer that poor girl was found in,' said Alice Hamley, the Rector's wife.

'What makes you think it might be?' Melissa parried.

'Well, we all know he had one stolen, don't we?' said Mrs

27

Foster eagerly. 'Trumpeted it all over the village he did, going on about police indifference and incompetence. Anyone'd think he'd lost a family heirloom instead of a piece of old junk.' Her pale eyelashes fluttered and her plump cheeks flushed rosy red with excitement. 'Still, the police were at his house late on Friday afternoon, weren't they, so they're taking an interest now all right.'

'They have to check everything for elimination purposes. It doesn't necessarily mean—'

'I dare say,' Mrs Foster interrupted. 'But what I'd like to know is, why would anyone want to steal a rusty old thing like that, if it wasn't to hide something in?'

'It was probably worth a few quid to anyone who could strip it down for scrap.' Melissa had no particular liking for the Fords, but she had some sympathy for their predicament and was reluctant to encourage further specu-lation.

'Ah, then I expect it was those gipsies the Major was on about,' said Miss Brightwell, who lived in a cottage behind the church. 'They do that sort of thing, don't they? Then they dump what they can't use. I've just remembered,' she went on, her pale face under its crown of wispy white hair becoming suddenly animated. 'One of the women knocked on my door the other day, trying to sell things. If you ask me, it was just an excuse to have a good look round to see if there was anything worth stealing.'

'I expect it's the same one who called on me,' said Mrs Yorke, who lived a short distance from the Fords' cottage. 'She was selling lace – hand-made, so she claimed. I didn't really want any, but I bought some little mats to get rid of her. She was so pleased – she offered to read my hand for nothing, but I didn't have time. Anyway, I don't believe in that sort of nonsense.'

'Quite right too!' said Mrs Foster. 'Those people are so artful – all smiles and telling you what a lucky face you have, and if you turn your back for a second, they're sneaking in to pinch your silver.'

'I don't think that's quite fair,' said Alice gently. 'It isn't as if there's been any other theft in the village – and she could hardly have put a freezer in her handbag, could she?' she added with a smile.

'She could have gone back and told her menfolk about it,' retorted Mrs Foster with an offended sniff at the mild reproof that seemed to say, *You might be the Rector's wife, young lady, but you don't know everything.*

'But according to the Major, the freezer wasn't put out for collection until quite late on Monday evening, so she could hardly have known about it,' Melissa pointed out.

'That's right, he got two of the Woodbridge brothers to do it,' said Mrs Yorke. 'I heard him discussing it with them as I walked past on my way to the shop – and later on I actually saw them doing it.' She thought for a moment, then went on, 'That must have been after nine o'clock as it was beginning to get dark. There was quite a bit of banging and shouting going on . . . I had the impression they'd had a few pints in the Woolpack beforehand and I don't think Madeleine was amused at having that pantomime going on at her gate.'

'And I suppose the Major was adding to the confusion by shouting orders,' said Melissa with a chuckle.

'I never saw him,' said Mrs Yorke. 'Doesn't he go to some meeting or other on a Monday? Come to think of it, I haven't seen him – or his wife – since.'

'Neither have I,' said Mrs Foster. Her voice fell to a shocked whisper as she added, 'You don't suppose they've been arrested, do you?'

This preposterous suggestion, apparently made in all seriousness, was received with indulgent smiles and covertly exchanged glances all round. Mrs Foster's macabre imagination was well known and her verdict on any matter under discussion generally taken with a good pinch of salt. It was a signal for the gathering to break up and everyone to go their separate ways. Only Alice Hamley lingered outside the shop for a quiet word with Melissa.

'I feel so *sorry* for the Fords,' she said in her gentle, earnest manner. 'It must be horrid for them to be mixed up in something like this. Surely, they can't be under suspicion?'

'No, of course not, but I'll bet they're terrified people will think they are,' Melissa replied. 'That's probably why they're keeping their heads down.'

'I think I'll ask John to call and reassure them.'

'I'm not sure they'd appreciate that ... you know how touchy they are. You're such a charitable soul, Alice – don't you think that if it had happened to someone else, Madeleine Ford would be the first to drop hints about there being no smoke without fire?'

'I suppose so,' Alice admitted with evident reluctance. There was a troubled expression in her blue eyes and she ran her fingers through her short blond curls.

'Well then. It won't hurt them to know what it feels like to be under a little cloud for a day or two. It'll soon blow over, once the police have cleared up the case.'

'You think they'll find out who did it?'

'Sure to, once they know who the girl really was. They think she was using an assumed name, so she was probably hiding from someone, maybe someone she was afraid of. Find out who that was and you've almost certainly found the killer.'

Alice shuddered, evidently imagining all kinds of horrors. Then she looked down at the copy of *The Times* she was holding and her mind switched back to reality. 'I must be getting back,' she said. 'John likes to glance through this before he starts the day's work.'

When Melissa reached home she found a message on her answering machine. She pressed the 'Play' button and heard Bruce Ingram's voice saying, 'Any joy? Please call back asap.'

'Cheek!' she muttered as she reset the machine. 'I'm not your dogsbody, young man. You can jolly well wait.'

Ten minutes later the telephone rang. Once again, Bruce was on the line. 'Didn't you get my message?' he asked.

'I did, and I'm ignoring it while I drink my coffee and do the crossword,' she retorted. 'What's so urgent anyway?'

'Now, don't be awkward,' he coaxed. 'All I'm asking is, was it or wasn't it?'

'If it's the Major's freezer we're talking about, it was. Now, will you go away and leave me in peace?'

'Just as you like. I was going to invite you to join in the action . . . but have it your way.'

'What action?' Knowing Bruce of old, she was instantly suspicious. 'What are you up to, for goodness' sake?'

'Like I told you, I'm ahead of the pack.' He dropped his voice, evidently anxious not to be overheard. She recognised the tactic; he scented a scoop and had no intention of sharing it with any of his colleagues. 'There's a gipsy encampment in the area, right?'

'Right.'

'And gipsies deal in scrap metal, don't they?'

'Among other things . . . yes.'

'So that's where the police'll be focusing their inquiries. And that's where I plan to be in half an hour or so. Why not come along and see the fun? We might even witness an arrest.'

'What makes you think . . . just a minute.' Melissa's brain was working at peak revs. 'There's something else behind this, isn't there?'

'Well . . . in a manner of speaking. Look, I can't explain now. Meet me in the car park in Hucclecote in fifteen minutes and I'll tell you on the way.'

'If you think I've got nothing better to do—' she began, but he cut her short.

'If my suspicions are correct, it might even give you an idea for a plot,' he urged. 'Come on, it won't take long.'

'Oh, very well,' she said resignedly. 'It had better be good, that's all.'

Iris, a lean, sunburned figure in a faded cotton skirt and T-shirt, was in her garden dead-heading roses as Melissa emerged from her cottage. At the sound of the garage door being opened she looked up and called out, 'Hello, where are you off to?' On hearing about Bruce's mysterious errand she gave a dismissive cackle and said, 'Wasting his time . . . and yours. Probably long gone by now.'

'Who – the gipsies?'

'Who else? Why Hucclecote anyway? They were on the Cirencester road.'

'That's true.' With her key in the garage door, Melissa hesitated. 'Maybe he knows where they've gone.'

Iris shrugged. 'Rather you than me,' she said and returned to her roses.

As she swung the Golf into the car park where they had arranged to meet, Melissa spotted Bruce's bright red Escort and pulled up alongside. 'Where are we heading?' she asked as she slipped into the passenger seat.

'Upton.' He started the engine and drove out into the road, heading back towards Gloucester. 'They're camped on farmland belonging to a friend of my Dad's.'

'Upton? But I thought—'

'Thought what?'

'Never mind. Aren't you going to tell me the great secret?'

He took his eyes from the road for a moment to give her a sly grin. 'I'm looking for a motor for an electric fan,' he said.

'You're what?'

'I've got this workshop rigged up in a shed in the back garden. It gets very hot so I need something to cool it down. I've got an old desk fan, but the motor's kaput, so—'

'But surely . . . oh, I see!' she exclaimed. 'These people break all sorts of electrical stuff down for scrap, don't they? You think the police will be searching the camp, you want to be in at the kill and you need an excuse for just happening to turn up at the same time.'

'Got it in one.'

'But why are you so keen for me to come along?'

'I thought it would be a good idea to have someone with me to confirm my story,' he said cheerfully. 'You do agree, don't you, that my shed gets stifling in the summer?'

'You are preposterous!' Melissa exploded. She turned to glare at him, but at the sight of his disarming, schoolboy grin could only laugh.

'I'm sure you'll find it an interesting experience.' he assured her. 'These people lead a very colourful lifesty, ⸱.'

They had turned off the main road and left the housing estates of Abbeydale behind them. A couple of miles along a country lane Bruce turned in through an open gate and followed a track that skirted some woodland. After a couple of hundred yards he pulled on to the verge and took a rough sketch map from his pocket. 'They're a bit further along,' he said after studying it for a moment. 'We'll walk the rest of the way.'

'I don't see any sign of the police.'

'Great. That means we're ahead of them.' He locked the car and they followed the track until a point where it divided. A few yards ahead it was closed by a gate and, after once again consulting his map, Bruce indicated the right fork, which led into the wood. A couple of minutes later they found themselves in a clearing where half a dozen painted wooden caravans were parked. Several horses, tethered to stakes, were quietly grazing and some brown-limbed children were squatting in a circle on the ground, playing with pebbles. A dog, tied to the wheel of one of the caravans, barked at their approach and a dark-haired woman seated on a chair with a low table in front of her, her hands deftly manipulating bobbins on a black cushion, looked up and gave them a bold, questioning look.

'I'm afraid you've made a booboo,' whispered Melissa. 'These are real gipsies ... Romanys ... not scrap-metal dealers.'

'Shit!' Bruce muttered under his breath. 'No wonder there's no sign of the Bill. Might as well go back.'

'No, wait.' Melissa took a step forward. 'Good morning,' she said with a friendly smile.

The woman eyed her warily, but returned the greeting. She had proud, aquiline features and swarthy skin, and her hair lay in two raven-black braids over her breasts. Gold hoops dangled from her ears and she wore several gold bracelets on her wrists. Her long dress was black and her brown feet on the dusty soil were bare. She fixed the newcomers with a fierce stare from eyes the colour of ripe chestnuts, waiting for one of them to speak.

'May I see your lace?' Melissa asked politely.

The woman laid down the bobbins and invited her, with a gesture, to approach. The half-finished piece was spread out on the cushion like a spider's web of extraordinary intricacy and delicacy. Melissa admired it in silence for a few moments, marvelling at the skill that lay in the strong brown fingers. 'It's beautiful,' she said at last. 'Do you have any for sale?'

The woman's manner underwent a subtle change and became almost friendly. 'Not here,' she said, 'My sisters are out on the road with all our stock. If you live nearby, one of us will call on you tomorrow.' The brown eyes were scrutinising Melissa as she spoke. 'You're a story-teller,' she said unexpectedly. 'That's an ancient art.'

'How did you know?' Melissa asked in amazement.

'It's written in your face. And you have a good man ... but not that one,' she added with a movement of her eyes in Bruce's direction. 'Cleave to the one who truly loves you.' She paused for a moment as if giving time for her advice to be digested, then said, 'Tell me where to find you.'

'I live in Upper Benbury, in the Cotswolds.'

34

The woman nodded. 'I know it.'

'My cottage is outside the village – it's not easy to find, but I could draw you a map.' Melissa took a pen and notebook from her handbag and gestured towards the van. 'Perhaps—'

The woman had read her thoughts and stood up. 'Come inside. There's a table you can use.' She climbed the wooden steps into the caravan and beckoned Melissa to follow. At the top she turned and said something to the children in a strange tongue. They left their game and clustered round Bruce, jumping up and down with small hands outstretched, clamouring for pennies. He cast a look of dismay at Melissa, who gave him a cheery wave in return.

The interior of the van was cool and dim after the bright sunlight outside and it took a few seconds for her eyes to adjust and enable her to appreciate the beautifully made, highly polished fittings, the lace curtains at the windows and the tiny kitchen at the far end with the stove chimney leading through the roof. Everything was spotlessly clean and designed to make the best use of every inch of space. The woman indicated a box seat and unfolded a table attached to one wall. She watched while Melissa, uncertain whether she could read and not liking to enquire, drew a plan with pictures of the church and the village green with its war memorial, and a series of arrows leading to Hawthorn Cottage, which she marked with a large cross.

The woman studied the drawing briefly before putting it into her pocket. 'I'll come tomorrow afternoon,' she said with a smile that softened the severe lines of her face and made it beautiful.

'I'll look forward to it. My name's Melissa, by the way. What's yours?'

'Rachel.'

'It's been lovely talking to you, Rachel. I'll go now and let you get on with your work.'

As she was leaving, Melissa noticed a fixture made like an

old-fashioned mahogany chest of drawers at right angles to the door. On its gleaming surface, covered with a runner of exquisite lace, was arranged a collection of ornaments flanked by two photographs in silver frames. One was a formal portrait of a family group showing what were evidently several generations, the men in dark suits standing stiffly erect behind a row of seated women in plain dresses relieved by lace collars, their children on their laps or sitting cross-legged at their feet. The second was a snapshot of a strikingly lovely young woman making lace. Her eyes were on the bobbins she held between her fingers, but her lips were curved in a faint, secretive smile, as if her mind was filled with pleasant thoughts far removed from her work.

'What a beautiful girl!' Melissa exclaimed.

'My husband's niece,' said Rachel. There was a new, harsh note in her voice that made Melissa glance at her. With a shock, she realised that the huge brown eyes were swimming in tears. Embarrassed, she turned back to the picture and saw something she had not at first noticed; threaded into the filigree work of the frame was a length of black ribbon.

'I'm so sorry, I didn't mean to upset you,' she said gently. 'What happened to her?'

'Ask the *gadgy* who took the picture . . . and then took her away.'

'She isn't dead, then?'

'Might as well be.' Without further explanation, Rachel descended the steps and Melissa, her bare arms prickling with gooseflesh as if a breath of cold air had passed through the caravan, was glad to follow her into the sunlight.

'Well, goodbye until tomorrow,' she said, but Rachel had already returned to her lace-making and made no reply.

Outside, the children were laughing and playing knuckle-bones with pennies. Bruce had moved away and was waiting for her at the point where the track divided. 'I see you managed to buy them off,' she remarked as she rejoined him.

'They were milling round me like a swarm of gadflies,' he complained with a rueful smile. 'Thank goodness I had plenty of change and a packet of toffees in my pocket. Any idea what that woman said to them, by the way?'

'She was probably telling them to make sure you didn't nick anything while we were inside the van.'

'Thank you very much. What kept you so long?'

'I was showing her how to get to my cottage . . . I might buy some of her lace as a wedding present for Iris and Jack. And then I was looking at some photographs.' On the short walk back to the car, Melissa repeated the sad story of the young woman who had left her tribe for an outsider and was now thought of by the family as dead. She stopped short as an awful possibility occurred to her. 'Bruce, you don't suppose she could be the girl in the freezer? That black ribbon – Romanys are supposed to have second sight, aren't they? Maybe they already know in their hearts that she's dead. Supposing this *gadgy* Rachel was talking about abducted her and then murdered her—'

'—looked for somewhere to dump her body, found the abandoned freezer and hid it in there,' Bruce continued excitedly. 'Mel, you could be on to something.'

'Let's not get too carried away,' said Melissa. 'It could be no more than a coincidence.'

'I suppose so,' he admitted, reluctant to abandon a possible headline-grabbing story.

'Just the same,' she went on, 'it might be worth mentioning it to the police. It's unlikely that girl's family reported her disappearance to the authorities and I don't suppose they read the papers, so they probably don't even know about the freezer murder.'

'You're right.' Bruce unlocked the car and they got in. 'We'll call in at the nick on the way home.'

Chapter Five

'What in Heaven's name possessed you?' demanded Harris. His anger and agitation fairly thundered along the wire and Melissa moved the receiver a couple of inches from her ear, contorting her features and baring her teeth in a scowl as if the two of them were face to face.

'There's no need to get so worked up,' she retorted. 'Anyone would think I'd wandered into a den of wild animals to hear you go on.'

'If the dead girl is the runaway niece, those people might know more than they care to admit.'

'Oh, for goodness' sake! They were heartbroken when she ran away from them . . . Rachel was in tears—'

'That doesn't mean a thing. They might have decided to punish her to redeem the honour of the tribe.'

'Are you suggesting that it was her family who murdered her?'

'How can you be certain they didn't? You don't know anything about those people or how their minds work. The way they see things, that girl brought shame on them by going off with some outsider.'

'I didn't know you were such an authority on Romany culture.' She tried to keep her tone light, but she was fast running out of patience.

'Don't be sarcastic,' he snapped back. 'Didn't it occur to you that woman might have thought you were from the police?'

'Why should she? Anyway, considering there was only her

and half a dozen kids there at the time, I wasn't exactly threatened. Do be reasonable, Ken. All I did was ask to see some lace – it was pure chance that I heard about the runaway niece. I don't think the family even knew about the murder and I certainly wasn't going to alarm Rachel unnecessarily by referring to it. I'm beginning to wish I'd never mentioned it to you.'

'It would have been better if you'd kept your nose out of it altogether.'

'I find that very offensive,' she said coldly. 'It so happens that I may have stumbled on an important lead in a murder hunt. I imagine one of the relatives will be invited to try and identify the dead girl, won't they?'

'Sure to,' he said curtly.

'And if they do, it'll take the police a step nearer finding her killer, won't it?'

It was late on Monday afternoon, some hours after her visit to the Romany camp with Bruce Ingram. While the two of them were waiting in reception at police headquarters to report their theory as to the possible identity of the freezer victim, Detective Sergeant Matt Waters had passed through with a colleague and given them a nod of recognition. In the more or less certain knowledge that her presence would in due course be mentioned to Ken Harris, she had decided to get in with her version first and called him at his office. A ticking-off and – almost certainly – another dig at her tendency to 'go poking her nose in' were to be expected, but not such a furious outburst as this.

'Well, won't it?' she repeated as he remained silent.

'Sure to,' he repeated grudgingly, 'but that still doesn't excuse your action.'

'Oh, stop sounding so pompous.'

'I suppose that cub reporter put you up to it?' he went on, ignoring the jibe.

'If you mean Bruce Ingram, he's hardly a cub reporter . . .

and he didn't put me up to anything. He told me what he was planning to do and asked if I'd like to go along. If I'd realised it was the Romanys he was interested in, I'd have told him he was barking up the wrong tree, but I assumed it was the other lot – the scrap-metal merchants – he was talking about. I was curious, so—'

'So you admit that it wasn't lace-buying you were interested in at all.'

This was intolerable. He was challenging everything she said as if she was a recalcitrant suspect and he still a policeman. 'I never said that was my *prime* motive in going—' she began, but he interrupted with a sardonic bark of laughter.

'No, we know what really motivated you, don't we – your insatiable curiosity. Well, curiosity killed the cat, remember? So in future, please don't go doing anything like that without consulting me first.'

The use of the word 'please' could not conceal the fact that this was a command, not a request. Melissa's hackles all but scraped the ceiling. 'If the best you can do is quote some tired old proverb at me, there's not much point in continuing this conversation,' she snapped. 'And if you think you have the right to approve in advance anything I propose to do, you can think again.'

'There's no need to take that attitude.'

'I don't care for your attitude either, and from now on I'll think twice before I tell you anything.' Without giving him a chance to get in another word, she slammed down the telephone.

To her chagrin, she realised she was trembling. This was the first serious row they had had for a long time, and all her righteous indignation could not conceal the fact that it had upset her. Her first thought was to seek out Iris and pour her woes into a sympathetic ear. She was halfway to the front door of Elder Cottage before she noticed Jack Hammond's car parked a short distance away.

'Damn!' she exclaimed aloud and retreated, slamming her own door behind her. Not that she had anything against Jack except that he was a man, had somewhat old-fashioned ideas about relationships between men and women and would undoubtedly side with Ken. Still seething, she marched into the kitchen, poured herself a glass of sherry, took it into the sitting-room and switched on the television. The early evening news had just started but she paid scant attention, moodily sipping her sherry and reflecting on the shortcomings of men in general and of Kenneth Harris in particular. The bulletin was drawing to a close when the final announcement made her sit up with a start.

'Here is an item that has just come in,' the newscaster was saying. 'We understand that the body of a woman discovered three days ago in an abandoned freezer some five miles from Cirencester has been identified as that of Hannah Rose, a member of a family of Romany gipsies presently encamped on land near Gloucester. And that's all for now. Our next bulletin will be—'

Mechanically, Melissa picked up the remote control and switched off the set. Hannah Rose. The girl who had gone missing from her job at the Crossed Keys called herself Hilda Rice. The similarity was too much of a coincidence – they had to be one and the same. She wondered which of Hannah's relatives had identified her and how much they had told the police. It might be very little . . . they probably mistrusted the police anyway and . . . at the next thought, Melissa's brain, prompted by something Ken Harris had said, went into overdrive. An image of Rachel, standing beside her as she admired Hannah's photograph, flashed on to her retina like a film projected on a screen. She saw once more the proud Romany features contorted by grief . . . and then heard the rasp of anger in the woman's voice when speaking of the *gadgy*, the outsider, who had taken her husband's niece away and whom her family probably now held responsible for her death. And she felt an uneasy premonition that, rather than leave the hunt for the girl's killer in the hands of the police, they might keep their own counsel and set about tracking down the man themselves, with the object of meting out their own brand of punishment.

She glanced at the clock. It was almost seven; over an hour had passed since the quarrel with Ken. Her anger and resentment had subsided, swept aside for the time being by the latest development in the 'Body in the Freezer' mystery and by the notion that the bereaved relatives might be bent on taking the law into their own hands. She could imagine them, tight-lipped in the face of the inevitable police questioning. 'She left us to work in a town,' they might say. 'We don't know where she went or who she went with. We haven't seen her from that day to this.'

And where had Hannah met the man who took the photograph . . . and then, if Rachel was speaking the truth, made off with his subject? Was it an abduction, or had the girl gone willingly? Recalling the dreamy expression on her face, the lips parted in a half-smile, Melissa guessed that she had already fallen in love with him. What tales had he told her, what promises had he made in order to entice her away?

Rachel had said very little, but she might now regret having revealed even that much to a *gadgy*, however sympathetic. Supposing she were to tell her menfolk about the visit? The thought that there was someone who could pass the information to the police, thereby frustrating their plans for vengeance, would not please them. They might ask themselves if there was a way of preventing it going any further. And Melissa had given Rachel her address . . .

For a moment, panic took hold. Then she gave herself a mental shake and began to rationalise the situation. Even without her own statement, or mention by the family, the police would have a shrewd idea that there was a man involved in Hannah's flight. No doubt they had already raised that very point, and even if the family had refused to answer, that silence would have confirmed their suspicions. Nothing Melissa could tell them would add to their knowledge. 'Pull yourself together, woman!' she said aloud. 'It's Ken Harris and his idiotic suggestions that's put the wind up you!' She went into the kitchen to start preparing her supper.

She had just finished eating when the telephone rang. In the hope that it was Ken calling to make his peace she hastily snatched up the receiver, but Matt Waters was on the line.

'Melissa? Are you busy?'

'Not particularly – what is it?'

'I wonder if I could call in for a word on my way home? It's about that photograph you referred to in your statement . . . the one of the dead girl.'

'What about it?'

'It's important to establish where and when it was taken. Her family aren't being very co-operative. It's always the same with these people; they look on the police as their natural enemies even when we're trying to help them.'

Maybe that's because they've got their own ideas on how things should be handled, she thought grimly. Aloud, she said, 'I'm not sure I can be of much help, but drop in by all means.'

'Thanks.'

It would be good to have company, even if only for a short time. She was beginning to regret her shouting match with Ken. His anger had, she knew, been prompted solely by his concern for her. His presence at that moment would be reassuring . . . she decided that she was almost ready to forgive him . . . provided, of course, that he apologised and promised not to be so bossy in future.

She prepared coffee and when Matt arrived they went into the sitting-room. 'I don't know what else I can tell you,' she said as she filled two mugs and handed him one. 'Everything Rachel said is in my statement. When I asked if the girl was

dead – because of the black ribbon round the photo frame –
she said "Might as well be" and never uttered another word,
not even "Goodbye". She'd already told me that some man
took the picture – she didn't say where or when – and then
"took the girl away" as she put it.'

'Yes, that's right,' Matt agreed. 'What I'd like you to do is cast
your mind back to that picture and try to remember anything
else that was in it . . . anything at all that might help us to
identify the location. Take your time.' He sat back with his
mug of coffee and waited.

Melissa closed her eyes and called up an image of the
interior of the caravan, the polished wooden locker with its
array of bric-à-brac and the two photographs in their gleaming
silver frames. She focused her inward eye on the picture of
Hannah, recalling each detail . . . the cushion with the lace
spread out on it, the bobbins, the fingers that held them and
the eyes with their faraway look, gazing down at the work yet
not seeing it, seeing instead something far more interesting,
something exciting and pleasurable enough to bring that
sensuous half-smile to the perfectly shaped mouth.

But it was the background that Matt was interested in.
Melissa had been so taken by the look on the girl's face
that she had paid scant attention to anything else . . . but
yes, little by little other details began to come back. There
was a dog, the dog that had barked when she and Bruce had
first approached the Romany's camp, sitting on its haunches
at Hannah's side. And some kind of group in the background,
out of focus, but identifiable . . .

'I think there were some men with horses,' she said after
a long pause. 'It was quite blurry . . . you couldn't see their
faces—'

'You're sure there were horses?' Matt's voice was sharp,
interested. 'How many?'

'Yes, quite sure . . . several. I only half took them in, but . . .
yes, definitely men with horses.'

'Well done. Now Mel, think again about the girl. What was she wearing?'

'She had on a brightly coloured dress that went down to her ankles. I remember that quite clearly because you could just see her bare feet.'

'Short or long sleeves?'

'Short. Definitely short. The sun was shining . . . it was probably quite a warm day.' It was amazing, Melissa thought, how much she had subconsciously absorbed and was able to recall.

'Was she wearing any jewellery?'

'She had long hair – I don't recall any earrings, but I believe most of the women wear them.'

'What about bangles?'

Melissa thought for a moment, then shook her head. 'Sorry, I can't remember, but it's quite likely. Rachel was wearing several. Were there any on the body?'

'No.'

'So maybe the motive was robbery?'

'That's one of the lines we're considering. I believe gipsies put a lot of their money into gold – even the men wear earrings.'

Melissa nodded absently, her thoughts still on the photograph. 'I've just remembered something else,' she said. 'Hannah was sitting quite close to the caravan and there was a white jug on the steps with some flowers in it . . . bluebells, I think.'

'Bluebells, eh?' Matt re-opened the notebook he had just closed and began scribbling again. 'That's a great help.'

'It is?'

'Sure. When do bluebells come out?'

'Let's see . . . late April, early May . . . oh, I get it. You reckon that picture was taken at the Stow Horse Fair?'

'I reckon so. And don't forget, the girl had been working under an assumed name at an hotel just outside Stow. There could be a connection. Thanks Mel, you've been a great help.'

'I hope you'll find the bloke she went off with.'

'Well, at least we know now where to start looking. Mind you, he's not the only suspect . . . we haven't ruled out the possibility that her own menfolk had a hand in her death.'

Melissa's heart sank. It was exactly what Ken Harris had suggested. When two experienced detectives had the same gut reaction, was it reasonable to take the opposite view? Yet her own conviction was just as strong. If Hannah had been killed by members of her tribe, Rachel must surely have known, yet nothing in her demeanour had indicated that she was harbouring such an awful secret.

'If you wouldn't mind calling in at the nick some time in the near future to make another statement?' Matt was saying.

'Of course. Would you like some more coffee?'

'No thanks, I must be getting along.'

As he got up to leave, they heard the sound of an approaching car. 'Sounds as if you've got another visitor,' Matt remarked.

A car door slammed and someone pounded on the knocker. Ken Harris was standing in the porch; he appeared taken aback at the sight of his former colleague.

'Matt – what are you doing here?'

'Official business. Melissa's been helping with our inquiries. Really helping – she's been brilliant. Thanks once again Mel – see you!'

As Matt got into his car and drove off, Melissa stood silently to one side while Harris stepped into the hall. She closed the front door and went past him into the sitting-room with her head averted, determined not to reveal her relief at seeing him.

'What was all that about?' he demanded.

'Matt wanted to know if I could remember anything to help identify the place where the photograph of the murdered girl was taken.'

'So why couldn't they get that information from the family?'

'I suppose it's because the family haven't shown them the photo.'

'What did I tell you? It's odds on they know far more than they're prepared to admit.'

'That doesn't follow. Matt says they're never very well disposed towards the police.'

'The opposite's true as well . . . and with good reason. What else did Matt say?' His manner was aggressive, but the expression in his eyes indicated hurt rather than anger.

'Nothing much. I imagine the number one priority will be to trace the girl's movements from the time she left, but we didn't discuss that. Look Ken, if you've come here to carry on a cross-examination, forget it.' Without a second thought, she decided not to mention the possibility of a revenge killing. It was probably her imagination working overtime . . . but even so, it would only set him off again. She picked up the tray of coffee things and headed for the door. He took it from her grasp, put it back on the table and pulled her into his arms.

'Don't be mad at me, love,' he said in a softer tone. 'It's only because you mean so much to me . . . I get worried—'

'And I get the feeling of being stifled,' she retorted. The familiar scent of his jacket, his breath on her cheek and the feel of his body pressed against hers made it difficult to maintain her attitude of justifiable resentment, but she persevered. 'You've no right to expect me to account to you for my every movement.'

'I don't expect that.' His voice was conciliatory, his hands gently massaging her back. 'All I'm asking is that you let me know before you go haring off on some mad-brain scheme. Suppose anything had happened to you in that camp? No one would have known where you were or where to start looking.'

Chemistry was beginning to have an effect. Melissa felt her resistance being undermined, but she was determined to hold out a little longer. 'And if I had told you, what would you have done?'

'I'd have told you not to be so daft, but—' Abruptly, he released her from the bear-hug and held her at arms' length, his lumpy features crumpled in a rueful smile. 'Knowing you, you'd have gone ahead anyway.'

She allowed herself a small, triumphant smile in return. 'That proves my point, doesn't it?'

He took her face in both hands and tilted it towards his. 'Oh Mel, why can't you stick to fiction and leave the real detective work to the professionals?'

'Something in the genes, I suppose.'

'You're an infuriating woman, do you know that?'

'I guess so.'

He heaved a sigh of mock despair. 'What am I going to do with you?'

No doubt other skirmishes lay ahead, but in this one Melissa sensed that he had tacitly conceded victory. It was time to let him off the hook and make peace. 'I can think of several things,' she said demurely.

He pulled her towards him again. 'Just at the moment,' he said, 'I can think of only one.'

Chapter Six

A s Matt Waters had requested, Melissa called in at police headquarters in Cheltenham on Tuesday to repeat as a formal statement her recollections of the photograph of Hannah Rose that she had given him the previous evening. The day was pleasantly warm with a hint of autumn in the mellow sunlight, the pavements dappled with gold by fallen leaves. Trees in the neighbourhood gardens, which a few months before had provided dazzling displays of pink and white blossom, were now laden with crab apples and rowan berries and alive with birds squabbling over the ripening fruit.

She had left the Golf in a tree-lined street a short distance away and as she headed back to it her mind was busy with some of the unanswered questions about the last hours of Hannah Rose – questions she was dying to put to Matt. She had hoped for an opportunity for another word with him, but although she had spotted him in a corridor he had given only a perfunctory nod in response to her greeting before disappearing into an office and closing the door. His expression had said, as clearly as words, that here she could expect no confidential titbits of the kind he occasionally revealed in private to her and his former superior officer.

Behind her, she heard rapid footsteps and someone calling her name. She stopped and turned to see Bruce Ingram sprinting after her.

'What brings you here?' he panted as he drew level. 'Oh,

I know you were in the nick,' he went on as her eyebrows went up, 'I happened to see you arrive, but I was on my way to the press briefing and didn't have a chance to get a word with you.'

'It seems I'm a key witness in the Hannah Rose murder enquiry,' she told him.

'No kidding! I suppose you heard they're questioning two men?'

Melissa stared at him. 'No, I didn't. When . . . who?'

'Yesterday evening. It was on the late TV news – I guess you didn't watch.'

'Er, no, I had an early night.' Melissa felt a glow in her cheeks. The memory of her reconciliation with Ken set her senses tingling. Fearing that her face might betray her she turned away from Bruce and walked on, fumbling in her pocket for her car key, but his mind was focused on other matters. As they reached Melissa's car, he put a manilla envelope he was carrying on the roof, placed his notebook on top, opened it and stood with his pen poised above an empty page.

'So what makes you a key witness?' he asked hopefully. 'Anything I can use, or have you been sworn to secrecy? Tell you what,' he went on as she hesitated. 'Have you got half an hour to spare later on? We could have a spot of lunch somewhere and compare notes.'

'You mean, you could pick my brains,' she retorted with a wry smile, knowing him of old.

'I'm sure you'd like to hear what we learned at the briefing,' he countered. 'It won't all be in the *Gazette*.'

The offer was too attractive to turn down. She glanced at her watch; it was half-past ten. 'I don't see why not – I've got a few things to do in town before I go home,' she conceded. 'What sort of time are you thinking of?'

'Say twelve o'clock. I have to dash now – I'd like to catch the evening edition.'

'Okay, it's a deal. Who's leading the investigation, by the way?'

Bruce screwed up his face as if he had bitten into a sour apple. 'The man we all love to hate,' he said.

She gave a knowing chuckle. 'You mean DCI Holloway?'

'Who else?' They both had first-hand experience of the humourless, recently promoted Detective Chief Inspector, Bruce during his brief career in the police, Melissa through her involvement in previous investigations. 'He's a sarcastic bugger,' Bruce went on, 'I think he's got his knife into me because I left the force to go back to journalism. Sees me as gamekeeper turned poacher, I guess.'

'Which you are.' Melissa unlocked the car and opened the driver's door. 'So where shall we meet? How about the Courtyard in Montpellier?'

'That gets pretty crowded with tourists at this time of year. We don't want to have to share a table.'

'In case one of your rivals happens to overhear?' she teased, knowing his passion for secrecy. 'Okay, have you got a better idea?'

'There's that pub at the top of Crickley Hill. We could sit out and admire the view.'

'That suits me fine – it's on my way home.'

'Great. See you there about midday. Cheers!' And he turned on his heel and hurried back the way he had come.

When Melissa turned into the car park at the Air Balloon a few minutes before twelve, it was already surprisingly full. Bruce, arriving shortly afterwards, pulled a face. 'Looks as if it's going to be crowded here as well,' he grumbled, but when they went inside they found the place practically deserted. 'Where is everyone?' he asked the barman.

'Walking on the Cotswold Way, most of them. They turn up first thing, leave their cars here and come back for lunch.' The man took their order for sandwiches and coffee and said, 'I'll bring it to your table.'

'Thanks. We'll be in the garden.'

They had it to themselves. For a few minutes they sat admiring the panorama of the Severn Vale, with the city of Gloucester in the foreground and the Welsh Hills on the horizon, a smudge of indigo against the hazy blue of the sky. Behind them rose the dramatic spur of Crickley Hill, the dense greenery on its slopes relieved by splashes of bronze and gold. A flock of swallows and house martins, perched on the roof of a nearby house, suddenly took off like flakes of charred paper blown by the wind and began wheeling madly above their heads, filling the air with their thin, shrill cries.

'They'll soon be getting ready to leave,' Bruce remarked. 'Amazing, isn't it, that something so tiny can fly nonstop from here to Africa.'

'Amazing,' Melissa agreed absently, thinking of Iris. She too was preparing to leave but, unlike the swallows, would not be returning.

The barman put their order on the wooden table in front of them, made a favourable comment on the view and the weather, and departed.

'Right,' said Bruce, reaching for a sandwich. 'Who goes first?'

'You're more up to date than I am, so tell me what you learned at the briefing. My contribution is pretty much guesswork.'

'Okay. The arrested men haven't been named so we can only guess who they are or where they were picked up.'

'Gipsies?'

'I reckon so. We tried to get old Prune-Face to confirm it, but he wouldn't be drawn. Anyway, the body was found on Thursday evening and the pathologist who carried out the post-mortem says the girl had been dead anything between three and five days. The body had been put in the freezer very soon after death, and because of the insulation it hadn't been subjected to the same variations in temperature as if it had been in the open, so he claimed he couldn't be more accurate than that.'

'And the cause of death?'

'Fractured skull, caused by a severe blow to the head. There was bruising to the face as well, probably inflicted during some sort of struggle just before death.'

'Have any more details emerged about what she was doing when she wasn't working in the hotel?'

'Quite a bit. They found lace-making equipment in her room and they reckon she spent some of her time there making the stuff. House to house inquiries have already turned up a few people she called on, trying to sell it.' Bruce reached for the envelope he had been carrying, drew out a sheet of paper and handed it to Melissa. 'Here's a photo of a piece she sold to someone in a village not far from the hotel.'

Melissa studied the picture with interest. 'The pattern is very like the one I saw Rachel working on,' she said. 'I take it this will appear in the papers in the hope that more people who bought from her will recognise it and come forward.'

'I'm hoping the *Gazette* will carry it in this evening's edition and it'll be in the nationals tomorrow. The police are naturally anxious to learn as much as they can of the girl's movements, especially during the period immediately before her death.'

'Are they issuing a photograph?'

'It seems not. The relatives are reported to be very distressed and couldn't be persuaded to part with theirs. The police are hoping they'll change their minds, but meanwhile the people at the hotel have co-operated to produce this E-FIT. The pathologist seems to think it's reasonably accurate, although features naturally change in appearance after death.'

He handed Melissa a second sheet on which was an impression of a girl's face. She studied it for several seconds, mentally comparing it with the photograph in Rachel's caravan. 'That seems a fair likeness, judging from my recollection of the photograph,' she said as she handed the pictures back.

'Of course, you had a good look at it, didn't you?'

'It's what took me to headquarters this morning.' Briefly, she told him of the details that, under Matt's patient questioning, she had managed to recall.

When she had finished, he said thoughtfully, 'Even if the picture was taken at the May horse fair in Stow, as Waters seems to think, it doesn't mean that's when – or where – the girl first met the bloke who took it.'

'I've been thinking about that. From the dreamy look on her face she was already in love with him, which suggests to me that she had known him for at least a little while before. These gipsy families are always on the move . . . maybe they'd met somewhere else and he was following her around.'

Bruce shook his head. 'Unlikely, I'd say – unless of course he's a professional doing a series on Romany folk and their way of life, or something like that.'

'Perhaps one of the county magazines has commissioned – or been offered – a piece on those lines.'

'I haven't heard talk of it, but I could ask around.' Bruce sipped thoughtfully at his coffee and then said, 'I suppose they could have met at the previous fair – it's held twice a year.'

'Of course – May and October. Suppose they met last October and arranged to meet again the next time the family was in Stow. Maybe they'd been thinking about each other all winter . . . then when they met up again, decided to run off together. Maybe she was tired of the nomadic way of life and saw him as a means of escape—'

'And then found it didn't work out and came back to Stow, hoping to join up with her own people again next time they were in the area. They probably follow the same route every year, working on the same farms and so on. In that case, she would have known where to find them. Maybe that's where she was heading when she left the hotel after finishing her work on Monday.'

'If she was planning to rejoin her folks that day she wouldn't have left all her things – especially her lace-making equipment – behind,' Melissa objected. 'Everything points to her intending to come back from wherever she was heading for. Besides,' she went on, 'I believe some Romany tribes have very strong traditions about what they call *marimē*, which is their word for "pollution". By going off with a *gadgy*, Hannah might have become a pariah to her family.'

'So maybe she was so secretive because she was scared of being found by them.'

'It's possible, I suppose . . . but then, why stay in a place where she might run into them?'

Bruce polished off the last of his sandwiches and sat back. 'Perhaps she was trying to find the man she went away with in the first place,' he suggested.

'And if she found him and if he has a wife living in the neighbourhood, that could be a motive for killing her. Then he'd have wanted somewhere to hide the body. He could have found the freezer and . . . by the way, was there any suggestion at the briefing that he might be responsible?'

'That's something else our friend refused to comment on. He wants to contact him, naturally, even if only to eliminate him from the inquiries. I daresay Hannah's family wouldn't mind a few words with him as well,' Bruce added grimly.

His meaning was obvious. Melissa's mind went back to the alarming possibility that had flashed through her mind after watching the television announcement that the dead girl had been identified as Hannah Rose. She sat mechanically turning her empty coffee cup between her hands and said, half thinking aloud, 'There's a lot of ill-feeling against him among the family – I could sense it from the way Rachel spoke. Whether or not he actually killed Hannah, they'll hold him responsible. Matt said they aren't being very co-operative—'

They exchanged glances. 'You reckon they'll try and get to him first?' said Bruce.

'I wouldn't be surprised.'

Once again they fell silent, their minds busy with this line of thought. After a moment Melissa asked, 'Did the PM report say anything about sexual interference?'

'She was what is euphemistically known as "sexually active", but there was nothing to suggest she'd been raped.'

'Any theories as to how – or when – the body came to be in the freezer?'

'Only that it was put there pretty soon after death, because of the state of post-mortem lividity. The lid was closed when the kids found it. If they hadn't opened it, it might have been weeks or even months before the body was discovered.'

'Maybe that's what the killer was banking on. Have the police any idea how long the freezer had been in that ditch?'

'They won't say, but they're appealing for anyone who regularly walks in the area to come forward.'

'We know she was found on Thursday evening.' Melissa began counting on her fingers. 'Five days takes us back to . . . let's see, Sunday. But the freezer was in the Fords' garage until Monday evening, when it was put out for collection on Tuesday. It disappeared some time after ten o'clock on Tuesday morning.'

'So either the killer knew it was there and turned up at dead of night to dump Hannah's body, or it was put there after the freezer was taken. No one in their right mind would turn up with a corpse for disposal in broad daylight.'

'Agreed. So the most likely explanation is that it was nicked by two of the travellers that Dudley was complaining about. They must have been cruising round the villages looking for whatever they could lay their hands on. Maybe they nicked the freezer and then – after one of them killed the girl – decided it was the perfect place to hide the body.'

Bruce nodded. 'Everything points to the police working on a similar theory. My guess is that the gipsy camp is where the arrests were made.'

'And of course,' Melissa said with a mischievous smile, 'the Bill hit on the right group of gipsies.'

'True,' he conceded, 'but if we hadn't made that mistake—'

'If *you* hadn't made that mistake—'

'Okay, point taken. What I'm saying is, because we went to the wrong camp, you saw the photograph and were able to point the police in the right direction. We should get a citation,' he finished with a grin. Then, his expression once more serious, Bruce leaned forward, planted his elbows on the table and rested his chin in his hands. 'The thing we have to decide now is, what do we do next?'

Scenting danger, Melissa reached for her handbag. 'You please yourself, I'm going home,' she said. 'I've got work to do. If I don't get down to it I'll never meet my deadline and my agent will give me hell, so forget about the "we", will you?'

'Just a figure of speech. What I mean is, what line do you reckon the police will follow now? They obviously don't believe they've got the case sewn up yet.'

'Oh come on, you know the way they work as well as I do – better, in fact. If they've got enough evidence to charge the two suspects, that's what they'll do. If they haven't—'

'—they'll be running around like headless chickens looking for it,' Bruce interposed. 'And I want to keep one jump ahead of them.'

'If you want to play detective to get your scoop feel free, but leave me out of it,' Melissa said firmly. 'I've already had a run-in with Ken Harris over yesterday's little excursion.'

'Kenneth Harris, the PI? What's it got to do with him?'

It was a question Melissa had asked herself on more than one occasion and to which she had still not found an entirely satisfactory answer. She muttered something about the inadvisability of meddling in police inquiries, but Bruce had already lost interest. He was frowning, evidently thinking furiously.

'Motive,' he said. 'There doesn't seem to be any conceivable reason why anyone from the travellers' camp should have killed that girl. She wasn't of their tribe . . . the hotel she was working in isn't the kind of place they go—'

'It seems pretty clear what she did in the daytime, but who knows where she went or what she did in the evenings . . . apart from being "sexually active" as you put it,' Melissa pointed out. 'She could have been picked up by one of them . . . in a pub, or maybe at a bus stop . . . anywhere . . . for casual sex . . . and then maybe threatened to blow the whistle on some scam they were up to.'

'I can't see it. These people know all the tricks . . . they're past masters at fooling the police. What could a girl like that have to use against them?'

'Maybe one of them is some kind of pervert.'

'In that case, there would most likely have been other, similar killings, and so far as I know there haven't been any recently. No, I reckon that photographer is more likely to be the killer – it seems more logical. If only we could find out who he is.' Bruce stared unseeingly across the Vale and into the distance, gnawing his lip in frustration.

'He might live in Stow. In that case, someone local may have seen him taking the picture. He might even be a regular at one of the pubs in the town.'

The suggestion had an immediate effect on the journalist. He sat bolt upright, wearing what Melissa always thought of as his 'eager terrier' expression. 'That's an idea!' he exclaimed. 'He might even have been seen with Hannah.'

'He might indeed. And it's more than likely DCI Holloway is thinking on the same lines,' Melissa added, goading him. 'So if you want to keep ahead of the opposition, you'd better go and turn some of your well-known charm on the local barmaids.'

'Do I take it you aren't interested in a combined operation?' Bruce appeared disappointed, but resigned.

'Got it in one,' she said. 'Thanks for the sarnies and coffee, Bruce . . . and good hunting!'

Chapter Seven

As Melissa approached the turning to Hawthorn and Elder Cottages, a bright green Mini emerged and headed towards her on the wrong side of the narrow lane. She hastily swerved into a convenient gateway, glaring at the oncoming driver and receiving in return a friendly wave from a plump, beringed hand through the open window. The car was unfamiliar, but she recognised the owner of the hand: Gloria Parkin, the exuberant young matron who had a regular round of cleaning jobs in the parish and – besides being an incredibly energetic and efficient worker – could be relied on to keep all her 'ladies' up to date with the latest gossip. As she drew level she popped a smiling face framed in a frizz of blond hair out of the window and said, in her rich Bristol accent, 'Morning Mrs Craig! Lovely morning, innit?'

'Lovely,' agreed Melissa. It was impossible to remain annoyed with Gloria for long. 'New car?' she added, eyeing the Mini.

'Just borrowed. The red one got dented so my Stanley's letting me use this while he has it mended,' Gloria explained. Her husband ran a lucrative and – on the whole – reasonably honest dealership in second-hand cars, and one could never be sure in what marque she would turn up next.

'Oh dear, did you have a prang?' *It would hardly be surprising, the way you drive*, was the unspoken thought that followed Melissa's question.

Gloria giggled. 'Nothing serious, just hit a post that were too close to the corner.' She squinted up at the sky and added,

'Think it's goin' to rain presently. Terrible about that gipsy girl, innit?' she went on inconsequentially. 'I were just saying to Miss Ash, my Stanley reckons he saw—' She broke off as another car appeared behind her, braked and gave a blast on the horn. 'Impatient, innee?' she said with a grin. 'Have to go now, tell you tomorrow.' She rolled up the window and drove off. Melissa watched in her mirror as the Mini, still in the middle of the road, staggered up the hill with the other car on its tail. She wondered in a kind of amused despair how it was that Gloria had never had a serious accident. It was probably because she rarely drove above twenty miles an hour.

Melissa had just put the Golf away and was about to enter her cottage when a voice called 'Yoohoo!' Glancing upwards she saw Iris leaning out of the window of her first-floor studio. 'Got a minute?' she called.

'Sure.' Iris shut the window and reappeared moments later at her front door. She was wearing a loose smock, its long sleeves rolled up over her thin brown arms and its front liberally streaked with blue paint, some of which appeared to have been transferred via her stained fingers to her short, mouse-brown hair.

'Glad I caught you,' she told Melissa. 'You had a visitor.'

'Oh? Who was it?'

'Some gipsy woman. Had a bag full of stuff she tried to sell me.'

'Lace?'

'No idea. Too busy to look at it. Sent her packing.'

'Did she say she'd call back?'

'Said something about having arranged to call on you. Didn't believe her. Said I didn't know when you'd be home.'

'She was telling the truth. Her name's Rachel. I met her yesterday . . . I was going to tell you all about it, but I never got the chance. She wasn't supposed to come until this afternoon. Did she leave any message?'

Iris shook her head and a tortoise-shell slide became dislodged from her springy hair. She grabbed it and clipped it back into place, managing as she did so to leave a blue smudge across one cheek. 'Seemed a bit up-tight,' she said. 'Red round the eyes. Might have been crying.'

'I daresay she had, poor woman. I'm pretty sure the freezer victim was her husband's niece.'

Iris's jaw dropped. 'Good Lord! How do you know?'

'It's a long story. I'll tell you when you've half an hour to spare.'

'Can't stop now – come for a cuppa about four.'

'Thanks, I will.' Melissa returned to her own front door, her sense of disappointment only partly due to the fact that a chance of buying something truly original as a wedding present for Iris and Jack had been missed. Rachel had appeared to be in some distress; that was surely confirmation – if any were needed – that the dead girl was a member of her family. The family who, to quote Matt's words, weren't being very co-operative. But it was possible that Rachel, in the course of conversation with Melissa whilst displaying her wares, would have revealed – inadvertently, perhaps – something of significance that direct questioning by the police had failed to uncover. Somewhat unreasonably, Melissa found herself blaming Bruce for the lost opportunity.

As she closed the door behind her, she noticed clouds building up on the horizon. Recalling Gloria's prediction of rain and anxious that the precious onion crop, dried and ripened to perfection during the long spell of sunny weather, should not become soaked and muddied, she hurried indoors to change into working clothes. She was in the garden, busy trimming the glossy brown globes before loading them into trays which she arranged on shelves in the lean-to shed at the back of the cottage, when she heard a hesitant voice call, 'Mrs Melissa'. Looking round, she saw Rachel standing on the other side of the fence, a canvas hold-all clutched in front of her with both hands.

Melissa put down the tray she was carrying and hurried across to greet her visitor, exclaiming, 'Rachel! I'm so glad you came back.'

The gipsy made a striking figure, with her black braids looped round her head like a coronet and a bright red shawl draped over the same long black dress she had been wearing the previous day. She held herself straight-backed and carried her head proudly erect on her long, graceful neck. Apart from the slight redness round the eyes that Iris had remarked on, her features were composed.

'Do come in. I'm sorry I was out the first time you called, but I wasn't expecting you so early,' Melissa explained as she ushered her visitor through the front gate, along the path to the back door and into the kitchen.

'We're moving on this afternoon,' said Rachel in a flat, expressionless voice. She stood in the middle of the room, her dark eyes darting appraising glances in all directions.

Melissa pointed to the table. 'Why don't you spread your lace out there while I put the kettle on – I daresay you'd like a cup of tea?'

The gipsy seemed faintly surprised at the offer, but she nodded acceptance and began unloading her hold-all. 'Are you looking for anything special?' she asked as she brought out piece after piece, each more delicate and intricate than the last, holding it up for inspection and then letting it fall, until the table was covered in folds of soft, creamy cotton. 'They are all hand made, except for the edges – I do those on a machine,' she explained.

'They're beautiful,' said Melissa. 'My friend is getting married and I'm looking for a wedding present for her.' She picked up a circular table-cover that had caught her eye and spread it on top of the others. It felt as light as thistledown in her hands. 'She'd love this one. How much is it?'

They agreed on a price; Melissa chose another piece for herself and took her purse from a drawer. It was fortunate, she thought as she handed over the money, that she had drawn cash that morning. It was unlikely that a cheque or credit card would have been acceptable. Seeing Rachel's eyes on the purse, she had a momentary feeling of unease. Ken Harris's warnings about the devious ways of gipsies flashed through her head, but she dismissed them. She had read something of their history and knew of the persecution they had suffered down the ages. Nonetheless, she was careful to return the purse to the drawer before making a pot of tea and fetching cups and saucers while Rachel repacked her hold-all. She made the tea, poured it out and brought it to the table. Rachel accepted the proffered cup with her left hand and at the same time reached out to grasp Melissa's own hand with her right.

'As you've bought some of my wares, I'll read your palm for nothing,' she said.

Melissa had little faith in palmistry, but she was too taken aback to refuse. In any case, she told herself while the gipsy scrutinised the lines on her hand, frowning in concentration, it would do no harm and it would be something to tell Iris later on. She recalled how Rachel had claimed to read in her face that she was 'a story-teller' and gone on to say, 'cleave to the one who truly loves you'. The memory gave her a mild *frisson* and a tingling sensation in her fingers, as if an electric current was passing from the other woman's hand to her own.

'You have known sorrow,' said Rachel abruptly, looking searchingly into Melissa's eyes. 'Loss of a loved one. Rejection by those who loved you.'

Melissa felt her pulse give an unexpected blip, but although the assertion was uncannily accurate she said nothing in reply except, 'Go on.'

'You have a child,' Rachel continued. 'Living, but far away

now.' She spoke with calm authority and without appearing to want confirmation, although the dark eyes sought Melissa's after every statement. 'The future is bright, but the past will one day seek you out. After that there will be peace.' Abruptly, she released the hand she had been holding in a firm but gentle grip and began to drink her tea.

Impulsively, Melissa said, 'I believe that you too have known sorrow.'

The huge brown eyes filmed over. Rachel's voice was unsteady as she replied, 'You have heard about Hannah? From the newspapers, I suppose?'

Melissa nodded. It would, she knew, be unwise to reveal her other sources. 'You said something about a *gadgy* who enticed Hannah away. Do you think this man killed her?'

'Even if he did not, the blame for her death lies at his door. If she had stayed with her own people, she would still be alive. He bewitched her with his tales.' There was a bitter, angry rasp in the gipsy woman's voice and a fierce glitter in her eyes as she spoke.

Melissa experienced a sharp stab of apprehension, but she tried to keep her tone casual as she asked, 'What sort of tales?'

'Of the faraway lands he used to visit. Lands where our forefathers came from, many centuries ago. When Hannah was a child her grandmother used to tell her how they came from the East and wandered the earth, driven from place to place by those who did not understand their way of life. She made her grandmother repeat the tales over and over again, always saying that one day she would visit those lands for herself.'

Rachel put a hand over her eyes, momentarily overcome by grief. When she was calm again, Melissa said, 'I have read about your people. The book said there were some lands – Hungary, for example – where the rulers were less harsh and showed them some compassion.'

'You are right. That is the place above all others that Hannah wanted to see.'

'Do you think that is where she went with the *gadgy*? Do you know who he is . . . does his job take him there?'

It was one question too many. Rachel's features seemed to turn abruptly to stone and without replying she stood up and went to the door. 'It is time for me to leave,' she said.

Recognising that she would reveal nothing further, Melissa politely escorted her to the gate. 'There's no bus into Gloucester this afternoon,' she said. 'How will you get back to your camp?'

'On foot, the way I came. It is not far.'

'It's over five miles,' Melissa pointed out, 'and it may rain. I'll give you a lift if you like. Are you sure?' she went on as Rachel determinedly shook her head.

'Five miles is nothing to a Romany gipsy and we pay little heed to the weather. Farewell, and thank you.' She took a couple of paces, then turned back and said, 'Remember my earlier words. Cleave to the one who truly loves you. And I wish your friend a long and happy marriage.' She strode away, her earrings glinting in the sun and her shawl making a splash of brilliant scarlet against the stone wall that separated the track from the sloping pasture beyond.

Melissa watched until she vanished round a bend, then slowly returned to finish putting away her onions before going back indoors. Her thoughts were racing and she was relieved when four o'clock came and it was time to go next door for the promised 'cuppa'. It would be good to talk things over with Iris before deciding what to do about the new information that Rachel had revealed.

Iris, naturally, was anxious to know exactly what was going on, and between sips of herbal tea and bites from home-made nut cookies, Melissa related the entire story so far, including her show-down with Ken Harris and her latest meeting with Bruce. At the mention of the reporter's name, Iris pulled a face.

'Watch it!' she advised. 'He'll lead you into a scrape if you aren't careful.'

'No he won't. I've already told him I don't want to get involved any further. Just the same,' Melissa went on, 'I think I'll put him in the picture about Hannah wanting to go to Hungary. It might narrow his search for the chap she went off with . . . the way Rachel reacted when I asked about his job makes me think he might be a long-haul truck driver who does runs to Eastern Europe.'

'Aren't you going to tell the police?' demanded Iris as Melissa broke off to take a bite of her cookie.

'Of course,' Melissa said with a sigh.

'What's the problem?'

'If Matt Waters hears about it, he's sure to tell Ken that the information came through me. And Mister Bossyboots will demand to know how I came by it, and—'

'—and then he'll know your gipsy lady has been here,' Iris finished. She gave one of her witch-like cackles, her grey eyes sparkling with impish glee.

'Don't laugh, it isn't funny,' Melissa scolded. 'After the bust-up about my going to the Romany camp, he'll go ape—'

Iris grew serious again. 'Let him,' she advised. 'Can't let these chaps boss us around all the time. Jack would like to vet my clients. Gets worried in case one of 'em tries it on.' Some of Iris's most lucrative commissions were for paintings of the houses of wealthy property-owners. 'He'd like me to work from photos,' she added scornfully. 'Such rot . . . can't get the feel of a place from a photo.'

'That's not quite the same thing. Still, there's no way round it. If I don't tell the police, and the gipsies find that truckie first and beat him up – or worse – I'll feel responsible. I'll just have to risk Ken's wrath.'

'How about calling *Crimestoppers*? No need to give your name then.' The grey eyes were mischievous again.

Melissa laughed and shook her head. 'It's tempting, but I think on balance I'd better do things properly. If I could get a word with DCI Holloway himself, Ken might never find out.'

'So what if he does? You scared of him or something?' Iris taunted.

'Certainly not!' said Melissa indignantly. 'Just the same, I'd rather not have another fight with him just yet.' She pushed aside her empty plate, finished her tea and stood up. 'I'll go home and call the incident-room right away. Oh, by the way,' she added as she reached the door. 'I met Gloria just now and she said something about her Stanley having seen something or someone to do with the case.'

'That's right – forgot to mention it. Says he saw a gipsy in a pub in Gloucester trying to sell stuff to the customers.'

'Was it lace?'

'Gloria didn't say. The landlord threw her out ... got a right mouthful in return by all accounts.'

'I wonder if anyone's told the police about that?'

'No idea.'

'It might have been Hannah. Oh well, I'm sure to hear all about it from Gloria tomorrow. I'll let you know if I hear anything new.'

As it happened, neither DCI Holloway nor Matt Waters was available when Melissa made her call to the police. A woman officer noted the information, took her name, thanked her and said one of the detectives on the case would be in touch.

Next, she called Bruce Ingram. He was out of the office, but she managed to reach him on his mobile phone at a pub not far from the Crossed Keys. He received the news of Hannah Rose's desire to visit Eastern Europe with evident excitement.

'Thanks Mel, that could be a really useful lead,' he said. 'Have you told anyone else?'

'The police, naturally.'

'Yeah, I suppose you had to.'

'Have you picked anything up yet?'

'Not so far. I've tried a couple of pubs near the hotel, but no one I've spoken to remembers anything about a bloke with a gipsy girl, or even a gipsy on her own selling lace. The police have already been here anyway, asking the same questions. I have to leave it for the time being, I've been assigned to another story.'

'Maybe the E-FIT and the picture of the lace will jog a few memories. Why don't you leave it to the police from now on?'

'No chance. Think what a story I'd have if I found that truck driver. "My Life on the Road with a Doomed Romany" – how's that for a headline?'

'Very Gothic,' Melissa said drily. 'Well, it's up to you. Best of luck.'

'Cheers!'

Finally, she called Harris Investigations and learned from Ken's assistant, Tricia Jessop, that he had been called away on a case and had left a message that he would be out of town for a couple of days. 'I tried to call you just now, but your line was engaged,' Tricia explained.

'Fine, no problem,' said Melissa. She put down the phone with a feeling of relief. With any luck, the news of Rachel's visit might never get back to him. Then she mentally scolded herself for being a coward. 'What's it got to do with him anyway?' she said to herself.

The answer, although she did not know it at the time, was, 'Quite a lot.'

Chapter Eight

Soon after five o'clock, the bank of cloud that had been slowly spreading from the west slid quietly across the sun. The temperature sank, the golden autumn light faded to sombre grey and within a short time a steady, soaking rain was falling on the thirsty earth. Melissa's relief at seeing the drought broken at last was tempered with concern for Rachel. Picturing the gipsy trudging the lanes with her hold-all, water streaming down her face and dripping from her black braids, her scarlet shawl saturated and her long skirt clinging wetly round her legs, she wished she had been a little more pressing with her offer of a lift. Then she reminded herself that it was three hours since Rachel had set off and the walk back to the Romany's encampment should have taken little more than two. It crossed her mind at the same time that although the gipsies were still living in horse-drawn caravans, they almost certainly had some motorised transport as well. Despite Rachel's claim to have reached the village on foot and her declared intention of returning the same way, Melissa found herself wondering whether that was really the case and whether she had been wise to accept without question everything Rachel had told her. She could imagine all too well what Ken Harris would have said. *That's just the sort of yarn these people spin. It's ten to one she had a car – probably neither taxed nor insured – parked somewhere outside the village.* Then she reproached herself for her mistrust. It was true that the gipsy had been unwilling to reveal anything that might help to identify her young relative's abductor, but that in itself was no reason to suspect her of lying about anything else.

There was, however, some reason to feel uneasy about what lay behind the reticence. The more she thought about it, the more convinced Melissa was becoming that Hannah's relatives were intent on settling their own score. If, as she had been led to believe, she would soon be receiving a call from one of the officers investigating Hannah's murder, she would do her best to sell the idea that whoever had taken the girl away in the first place was in serious danger from men living on the fringe of society who were hell-bent on exacting a private revenge for the wrong done to one of their number and – by extension – to the whole family. Rachel had mentioned that her people were moving on that afternoon, but although she had given no indication of how far or in which direction they would be travelling, there was little doubt in Melissa's mind that they would remain within striking distance of the place where Hannah had last been seen until, one way or another, her killer had been brought to book.

When, soon after six o'clock, the call came through, it was Detective Sergeant Waters on the line. 'Thanks for the info you passed to us, Mel,' he said. 'Will it be okay if I call in for a quick word later on? I'll be coming quite close to your village on my way home.'

'Sure, Matt.' It was a relief to know that DCI Holloway was not following up her call in person. He was unlikely to have taken her fears seriously; he prided himself on dealing in facts and not allowing himself to be swayed by hunches for which no practical justification could be produced – especially when the source of the hunch was female.

'Say around seven?' Matt suggested.

'That'd be fine.'

'Right, see you then.' There was a pause before he added,

somewhat diffidently, 'If you've nothing else arranged, perhaps you'd care to go out for a drink after we've had
our chat?'

The invitation took Melissa by surprise. She had come to
know Matt several years ago through her involvement in
a case on which Ken Harris had been engaged. The two
men had kept up their friendship after Harris's retirement
from the police and the three of them had shared the odd
social occasion, but this was the first time Matt had asked
her out. She knew nothing of his private life, apart from the
fact that he was a widower living on his own and that his
high personal regard for his superior officer was in no small
part due to the support the former DCI Harris had given
him during his wife's last illness. It would be totally out of
character for him to repay that support by making a pass at
his friend's lover behind his back. There must be an ulterior
motive; it would be interesting to know what it was. So she
kept her tone light and matter-of-fact as she replied, 'Thank
you, that'd be nice. See you later.'

It was almost eight o'clock when Matt arrived at Hawthorn
Cottage. He apologised for being late without giving an explanation, followed Melissa into her sitting-room, declined her
suggestion of coffee and settled down with his notebook.

'I understand from PC Sheldon's report that you have
reason to believe the dead girl was anxious to travel to
Eastern Europe, and that the man she ran away with could
be a long-distance truck driver?' he began.

'That's right.' Without mentioning Rachel's visit, Melissa
recounted what she had learned of the girl's fascination with
her grandmother's stories of their people's history and the
lands where they had originated, together with her aunt's
claim that the man had 'bewitched' her with tales of his
own. 'I'm very much afraid they mean to do him harm,'
she went on earnestly. 'That's why I believe it's vital that

the police find him before they do and why I called the incident-room as soon as I realised—' She broke off, aware that the intensity of her feelings was beginning to show.

Matt opened a folder he had brought with him and was scanning the top sheet in it while she spoke. 'I don't see any reference to the man's possible occupation in your original statement,' he remarked. 'Or the supplementary statement you made this morning, after our talk yesterday.' His steel-blue eyes fixed her with the searching gaze that seemed to be a part of every police officer's stock-in-trade.

Melissa shifted uncomfortably in her chair. 'It didn't occur to me at the time,' she said lamely.

'And what about the grandmother's tales and the girl's apparent wanderlust?' Matt persisted. 'You didn't tell us about them either. Why was that?'

'Because I only learned about them this afternoon,' she admitted reluctantly.

Matt's eyebrows lifted. 'How did that come about?'

It had been naïve to suppose that she could conceal her invitation to Rachel. It would get back to Ken, of course, and he'd be scathing about it, wanting to know if she had missed any items of value and generally laying down the law about the folly of inviting vagrants into her home. It would lead to another spat, but there was nothing she could do about it now. So she met Matt's gaze with a hint of defiance as she replied, 'When Bruce and I visited the Romany camp, before any of us knew about Hannah's murder, I watched Rachel making lace and asked if she had any to sell. She had none there at the time and I arranged for her to call this afternoon and bring some to show me. We got talking, and—'

'You're saying she came here at your invitation?' Matt interrupted, his voice expressing both surprise and disapproval.

'That's right.' Melissa was about to launch into an explanation of her search for a wedding present for Iris, but checked herself. Didn't she have a perfect right to issue invitations to whoever she chose? Why should she have to justify everything she did?

'I see.' Matt closed the folder and made a note in his book. 'Do I take it, then, that the girl's aunt told you she had run off to Eastern Europe with a truck driver?'

'On the contrary, she clammed up as soon as I started asking questions about the man and his job. It was what she told me earlier in the conversation that put the idea into my head. It occurred to me that meeting someone with first-hand knowledge of the countries where her ancestors came from would have fired Hannah's imagination and made it a doddle for him to persuade her to go with him. Don't you agree?'

'It's certainly worth considering.'

'And another thing,' Melissa hurried on, 'the fact that her own family still travel in horse-drawn vans when almost all the others have these fancy motor caravans, and move around much faster, might have made the opportunity to go further afield even more inviting.'

'You may well be right.' The detective made a few more notes. 'Thanks Melissa, I'll pass this on to Mr Holloway.'

He was in the act of closing his notebook when Melissa put a hand on his arm. 'Matt, you will impress on him that Rachel's family are looking for the man as well, won't you?'

'Have you any proof of that?'

'Not proof, no, but it would be the obvious thing for them to do. I've read something about their customs . . . they have their own courts, their own traditional ways of punishing those who've harmed any of their people.'

'Aren't you being a little melodramatic? This is the twentieth century, not the Middle Ages. And in any case, this chap – whoever he is – might not have seen her for months – might even turn out to have been abroad when the girl was killed.'

'But don't you see, that wouldn't make any difference to the way they feel towards him. Even if he has an alibi, even if he can prove he's done nothing to harm Hannah, they still hold him responsible.'

'Did this woman say so?'

'Yes, she said something like, "Even if he did not kill her himself, the blame lies at his door." And you should have seen the anger, the *hatred* in her eyes when she spoke. I'm seriously concerned that those people will attack him if they find him before you do.'

'I'll certainly mention your suspicions, but unless they've actually been heard to utter threats against him, there's not much we can do.'

Melissa gave a sigh of resignation. 'I suppose not. What about the two men you're holding? Have you got anything out of them?'

Matt hesitated. 'I shouldn't really tell you—' he began, but Melissa broke in eagerly.

'Oh come on, you'd tell Ken if he was here.'

'And you'd soon worm it out of him, no doubt,' said Matt with a chuckle. 'I'll have to bear that in mind in future.'

'Please!' Melissa coaxed.

'As long as you promise not to pass it on to that journalist friend of yours until it's been officially released?'

She was on the point of retorting that it was more likely to be Bruce who fed her titbits of information that the papers didn't print, rather than the other way round, but decided that would hardly be circumspect. 'I promise,' she assured Matt. 'So what's new?'

'We've turned up some fresh evidence and applied for permission to hold the two of them for further questioning. That's what made me late.'

'What evidence was that?'

'When we searched their van we found some jewellery that looked as if it might have belonged to a gipsy woman and one of our lads was sent to the Romanys' camp to see if Hannah's family could identify it. All the caravans had gone and it took him quite a while to catch up with them.'

'Yes, Rachel told me they were moving on. Where are they camped now?'

'On a farm somewhere near Chipping Campden. Seems they go there every year to do tree and hedge trimming and the like. They tend to stay in the area until the end of October for the Stow Fair.'

Melissa nodded eagerly. 'Which we've already established is where Hannah met the man she eloped with.'

'We haven't *established* anything about him,' Matt pointed out. 'Everything about him is pure guesswork at the moment. What is certain is that Hannah's aunt and uncle positively identified the earrings and bracelets we showed them as belonging to their niece.'

'How did they react . . . the relatives, I mean?'

Matt shrugged. 'They got pretty stroppy when our chap explained that we have to keep the stuff as evidence. They demanded its return there and then . . . it got quite heated at one stage.'

'What about the two in custody . . . does this mean you've got enough to charge them?'

Matt shrugged. 'Mr Holloway seems to think we've got a case, but to my mind it's all too circumstantial. These blokes are sticking to their story that the body was in the freezer when they opened it and so far we've uncovered nothing to disprove their claim. They admit knowing the girl and having sex with her on more than one occasion, but they flatly deny killing her. As for taking the jewellery, their attitude is . . . what does a dead girl want with gold earrings and the like?'

'That's pretty callous,' Melissa commented. 'Matt, you will go on looking for this truck driver?'

'We don't know for certain he's a truck driver,' Matt pointed out. 'But of course we'll continue our efforts to trace him, whatever his occupation. We're anxious to get a complete picture of Hannah's movements prior to her death and this guy may be able to help us. But I have to be honest with you, Mel, we haven't the man-power to follow up every lead in person. What we're doing is appealing to the public for information.'

'Surely you could at least contact long-distance hauliers—'

'I've no doubt Mr Holloway will consider that possibility.' Melissa thought she detected a trace of weary reproof in Matt's tone, as if he considered that she had been pushing her ideas a shade too hard but was too polite to say so. Her confidence was only partially restored when he added, 'We'll certainly report what you've told us at tomorrow's press briefing and make an appeal on radio and TV. Hopefully, either the man himself, or someone who can identify him, will come forward.'

'Why wait till tomorrow? If you call in right away, you might be in time to get it on tonight's TV news.'

Matt's face was a study as he pulled out his mobile phone and made for the front door. 'Anything for a quiet life!' he said resignedly. 'Give me five minutes and then we'll go and have that drink I promised you.'

Chapter Nine

Rocky Wilkins strode naked out of the bathroom into the bedroom, towelling himself with grunts of satisfaction. It was good to be home, to look forward to a few days of Julie's cooking followed by an evening drink in his local and the comfort of his own bed, instead of the fry-ups in motorway service restaurants and dossing in the cramped bunk in his cab. Being a long-haul truck driver had its advantages, especially since he'd bought his own outfit and gone solo, but it got lonely at times. He hadn't even managed to pick up a decent bit of crumpet on this last trip. Still, if Julie was in a good mood, he might get a bit of legit – if not very exciting – sex. *If* she was in a good mood . . . but you could never bank on it these days. Never had been able to, when he came to think about it . . . didn't seem to think it was important or understand how much it meant to a man. He reckoned that if he didn't touch her from one week to another it wouldn't bother her – although she got jealous as hell if she caught him so much as looking at anyone else. Still, she cooked like an angel, never complained if he brought his mates home and kept the house like a new pin. You couldn't have everything – not from one woman, anyway.

Thinking of sex made him cast his mind back with nostalgia to the fun he'd had with that little gippo number he'd taken along on a trip to Eastern Europe in the spring. She'd been something special. What was her name now?

Hattie ... Harriet ... no, Hannah, that was it. Hot as hell with her red lips, come-hither eyes and soft brown limbs, and the black hair that tumbled round her shoulders and curled invitingly in other, secret places, soft as velvet under his touch. A nice little earner she'd turned out to be too. It was a pity it had to end the way it always did; of all the women he'd picked up – and disposed of – during his travels, she was the one for whom he felt the odd pang of regret. Mostly, he'd have been hard put to it to recall their faces – leave alone their names – once he'd done with them, but Hannah stood out in his memory like a peacock among starlings.

She'd come knocking on the door one day, last October or thereabouts – hard to believe it was almost a year ago. He was at home between runs and alone in the house. Remembering the arch glances she shot at him from under those long silky lashes, he reckoned he could have had her there and then, only he knew Julie would be back any minute and there'd have been trouble if he'd invited the girl over the front doorstep. So he'd kept her out in the porch while she showed him the lace she was selling, taking the filmy bits and pieces out of her hold-all and lifting them up for him to see, holding them in front of her in that sexy way she had, as if she were about to do the dance of the seven veils with them. Just thinking about it was enough to give him the start of an erection.

He hadn't been able to resist chatting her up a bit, while keeping a wary eye out for Julie's return. He guessed she was from one of the gipsy families who congregated in the area twice a year for the horse fair and asked her casually where she and her people came from, expecting her to say Stratford or Nottingham or whatever place they stayed in last. Instead, she said, 'Hungary' and went on to spin some yarn about how her ancestors spent hundreds of years wandering across Europe before getting to England.

When he told her he'd only got back a couple of days earlier from a run to Budapest, and pointed to the truck that he kept parked in the lay-by across the way, she reacted like a child taken to see Father Christmas, peppering him with questions about the country and the people.

He'd just finished processing some black and white pictures he'd taken along the way and he went and fetched them to show to her. She was so entranced that he gave her one to keep. Then she asked his name and he told her it was Petroc, not bothering to mention that no one ever called him anything but Rocky. That had really excited her; she'd given a little squeal and exclaimed, 'Is that Hungarian? Do you have Romany blood?' He hadn't denied it; it seemed a shame to disappoint her although the truth was that his mother was from the West Country and had insisted on naming him for some obscure Cornish saint. Then Hannah asked to read his palm and wouldn't take no for an answer, grabbing one of his stubby-fingered hands between both her small brown ones. He'd been happy to let it lie there while she jabbered on about how his Romany heritage had made him choose a life of long journeyings, until he spotted Julie turn into the lane on her bike and hastily pulled away, grabbed a set of lace mats at random, paid for them and sent the girl packing.

He never expected to see her again, but towards the end of May, happening to be at home between jobs and knowing the gipsies would be gathering for the spring horse fair, he drove to Stow with his camera, parked the car and wandered around among the caravans and the nags in search of some interesting shots. Quite by accident, he came across a van parked in a lay-by on the edge of the town . . . and who should be sitting outside in the sunshine but Hannah, making lace on a cushion. He could still see the look of surprise and wonderment on her face when she spotted him. The shot he took of her turned out to be one of the best he'd ever done and he went back the next day to give her a print, but this time there was no chance of a word with the girl herself. There'd been an older woman hovering in the background and then a fierce-looking bloke – probably her Dad – had appeared from nowhere, snatched the photo and ordered the girl into the caravan. Rocky remembered the look the man had given him . . . there was a real 'hands-off-my-daughter' warning in the fierce black eyes.

The sound of a key in the front door broke into his day-dreaming. Julie was home. He hurriedly finished drying himself and reached for the cologne, splashing it generously all over his smooth, muscular body. He was on the point of pulling on his underpants, but on the off-chance that pleasure at seeing him home after several nights away would put her in a compliant mood, he threw them aside, marched out on to the landing and called down the stairs, 'I'm up here love. Come and see what I've brought for you this time!'

She was happy enough to see him, kissed him warmly and told him she'd made his favourite steak pie for supper, but otherwise her mood was far from compliant. She was pushed for time, she told him, on account of having to go to a meeting later on. She tried to make up for it by asking him about his latest trip while doing the vegetables to go with the pie, but when he suggested going out for a drink after the meeting she made the excuse that she didn't know how long it would go on and she was already tired after a long shift at the supermarket, serving behind the delicatessen counter. So Rocky, feeling distinctly hard done by, went to the pub on his own.

Tuesday was always a quiet evening in the Golden Bell and this evening there was no one there he knew apart from Rosie, who had served behind the bar for as long as he had been a regular there. During that time there had been more than one change of licensee and the present couple had smartened the place up quite a bit and made a few alterations, but they'd been sharp enough to realise that Rosie was almost as much a fixture as the pump handles. She was a great character and the locals loved her, sixty if she was a day but with a figure still good enough to make a man's eyes light up . . . and she knew how to make the best of herself. Always ready for a laugh, especially with the men, was Rosie. It was generally reckoned she'd been around and enjoyed herself in her time. Rocky suspected that Julie didn't approve of her although she never actually said anything; it was more the way she looked down her nose at some of the back-chat that went on. He had to be a bit careful what he said to Rosie when Julie was with him. But tonight he was by himself and he didn't have to worry.

'You're a real sight for sore eyes tonight, Rosie my love,' he said while she drew his pint. 'Look younger every time I come in, you do. What's your secret then?'

Rosie beamed and her brown eyes beneath the carefully mascara'd lashes sparkled. 'Maybe it's sweet talk from the likes of you,' she said roguishly. She set the brimming tankard on the bar, took the money and gave him his change, brushing her fingers against his in that suggestive way she had. She might be going on for twice his age, but he could easily fancy her. 'So where's your good lady tonight?' she asked, her bold eyes twinkling.

'Off to some meeting.' He took a long pull of beer and wiped his mouth with the back of his hand. 'Planning the harvest supper, so she said. I asked her to join me here when it was over, but she thought it might go on a bit.'

Rosie clicked her tongue in sympathy. 'Ah yes, those church folks do like their bit of chat, don't they? You wouldn't think there was that much to talk about . . . it's the same people who organise the supper every year.'

Rocky nodded, his face buried in his tankard. 'You'd think

they could do it in their sleep, without all these meetings,' he commented when he came up for air.

'And tonight your first night home for nearly a week, too. What a shame. She could've found something much better to do with her time.' Rosie gave a suggestive wink and, as if by way of compensation for what she plainly saw as a serious lack of consideration on Julie's part, planted her folded arms on the bar and treated him to a glimpse of her generous cleavage.

Rocky eyed it appreciatively. 'Been any excitement round here lately?' he asked casually.

'Only the freezer murder. I guess you read about that.'

Rocky shook his head and took another long draught of beer. 'Haven't seen a paper for days.' He pushed the empty tankard across the bar for a refill, his eyes still feasting on the expanse of swelling flesh.

'Someone topped a girl and hid the body in an old freezer,' Rosie explained as the beer gushed and foamed from the pump. 'Some kids found it. Been dead several days, so they say.'

'Near here, was it?'

'Langley Woods, about twenty miles away . . . but they seem to think the girl had been working in a hotel in Stow.'

'Any idea who did it?'

'I believe they've arrested a couple of gippos, but there's something in tonight's paper about the police wanting more information. Here.' She reached behind the bar, picked up the evening edition of the *Gazette* and gave it to him. 'Read it for yourself. Excuse me.' She moved away to serve some customers who had just entered.

Rocky glanced round the bar to see if there was a familiar face, but found none. He took the paper over to an empty table in the far corner and sat down to enjoy his second pint.

*　　*　　*

'Where d'you fancy going?' asked Matt as he held the passenger door open for Melissa to get into the car.

'There's a pub on the way to Andoversford – the Golden Bell, I think it's called – that's recently changed hands.' She settled down and clipped on her seat belt. 'It was getting a bit run down, but I read in the *Gazette* the other day that the new owners have smartened it up. Shall we try it?'

'Why not?' He started the engine and drove slowly along the track towards the lane. Jack's car stood at the door of Elder Cottage and the downstairs lights were on. The sitting-room curtains were not yet drawn and Melissa had the impression that Jack had only just arrived. He was in the act of handing his coat to Iris, who took it and left the room while he sat down in a chair with his back to the window. There was no physical contact between the couple, yet the brief glance they exchanged during that moment was enough to reveal the depth of intimacy between them. Melissa sat without speaking as Matt headed along the lane towards the main road, reflecting – not without a trace of envy – on the subtle change she had observed in her friend since her engagement. Outwardly, she was unchanged, but underlying the prickly personality, impish humour and laconic turn of phrase was a new air of confidence – the confidence of a woman at peace with herself; a woman who, having considered long and hard beforehand, had taken a momentous decision and was untroubled by the smallest doubt.

Matt broke into her thoughts by saying, 'I've been thinking over what you were telling me about the dead girl's ancestry. There was a black and white photograph among her possessions in the hotel that from the style of architecture might have been taken in some East European or maybe Russian city. Her relations deny having seen it before. Not that it's been much help . . . we haven't been able to identify the location and there's nothing on the back to tell us when it was taken or where it was processed.'

Melissa's interest was immediately aroused. 'That's unusual, isn't it?' she commented. 'Most commercial processors put some kind of coding on the back of their prints.'

'Exactly. It suggests that whoever took it did his or her own processing. Plenty of people do.'

'So we could be looking for a long-distance truckie whose hobby is photography?'

'We?' Matt took his eyes off the road for a moment to give Melissa a keen glance. Although the light was failing rapidly, there was still enough for her to read concern in his expression. 'I hope you aren't thinking of doing any unofficial sleuthing on your own, Mel.'

'No.' *Not on my own . . . but if I pass this latest titbit to Bruce, who knows? It's obvious that finding this man isn't getting top priority from the police.*

'Good.' Matt's voice held a note of finality, as if the monosyllable was something more than a mere expression of approval. Melissa felt a sneaking suspicion that there was more to this invitation than a friendly gesture or expression of thanks for her help, but all she said was, 'Take the next turning to the right and then left at the T-junction. The pub's about two miles along.'

'Thanks.' Having completed the manoeuvre, Matt said casually, 'D'you find the time drags when Ken's away?'

The suspicion grew a little stronger, but all she said was, 'Not particularly. I've always got plenty to do. I'm working on a book and just now I'm trying to get the garden straight before the really cold weather sets in.'

'Ah yes, always something to do in a garden, isn't there? Mine always seems to be one jump ahead of me.'

No reply seemed to be called for and there was another silence until Melissa said, 'There's the pub,' and pointed ahead at the illuminated sign that shone like a miniature moon in the gathering dusk.

The car park was almost empty and there was no one else about as they made their way to the entrance, their path illuminated by mock-Victorian street lamps that cast a warm glow on the creamy gravel. The roof of the ancient building had been newly thatched, the doors and windows freshly painted and the name The Golden Bell in gilded letters mounted on the wall above the stone porch. Well-tended tubs of geraniums, still blooming bravely despite the autumnal nip in the air, were ranged along the front of the building. Matt gave an appreciative nod.

'Looks promising,' he commented. 'Let's hope the beer's as good as the surroundings.' He pushed the door open and stood aside for her to enter.

The impression inside was of warmth and an almost clinical brightness. The stone walls had been cleaned and repointed, the oak beams across the low, whitewashed ceiling treated with preservative and the floor covered in a brand-new crimson carpet. A log fire burned in a wrought-iron basket beneath a massive stone chimney-piece, the flames reflected in a myriad highly polished surfaces: the legs of the chairs, bar stools and tables, the collection of copper kettles ranged on either side of the stone hearth and various copper and brass artefacts dotted around the walls. Concealed loudspeakers played anodyne 'mood music' of the kind Iris used as a background to her yoga classes.

'Very nice,' said Matt, glancing round. 'Could do without *that*, though,' he added in an undertone, jerking his head upwards at the nearest speaker.

'Can't get away from it nowadays,' Melissa agreed resignedly.

A vase of scarlet and yellow dahlias stood on the bar, their brilliance almost eclipsed by the flamboyant colouring of the woman who was filling a tankard with beer while being chatted up by a heavily built, leather-jacketed man. He was leaning on the counter openly admiring her cleavage while bemoaning the fact that his wife had deserted him on his first evening home for a week. There were only a handful of other customers: a couple of ruddy-faced men, probably farmers, and a dowdy-looking middle-aged couple with a dog who sat silently contemplating two half-consumed drinks.

Melissa asked for a spritzer and, at Matt's suggestion, went over to a table near the fire. As she sat down, she saw the barmaid hand a newspaper to her flirtatious customer, who came and settled with it in the opposite corner. He had a round, slightly pugnacious face, not especially handsome but with a brooding, sensual quality that many women would find attractive. She decided that he might serve as a model for a character in a future novel and she observed him covertly, noting the carefully styled brown hair, the rather prominent eyes set in lightly tanned features, the strong hands sprinkled with brown hair and the square-cut fingernails. His checked shirt was open at the neck beneath the unbuttoned leather jacket, revealing a narrow leather thong that hinted at the presence of a medallion nestling seductively on his chest; his fawn slacks were sharply creased and his leather moccasins looked brand-new. He was probably awash with the latest thing in body lotion as well. It was easy to imagine him scanning the colour supplements, looking for the latest trendy gear to impress likely females. An undoubted womaniser who'd do his best to score with whoever took his fancy, even if the signet ring on his left hand meant that he had a wife. Not hard up for a bob or two either, judging from the heavy gold wrist-watch that caught the light as he raised the tankard in his left hand. Over the rim, he caught Melissa's eye and winked. Disconcerted, she hastily looked away.

Matt arrived with their drinks. He settled in the chair beside her, raised his tankard of ale and said, 'Cheers,' and she raised her own glass in reply. He took a long pull and gave an approving nod. 'That's the real McCoy – knocks spots off all the mass-produced rubbish that passes for beer in some pubs. How's your spritzer?'

'Fine, thanks.'

'So what have you got lined up for the next few days?'

'While Ken's away, you mean?' He looked slightly abashed, and she went on, 'Matt, I have a feeling there's something behind this little jolly.'

'I don't know what you mean.'

'I think you do. Either you're about to give me some sort of lecture, a semi-official warning' – here she paused deliberately to gauge his reaction and saw his grip on the handle of his tankard momentarily tighten – 'or you're taking advantage of your best friend's absence to make a pass at me.' Matt hurriedly put down his drink, his eyebrows shooting up in alarm, and Melissa burst out laughing. 'Don't worry, that wasn't a serious suggestion . . . but I'm on the right track, aren't I?'

'Well—' For once, the slightly stolid police sergeant appeared disconcerted. Melissa sipped her drink and waited. It was her turn to use the steady, unwavering gaze technique and after a moment he shrugged and said, 'It's pretty obvious to both Ken and me that you're more than a little interested in this freezer murder . . . and your curiosity has got you into some pretty hairy situations in the past—'

'Just a minute!' From being mildly amused, Melissa felt her hackles rising. 'Did Ken put you up to this?'

'Put me up to what?'

'Warning me off? Telling me to be a good girl and stick to my desk and my garden while he's not here to keep an eye on me. Is that it?'

Matt made a gesture of capitulation. 'I told him you'd see through it,' he admitted. 'Don't be angry with him, Mel . . . it's only because he cares about you. He—'

'He wants me to ask him for an exeat every time I go out of the house.'

'Oh come on, that's a bit of an exaggeration—'

'All right, it is, but I'm not going to have him – or you – telling me what to do. Anyway, what's the problem with this particular case? You've got your killers . . . all I'm saying is you should be concerned for the safety of the man the girl ran away with and—'

'—and if we don't throw every available man into the hunt for him, you'll try and track him down yourself,' he interrupted. 'That's what you have in mind, isn't it?' This time, his eyes met hers squarely and accusingly.

'I never said so.' It was her turn to hedge. She glanced away from Matt and her eye fell once more on the man opposite. He was in the act of refolding the newspaper the barmaid had given him and as she watched he got up and left, dropping it on the bar in passing with a curt word of thanks. It struck her that he appeared put out, as if something in the paper had upset or annoyed him. It was just such an idly observed reaction that would normally set her imagination on the track of a new twist to a plot, but at the moment she was feeling too irritated at the apparent conspiracy between her lover and his former colleague to give it a second thought. She picked up her glass and drained it. 'Well, you've said your piece. Shall we go?'

'You're angry, aren't you?'

'I don't like being told what to do. You can tell Ken you did your best—'

'—and got a flea in my ear.' Matt gave a rueful grin and stood up. 'Okay, Mel . . . but do be careful. At least, promise me one thing.'

'What's that?'

'If you do happen to stumble on something, let us know at once.'

'Of course – don't I always?'

Shortly after they turned out of the car park and headed

back towards Upper Benbury, Melissa noticed a man standing at the roadside, leaning over a gate. She had only a fleeting glimpse of his back, but there was something familiar about the hunched shoulders and lowered head. She was almost certain it was the man she had noticed in the bar.

Chapter Ten

Julie Wilkins set out for the meeting of the organising committee of Carston Village Hall in an uneasy frame of mind. The way Rocky's mouth had set in a hard, sullen line when she not only declined to have sex with him immediately she arrived home, but also announced that she would be going out after supper, meant that he would probably spend the evening in the Golden Bell, most likely pouring out his imaginary troubles to that awful brassy blonde who was old enough to be his mother but who made eyes at him whenever he set foot in the place. Not that Julie could blame her in a way; her Rocky was good-looking enough to turn any woman's head . . . but really, at her age . . . you'd think she'd save it for someone a bit older. Still, there it was, some women seemed to enjoy flashing it around, although what the attraction was in what Julie's mother had always delicately referred to as 'The three Es' – or, if she was feeling daring, 'Ess Ee Eks' – was a mystery to her. The other girls on the deli counter at the supermarket where Julie worked made out they enjoyed it and seemed to think there was something odd about anyone who didn't. For her part, she simply couldn't understand what they found so attractive in a few seconds of clumsy pawing of their private parts followed by a man's dead weight half crushing the breath out of them while he heaved and shoved and grunted for a few minutes before rolling off and falling into a catatonic slumber.

Marriage, as envisaged by Julie before her wedding, would

bc an extension of her favourite childhood game of playing house. Domesticity delighted her; her one ambition as she grew from adolescence to womanhood was to have her own home where she could clean and polish, bake and sew, wash and iron and generally keep everything spick and span. She had resigned herself to Rocky's demands in bed, looking on them as the price to be paid for the fulfilment of her dream. Right from the start he was earning good money as a driver with a local haulage company; what he gave her plus what she earned in her part-time job meant that they had a comfortable home and wanted for nothing. And once he had his own outfit and began landing contracts that took him farther afield, they were even better off. It also meant that he was often away for several days, sometimes a couple of weeks on end. Although at such times Julie missed the cooking and cleaning and waiting on him that she enjoyed so much, it was bliss to have the bed to herself.

She missed the evenings out as well. Rocky loved company and it gave her enormous pleasure to be seen with him because his good looks and his charm meant that other women envied her. She had to keep an eye on him, though. Quite often she had to step in sharpish when some wannabee Armani model with a couple of vodka and tonics inside her started fluttering her eyelashes at him. She hoped there'd be no unattached females in the Bell this evening. Rosie would be behind the bar as usual of course, but she was only an irritant, not a serious threat to anyone's marriage. With an effort, Julie dismissed the matter from her mind in order to concentrate on ideas for the harvest supper.

When she reached Carston Village Hall she found her fellow committee members clustered round a table on which someone had spread that evening's edition of the *Gloucester Gazette*. They were peering down at it, shaking their heads, making tutting noises and – almost reluctantly, it seemed – declaring that they had 'Never set eyes on her'. As Julie approached the group, the chairwoman, Mrs Grantley-Newcombe, was saying with a sigh, 'Well, it doesn't look as if she ever came to Carston.' Then she spotted Julie. 'Ah, there you are, Mrs Wilkins. That's fine, we can start our meeting now we're all here.'

'I'm sorry I'm a bit late. Rocky just got back from a trip up North,' Julie explained. 'Had to give him his supper before I came out. He was none too pleased at being left on his own, but I told him I couldn't let the committee down. What's all the excitement about?'

Mrs Grantley-Newcombe reopened the paper, which she had been in the act of refolding, and held it out to Julie. 'There,' she said, jabbing at the page with a bejewelled finger. 'The latest in the "Body in the Freezer" murder.'

Julie did not share the general *penchant* for the macabre and sensational, but out of politeness she took the paper and made a show of interest in the report, aware that everyone was watching her. Reluctantly, she glanced at the likeness of the dead woman that stared up at her, shuddering a little and screwing up her mouth in distaste. She was about to hand it back when something made her take a closer look. It was only an artist's impression, but it struck a chord. She studied it, frowning, for several seconds, trying to think where she might have seen that face – or one very like it – before.

'It says she's been going round to people's houses, trying to sell lace,' said Mrs Grantley-Newcombe. 'I don't suppose she called on you, by any chance? The police are appealing for witnesses.'

At the mention of lace, Julie gave a little gasp and clapped a hand to her mouth. Immediately, she became the centre of attention.

'You've seen her?' 'Where?' 'When?' 'You must tell the police!' Questions and commands came thick and fast, tinged with a certain jealousy that someone who did not actually live in Carston, but in one of the outlying villages in the scattered parish, should have been so favoured. The only person who did not appreciate the turn of events was Julie herself. She hastily sat down, her heart thumping and her hands trembling.

'I don't know for certain . . . it may not be the same person at all,' she said in an unsteady voice. Desperately she played for time. 'It was a long time ago, several months in fact.' Under eager questioning, she admitted seeing a woman in a scarlet shawl walking in front of her along the lane. 'It was months ago,' she repeated.

'So what makes you think it was the same woman?' someone asked.

'I don't know, really, I think it must have been the shawl . . . gipsies wear shawls, don't they . . . and she was carrying a sort of hold-all. I just had the impression—' Julie's voice grew stronger as it became clearer in her mind what line she must follow, '—that she might have been selling something. It could have been lace . . . she might even have called at my house, only of course I wasn't at home . . . I was just coming back from work, you see.' *But Rocky was at home, wasn't he . . . and you know he spoke to her . . . and bought some of her lace.*

'But you'll tell the police anyway, won't you dear?' said Mrs Grantley-Newcombe.

'Yes of course, but as I said, it was a long time ago . . . some time last year now I come to think of it. It was probably someone quite different—' *Oh no it wasn't, it was the same girl, you know it was.*

'Well, we're all here so we can start now,' said Mrs Grantley-Newcombe for the second time and the discussion, in which Julie forced herself to join, turned to matters of more immediate importance such as whether they should serve braised pork or chicken casserole with the jacket potatoes, what choice of desserts they would offer and how many bottles of wine they should order. Somehow, she managed to get through the meeting without drawing any further attention to herself and to respond naturally when Mrs Grantley-Newcombe reminded her, as they were stacking the chairs and checking that all the radiators were turned off at the end of the meeting, of her promise to inform the police of her possible sighting of the murder victim. She exchanged cheerful goodbyes with everyone as they went their separate ways and her hands were steady on the wheel as she drove the short distance home.

It was not until the front door closed behind her that the fear of impending disaster, resolutely thrust into the back of her mind for the past couple of hours, rose like a tidal wave and all but overwhelmed her. She began trembling so violently that she could hardly undo the buttons of her jacket. In the kitchen, thinking that a cup of strong tea would help to steady her nerves, it was all she could do to hold the kettle under the tap and when the water boiled half of it missed the teapot and spilled on the floor. The house was warm, but when she at last held a mug of scalding tea to her lips, her teeth were chattering so much that it was several seconds before she managed to swallow a mouthful.

It was only ten o'clock; Rocky was almost certainly down at the pub and was unlikely to leave for at least another hour. It was only a few minutes' walk away and normally she would have joined him there, partly for the company but also to make sure no woman was trying to get off with him. But not this evening, not with the terrible anxiety and doubt that was swamping her, driving every other thought from her mind. This evening she could only sit and wait, half desperate for him to come home and allay her fears, half in dread of what nightmarish revelations her questions might uncover.

She took her tea into the living-room and switched on the television, just in time to catch the news. She was about to change channels when she heard the announcer read the headlines; the freezer murder was the first item. She sat in a state of stark terror at the sight of the face gazing out from the screen like a grotesque mask, while the announcer said, 'It is believed that the dead girl, who is known to have had an interest in visiting Eastern Europe, may have been given a lift there some months ago by a long-distance truck driver based in the area round Stow-on-the-Wold. The same driver – or possibly another – may have brought her back to England. If so, the police would like to hear from them, or from anyone else who has information about the victim's movements.'

With a groan of despair, Julie switched off the set and buried her face in her hands, while past events unrolled in her memory like an old movie. A couple of years ago Rocky had converted the attic into a darkroom. A keen amateur photographer, he spent hours up there, processing his own films. He had joined a local camera club and won several prizes; some of his pictures had been published in the *Gazette* and proudly displayed by Julie to her colleagues and friends. Her pride in his success was tempered by her resentment at being forbidden to enter the darkroom, on the pretext that everything was arranged just so and he wasn't going to have it disturbed by a woman with a mania for tidying up and dusting everything in sight. Julie had accepted this without question at first, but when she mentioned it to the girls at work, one of them winked and said the real reason was that he didn't want her to see his dirty pictures. This suggestion she had hotly repudiated at the time, but the suspicion that there might be some truth in it had gnawed away at her mind until once, when he was away overnight, she had cautiously lowered the ladder that led to the attic and searched through his albums, almost holding her breath as she went through each one for fear of displacing it by a fraction of an inch. The search had revealed nothing sensational – hardly anything in fact, that Julie had not already seen. Rocky was always ready to show off his work. But then she had come across a series of shots he had taken at last October's fair in Stow. She had seen those as well . . . all except one, a picture of a gipsy girl sitting outside a caravan.

Julie had lost a lot of sleep over that picture, wondering who the girl was, why Rocky hadn't shown it to her, whether it was because there was something between them. She had never actually caught him out in anything that hinted at an affair, but there were times when she wondered what he got up to while he was away. He was so attractive and there was no doubt that he enjoyed the admiration of other women. That photo had aroused all her latent suspicions. She dared not risk his anger by revealing that she had been snooping among his things so she had tried to forget it, comforting herself with the knowledge that by now the girl was probably far away. Just the same, those striking Romany features were printed on Julie's memory as sharply as in the photograph. And now she knew the girl's name; it was Hannah Rose, she had been murdered, and the police wanted to speak to a local truck driver who might have taken her to Eastern Europe.

Rocky had been there more than once; he could be the man they were looking for. He could have been carrying on with Hannah all this time. And Hannah knew where he lived. Perhaps she had asked him for money, hinted that if she didn't get what she wanted she would come to the house and make a scene in front of his wife. Such a threat would have infuriated Rocky. Julie had good cause to remember the odd occasion since their marriage when he had lashed out at her after losing his temper over some comparatively trivial matter. She had carried the marks of his anger for several days and shuddered at the thought of what he might do if he felt seriously threatened. Had he then killed the gipsy in a fit of blind fury?

No, it couldn't be true. He might have a short fuse, could get a bit free with his fists if he was really upset – Julie had soon learned that there was a limit to how far she could go – but he would never seriously hurt anyone. She found herself repeating aloud, 'My Rocky is not a murderer,' over and over like a mantra, praying for it to be so. *Ah,* said a voice inside her head, *but how can you be sure? He knew that girl, he took her picture and never showed it to you. Who knows what else passed between them?* 'No!' she almost sobbed, thrusting the unthinkable into the depths of her mind. 'I don't believe it . . . I will not believe it!'

Suddenly calm, Julie finished her tea, rinsed her mug under the tap and stowed it in the dish-washer. She went mechanically through the familiar actions, emptying and rinsing the teapot and putting it away, wiping up the splashes of water and carefully wringing out the dish-cloth before folding it neatly and hanging it over the edge of the sink. She changed into her slippers, arranged her outdoor shoes side by side on the rack in the lobby by the back door and hung up her jacket in the hall cupboard. And all the time she was steeling herself for what she knew she must do.

She and Rocky never bothered with the papers and when the news came on the telly they would switch over to another channel. The only reason she knew about the freezer murder was because the girls at work had chatted about it, discussing the gruesome details with a morbid curiosity that disgusted her. Rocky had never referred to it and neither had she; the chances were that he knew nothing about it, hadn't seen that picture, couldn't possibly be aware of the danger he was in. If she were to tackle him about it and urge him to destroy the photograph, he would know that she had disobeyed him. Julie quailed at the thought of his anger. But if she were to act quickly, if she could lay her hands on it and destroy it before he came home, he would be safe.

Now there was only one idea in her head: that her Rocky must come to no harm. She would do everything in her power to protect him even if – and for a fleeting moment she faced up to the lingering doubt that would not, for all her prayers and protestations, be silenced – *even if he was a murderer.*

She stood for a moment at the foot of the stairs, gazing up at the trap-door beyond which she had been forbidden to go. She drew a deep breath and began to climb the stairs, gripping the banister rail, moving slowly but steadily as if drawn by some invisible magnetic power. On the landing, hardly aware of what she was doing, she reached out and pressed a switch. There was a click and a gentle whirring noise as the electrically-controlled ladder began to descend. Slowly it inched towards her; a black hole opened above her head and a layer of chill air fell round her face. There was a soft thud as the mechanism settled into place. Julie began to climb.

An eternity seemed to pass before she found what she was looking for, but at last she held the photograph in her hand. Time was racing past; Rocky could be home at any moment. Holding her breath, desperately hoping that she had left everything exactly as it was so that he would never suspect that she had been up there, she turned out the light and began to descend the ladder.

She was halfway down when she heard his key in the front door.

Chapter Eleven

There was no way she could conceal what she had done. The staircase was immediately opposite the front door; the moment Rocky stepped into the hall his eyes would be drawn upwards to the ladder and the open trap-door and she would be caught in the act of disobeying him. His anger would be terrible. Fear rose in a hard lump from the pit of her stomach into her throat and all but choked her. Every muscle in her body seemed to be paralysed; her legs turned to jelly. She waited, helpless, hearing the bellow of rage from the hall below and the slamming of the door that seemed to shake the house to its foundations, knowing only too well what to expect. Footsteps came pounding up the stairs. The incriminating photograph fell from her hand and landed on the floor while she clung to the sides of the ladder, mute and trembling, awaiting the first blow.

It never came. Instead there was a gasp, an oath and then silence. Julie dared to turn her head and glance over her shoulder. Rocky was standing as if transfixed with the photograph of the dead girl in his hand and a look on his face that she had never seen before.

'Christ!' he repeated, 'I'd completely forgotten—' He broke off and glared up at Julie. His expression darkened again, but he made no move to strike her. The hand that held the picture was not completely steady. 'How the hell did you know about this?' he demanded hoarsely.

Timidly, she descended the ladder and faced him. 'Don't

be angry with me Rocky,' she pleaded. 'There was a picture of that girl in the paper . . . Rocky, it's terrible . . . someone . . . she's been murdered . . . I was so afraid for you—' She put a hand on his arm, desperately jabbering on in the wild hope that to keep on talking would buy her time, time to calm his fury, make him see that she was on his side and was only trying to protect him. 'I remembered . . . I remembered seeing . . . I thought, if I was to burn the photo before—'

'You remembered? Are you saying you've seen this before?' He jerked his arm away from her clinging hand, his gaze travelling from her face to the picture and back again. Comprehension was swiftly followed by mounting rage. His eyes drove into hers like probes, viciously gouging out the truth. His hand went round her throat, forcing her backwards. 'How many times have you been up there, poking around among my things?'

Julie's teeth were chattering so violently that she could hardly reply. 'Only once, honestly Rocky. It was only because—'

'Because I said you weren't to, and you always want to know everything don't you, you nosy, meddling cow! You never learn, do you? Maybe this'll teach you to do as you're told!' He dealt her a stinging blow across the face with his free hand. A light flashed behind her eyes and her head sang. She put up her arms to protect it and he punched her viciously in the ribs. 'You bloody disobedient bitch!'

She staggered, fell against the wall and stood there with her eyes closed and her knees sagging, mentally bracing herself for further punishment, but nothing happened. After a few moments she opened her eyes again. Rocky was once more staring at the photograph. His anger seemed to be spent and his expression was troubled, a strange mixture of apprehension and bewilderment. Once again, she dared to put a hand on his arm and this time he allowed it to remain.

'I did it for you, Rocky,' she faltered. 'When I saw that

picture at the meeting I was so shocked . . . they were all talking about it . . . saying the girl's body had been found in a freezer and the police wanted to talk to a truck driver . . . I knew you'd seen her . . . she came to the house one day, didn't she? I was so afraid the police might find out and think—'

'Think what?' His voice had a dead quality; his eyes were still on the picture of the murdered girl.

'That you were the one who—' Her voice trailed away; for a moment, she could not bring herself to utter the words. Then the need to know the truth became stronger than her fear. 'Rocky, I don't believe you killed her, but if you did—' There was no reply and she raced on, hardly knowing what she was saying. 'If you did, I won't tell . . . I won't say a word . . . I'll say you were with me when it happened . . . I don't know when it happened but I'll say it anyway . . . but you didn't do it, did you? Rocky, please say you didn't kill her!' She was crying now, not from the bruises which in her agitation she hardly felt, but from sheer despair. More forcibly than blows, the realisation struck her that her orderly, settled life with the husband she adored was in ruins, that no matter what the truth was, what had happened was so terrible that nothing could ever be the same for them again.

He pushed the photograph into her hand, hardly seeming to notice her outburst. 'You're right,' he muttered. 'We must burn this. Go and put it on the fire; I'll get the negative.' He clattered up the ladder and she stood for a moment, watching as first his head and shoulders and then the rest of his body were swallowed up by the black hole in the ceiling. Then she went downstairs into the sitting-room, stirred up the fire and dropped the picture of Hannah Rose onto the flames.

He seemed to be up there a long time. There were sounds of movement overhead, then silence. At last she heard his footsteps descending the ladder, followed by the click and whirr of the mechanism and the thud of the trap-door settling into place. She was sitting on a stool in front of the grate with her back to the door when he entered the room, but she did not turn round. He reached over her shoulder and dropped a strip of negatives into the fire, causing a spurt of multicoloured flame. Neither spoke as the film distorted, blackened and shrank to nothing.

At last, Rocky gave a deep sigh and sank into a chair. 'Well that's that. No need for anyone else to know,' he said.

Still without looking at him she said in a small, dull voice, 'Tell me about her, Rocky . . . please.'

He was silent for several moments and she was about to repeat the question when he said, 'I was thinking, up there . . . what you did was for me—' It was the nearest he would come to an apology for the beating. Impulsively, she came and knelt on the floor beside him, her head on his lap. He stroked her hair and she grabbed his hand and kissed it.

'I love you so much Rocky,' she whispered. 'I'll do anything . . . say anything you want me to.'

'You promise?'

She raised her head, startled. 'Of course, but Rocky, you didn't—?' She dared not go on, but he read her thoughts.

'No,' he said harshly. 'I didn't kill her. Get that into your head, will you?'

She looked at him through a blur of tears. 'But you knew her, didn't you?' She swallowed hard before saying, 'Did you . . . you know—' The prudery inherited from her mother made the word stick in her throat.

'Have sex with her?' He shrugged, as if the question was unimportant. She bit her lip as he went on, his tone as conversational as if they were discussing the weather. 'Like I've told you a hundred times, a man needs it regular, but you never seem to want it. You say you love me, but—'

'I do, I do! And I do let you sometimes . . . it's just . . . I can't seem to—'

'Let yourself go? That's the trouble with you. Now Hannah,

she couldn't get enough of it. Not many inhibitions about that girl.' He gave a huge smile of self-satisfaction and with a little sob Julie buried her face in his lap again. 'She was dead keen to go to Hungary,' he went on. 'I had a load to deliver to a firm in Budapest so I took her with me. It was months – almost a year ago. I left her there. She was planning to join up with another band of gippos . . . said she was going to live in the land of her ancestors or some such crap.'

'So you didn't bring her back to England?'

'Didn't I just say so?'

'Someone must have.'

'So what? All I know is, it wasn't me. I never saw her again.'

'You swear it?'

'Course I do.'

She thought for a moment before saying hesitantly, her eyes averted, 'Rocky, it said in the paper the police want to talk to you . . . to the driver who took the girl to wherever it was. Are you going to—?'

She felt his body tense as he snapped, 'Am I hell?'

'But—'

'But nothing. All that time ago . . . what good would it do?' He made a grab at her hair, wrenching her head round to face him. His eyes were glaring, his chin jutting out. 'And you keep your trap shut, understand? Firms won't trust me with their loads if the cops show an interest in me.'

'If you say so, Rocky.'

'That's my girl.' He gave her shoulder a squeeze. 'And if you promise not to go nosing about in the attic again, we'll say no more. Tell you what, here's something to make you forget all about it.' He kissed her roughly on the mouth before pushing her on to the floor in front of the dying fire. Falling on his knees beside her, he thrust groping hands under her skirt, breathing heavily as he tore off her knickers and tights and flung them aside. She lay there without moving while he fumbled with his own clothes before throwing himself on to her, forcing her legs apart with his. Knowing that this was his way of saying that she was forgiven, she was content to let him do what he wanted.

Afterwards, hardly exchanging a word, they went upstairs to bed. Rocky was asleep within minutes, but his wife lay awake far into the night, fearful of what lay ahead.

Chapter Twelve

Fourteen-year-old Tommy, the youngest of the numerous Woodbridge offspring, had only last week maintained the family tradition of taking over from an elder sibling the responsibility for delivering the evening papers. Each day a driver from the *Gazette* brought them to the village shop, whence it was the task of the current holder of the concession to collect and distribute them to those households which had placed a regular order.

There had been no problems during Tommy's first week as sixteen-year-old Roger, who was handing over the job on the pretext that he needed more time and energy to devote to his social life, had cycled round with him each day. The following Monday – Tommy's first day of performing this seemingly straightforward task on his own – all had gone well, but things went awry on Tuesday and when he had finished he found himself with several copies left over. Assuming that this must be due to an over-delivery – a more acceptable explanation than that he had left a number of households without their daily ration of local news and gossip – Tommy had taken the easy option of quietly leaving the surplus among the unsold daily newspapers on the counter of the village shop while Mrs Foster's attention was – as he mistakenly believed – engaged elsewhere.

It was not until she returned home after her visit to the Golden Bell with Matt Waters that Melissa realised that her copy of the *Gazette* had not been delivered. A call to Iris revealed that hers was also missing. After a brief exchange on the shortcomings of the youngest member of the Woodbridge clan, they agreed that they were unlikely to lose sleep over the omission; Melissa would collect them the following morning, along with the national dailies. She and Iris performed this errand in turn, since the early departure of the school bus made it impracticable for any of the village youngsters to take on a morning delivery.

Melissa woke earlier than usual on Wednesday morning and after a shower and a hasty breakfast went straight to her study to work on her current novel. A key character was a retired army doctor with a guilty secret in his past life. Remembering that Madeleine Ford had been an army nurse, and anxious to make the setting of her story as authentic as possible, she decided to seek her help. Some background information and – with any luck – a few anecdotes that she could weave into the plot would help bring the action to life. It would also, she thought mischievously, be a change for someone who took such a keen interest in other people's affairs to find herself on the receiving end of a little probing into her own.

At nine o'clock, Gloria arrived to do her weekly stint of cleaning. She was fairly bursting with news.

'Have you seen last night's *Gazette*?' she asked as she peeled off her jacket, releasing an overpowering wave of exotic perfume.

'No, the boy forgot to deliver it,' said Melissa. 'Was there something special in it?'

'I'll say! There were a picture of that gipsy girl what got topped . . . it *were* the one what my Stanley saw in the pub a while ago . . . what I were telling Miss Ash about.' Gloria's toffee-brown eyes were round with excitement.

'Really? Do you mean the Woolpack, here in the village?'

'Nah, the Lamb and something in Gloucester, near my Stanley's showroom.' This was a euphemism for the patch of waste ground where the proprietor of Cathedral Cars displayed his current stock of used vehicles. 'He were having a drink one evening with one of his business associates,' Gloria went on, her tone undergoing a subtle change as if to emphasise the important nature of such contacts.

Melissa bit her lower lip to conceal a smile as she asked, 'Miss Ash said the girl was selling something. Do you know what it was?'

Gloria shook her crinkly mass of blond hair. 'Fraid not,' she sighed. 'Do it matter?'

'Not really. Is your Stanley sure it's the girl in the picture?'

'Quite sure. The barman ordered her out, but she must've hung around 'cos my Stanley saw her later outside with a bloke. She were getting into his car.'

Melissa felt a sharp surge of adrenalin. 'What sort of bloke . . . and what sort of car? Did your Stanley notice?'

Gloria shrugged. 'Dunno. It were quite late . . . nearly dark he said.'

'When was this?'

'He don't remember exactly. You reckon he should tell them at the *Gazette*?' Gloria glowed at the prospect of seeing a piece about her husband in the newspaper.

Her face fell slightly as Melissa said firmly, 'He should go straight to the police and tell them. It could be very important.'

'You reckon?'

'I happen to know the police are looking for the man Hannah went away with. It could be the man she was with that night.'

'Maybe he were the one what done it?' The brown eyes stretched even wider at the thought.

'I don't think so. They've arrested two other men for the murder, but they still have plenty of inquiries to make. This man might know something important to the case. If what your Stanley saw can help the police find him, I'm sure they'd be very grateful,' Melissa added shrewdly. She happened to know that Stanley Parkin had more than once been questioned about the origin of certain vehicles offered for sale by Cathedral Cars. So far, he had managed to maintain a clean record, but it would do him no harm at all to be seen voluntarily doing his duty as a law-abiding citizen.

Gloria was quick to grasp the implication. 'I'll tell him as soon as he gets home,' she promised.

'Fine,' said Melissa. 'I'm going into the village now and I may be gone for an hour or so. If I'm not back in time for coffee, you know where everything is.'

'Sure. See you later.' Gloria rolled up her sleeves over her plump arms and prepared to get down to work.

When Melissa entered the village shop she found Harriet Yorke on the receiving end of a prolonged and querulous complaint by Mrs Foster on the subject of paper-boys in general, and of Tommy Woodbridge in particular.

'You just can't rely on them,' she asserted. 'Only too happy to take their money every week, but never mind the convenience of the customer. The cheek of it, just too lazy to go all the way round and then dumping the left-overs in my shop. Thought I hadn't noticed but I saw him, only I never cottoned on to what he was up to till he'd gone. Just wait till he comes to collect the papers this afternoon – I'll give him a piece of my mind, I can tell you!'

'I don't suppose he left anyone out on purpose,' said Harriet. 'It's only his second week ... and the first on his own.'

Mrs Foster evidently took a less charitable view, for she gave a disparaging sniff and said, 'No doubt he'll have some fine excuse. Those Woodbridge lads are all the same. Can't say a word to them without getting a mouthful of cheek.'

'Have you any idea who else didn't get their paper?' asked Harriet who, judging by the copy of last night's *Gazette* in her hand, was evidently one of those so deprived.

'I didn't, for one,' said Melissa. 'And nor did Iris. I guess

Tommy just forgot about us as we live on the edge of the village.'

'In that case I don't suppose the Fords got theirs, for the same reason,' said Harriet. 'I'd offer to drop it in for them, only I've got a dental appointment and I'm a bit rushed.'

'That's all right, I'll take it,' offered Melissa. 'I'm on my way to see Madeleine as it happens. I'll bring it back if they got theirs.'

Harriet departed. Melissa bought a few groceries from a partially mollified Mrs Foster and left a few minutes later, bound for Tanners Cottage. Major Ford answered her knock and it struck Melissa that he looked far from well. Beneath a network of broken veins, his normally florid face was the colour of under-cooked pastry and his eyes were bloodshot. However, he greeted her with his normal, over-effusive courtesy.

'Good morning, Melissa. How nice of you to call.' He gave a courtly little bow and stood aside for her to enter. 'Do come in. Madeleine will be so pleased to see you.'

'Good morning Dudley. I was hoping to have a word with her if she's got a few minutes to spare. I'm after some information about military hospitals for my new novel . . . I believe she used to be an army nurse.'

'That's right . . . it's going back a bit, though. A lot of things will have changed.'

'That doesn't matter . . . it's how they were soon after the war that I'm interested in.'

'In that case, I'm sure she'll be delighted to help.'

'And I think you may have missed your copy of the *Gazette* yesterday evening,' Melissa added, holding it out as he closed the front door behind her. 'If so—'

The Major frowned and fingered his moustache. 'No, no, we got ours.'

'Ah, then this must be someone else's.' She tucked the paper into her shopping bag with the others. 'Never mind,

I'll return it on my way home. The new paper boy seems to have got in a muddle. I didn't get mine and nor did Iris or Harriet Yorke and we thought perhaps—'

'No, we got ours,' he repeated over his shoulder while striding ahead of her along the narrow, flagged passage that always seemed cold, even in midsummer. 'Maddy,' he said breezily as he ushered her through a door at the far end. 'A lady to see you.'

As always, Melissa was struck by the cluttered aspect of the Fords' sitting-room, with its low, oak-beamed ceiling, heavy antique furniture, dark velvet curtains and fussily patterned carpet. Every available surface was crowded with framed photographs, knick-knacks and curios from every country to which the Major's army career had taken them. It must, she thought, be a nightmare to dust, even for someone as energetic as Gloria.

Madeleine Ford was seated at a bureau under one of two leaded windows overlooking the garden. She appeared to be writing letters, but immediately put down her pen and stood up to greet her visitor in her customary gracious manner. Although it was only ten o'clock in the morning, her immaculately groomed appearance made Melissa uncomfortably aware of her own casual attire and lack of make-up.

'Do come and sit by the fire.' Madeleine indicated an old-fashioned, rather shabby sofa covered in floral-patterned cretonne. 'Dudley, take Melissa's coat and shopping bag. It's quite chilly this morning, isn't it?' she went on, sinking gracefully down beside her guest.

'Melissa thought we might have missed our evening paper,' said the Major as he obeyed the instruction. 'Seems that young scallywag Tommy Woodbridge left several people out, but I told her we got ours as usual.'

'That's right.' Madeleine gestured towards a low table where the previous evening's *Gazette* lay on top of a vast heap of newspapers and magazines. 'It was very sweet of you to think of us, though.'

'And she wants to quiz you about your experiences as an army nurse,' her husband went on. 'No giving away any trade secrets, mind!' he added roguishly.

Madeleine's enamelled features registered polite interest. 'I take it this is for one of your splendid novels? Naturally, I'll be glad to help if I can. Would you like some coffee?'

'That would be nice, if it isn't too much trouble. I don't know how Mrs Foster survives in that shop in cold weather – I got quite chilled standing there for just a few minutes.' Melissa stretched her legs gratefully towards the fire. Sinbad, who was sprawled on a shabby hearth-rug plentifully strewn with his own hairs, raised a languid head and studied the newcomer from rheumy eyes for a few seconds before falling asleep again.

'Dudley!' said Madeleine with a meaningful tilt of her carefully coiffured head in the approximate direction of the kitchen.

'Of course, dear.' He hurried out of the room and closed the door.

'Dudley looks a bit off-colour,' Melissa remarked. 'Has he picked up this bug that's going around?'

Madeleine leaned forward and poked the fire. 'I'm not sure what's the matter with him,' she said with a frown. 'He hasn't been sleeping too well lately and he seems to have lost his appetite. I want him to go and see Doctor Blake, but he absolutely refuses . . . says he'll only prescribe more pills.'

'It must be worrying for you.'

'Yes, it is. What with his blood pressure and his angina—' Madeleine put down the poker and sat upright with her hands clasped together. Outwardly, she appeared her usual poised and controlled self, but small white spots on her knuckles betrayed her unease. 'And of course,' she went on, 'he hasn't been helped by all the unpleasantness we've had to put up with recently from the police. We were practically treated like *criminals* over the death of that gipsy, just because some murderous ruffians hid her body in *our* old freezer.'

'Oh yes, that must have been *very* unpleasant for you.' Despite her sympathy for the woman's anxiety over her husband's health, Melissa could not completely hide her impatience with such a self-centred attitude. However, the hint of irony in her tone was totally lost on Madeleine.

'It was indeed,' she asserted, 'and I'm very much afraid this latest development is going to make things even worse.'

'Oh? What development is that?'

'Haven't you seen . . . no, of course you haven't, you didn't receive your paper last night.' Madeleine reached for the copy of the *Gazette* and handed it to Melissa. 'There, on the centre pages . . . that picture . . . Dudley tells me it's that . . . that *female* who had the impertinence to call on us, peddling some rubbish or other.' She made no attempt to hide her disdain.

'Really?' Melissa was staring at the artist's impression of Hannah Rose that Bruce had shown her the previous day. 'Are you saying this is the girl who was calling at houses round the village a little while ago?' The conversation in the shop the day after the discovery of Hannah's body had entirely slipped her memory, but now it came rushing back. Privately cursing herself for having been so exercised over the possibility of a revenge attack on the girl's abductor that she had failed to spot such an obvious connection, she exclaimed, 'Are you sure?'

Madeleine looked faintly affronted. 'Dudley tells me he recognised her immediately from the drawing,' she said, her tone indicating that Dudley's word should be enough to put the identification beyond doubt.

'You didn't see her yourself?'

'I was inside the garage, closing the door behind Dudley – he was just leaving as she arrived. He says he told her to clear off.'

'And she was selling lace?'

'I suppose she could have been . . . he didn't enquire. Really, Melissa, anyone would think you were a police officer, asking all these questions!'

'I'm sorry.' Melissa gave an apologetic smile. 'I do have a particular interest . . . I happened to meet the girl's aunt the other day. She's terribly upset over her death.'

Madeleine's raised eyebrow indicated a well-bred surprise at Melissa's choice of company, but all she said was, 'I'm not surprised, but what else does she expect if the girl is allowed to go round alone, knocking on doors? We've been wondering who else she called on. One hears of such dreadful cases nowadays of apparently normal people doing the most appalling things.'

'You're suggesting that someone enticed this girl into their house and then killed her?'

'It wouldn't surprise me in the least. As I said, if these people will persist in calling at the houses of complete strangers, they only have themselves to blame if they get into trouble.'

Melissa had difficulty in concealing her irritation at such a total lack of compassion, but all she said was, 'I take it Dudley will be informing the police?'

Madeleine made a hissing sound through her teeth. 'He insists he has to,' she snapped, 'although I can't see how it will help . . . he has no idea where the creature went after he spoke to her.'

'Dudley's absolutely right,' said Melissa. She spoke a little more forcefully than she intended, but Madeleine was too absorbed in her own feelings to take offence.

'And now I suppose we'll have reporters knocking at the door wanting interviews . . . and our names will be in all the papers . . . it's positively *demeaning*,' she continued peevishly. 'If only the men from the Council had come in the *morning* to take the freezer away, as they were supposed to do, none of this would have happened.'

You mean, the girl could have got herself murdered and her body hidden without any inconvenience to you, you selfish old witch! Resisting the temptation to speak her thoughts aloud, and making a superhuman effort to keep her tone reasonable, Melissa said, 'This could be a very important lead. I believe the girl called on Harriet Yorke as well, and Miss Brightwell. There are sure to be others in the village. And Stanley Parkin – Gloria's husband – thinks he saw her once in a pub in Gloucester. I'm sure *they* will be only too ready to do what they can to assist the police.'

Madeleine gave a resigned shrug. 'I suppose one has to do one's duty as a citizen,' she admitted with obvious reluctance.

'Quite. And it's essential to trace as many witnesses as possible. Dudley's evidence could be very helpful.'

'*Evidence*?' Madeleine's eyes stretched in alarm. 'Are you saying he might be called on to give *evidence . . . in court*?' Had it been suggested that the pair of them rode naked through the village on Walpurgis night, she could hardly have appeared more shocked.

Melissa managed to keep a straight face as she replied, 'Oh, I don't suppose for a moment it will come to that. Of course, if you were in the house when the girl called, they'll probably want a statement from you as well. Perhaps you and Dudley should go to headquarters together? I imagine that would be preferable to having the place swarming with detectives,' she added mischievously, and was gratified to see that this possibility seemed to horrify Madeleine even further.

The conversation was interrupted by Dudley's appearance with a tray.

'Here we are . . . coffee!' he announced, depositing his burden on the table. His eye fell on the open newspaper that still lay on Melissa's lap and he tut-tutted in disapproval. 'Really, old girl, you could surely have found a more wholesome subject to talk about than that unfortunate affair,' he said.

'You're absolutely right dear. I can't think how it came up,' his wife agreed.

'I think it was because I commented that you were looking a little peaky, Dudley,' said Melissa tactfully as she refolded the paper and put it aside. 'Madeleine mentioned that all the recent, er, unpleasantness hasn't done your blood pressure any good.'

'Oh that . . . nothing for us to worry about really. Have to tell the boys in blue, of course, about how that unfortunate young woman came to the house. Just the same, we'd be obliged if you'd keep it to yourself. Y'know what a lot of old gossips there are in the village . . . Maddy's terrified we'll have the press on our doorstep if it gets around.'

Melissa hid a smile at this blatant example of a pot calling the kettle black. 'I quite understand,' she assured them.

'Much obliged.' The Major distributed coffee and biscuits and then sat down. 'Now, what about that research you mentioned, Melissa? Perhaps I can help as well? I was in hospital a couple of times during my army career. In fact, Maddy helped to patch me up once, didn't you old girl? That's how we met – very romantic, what? Only don't you go putting us in one of your racy novels, *haahaahaa*!' His laugh, as always, put Melissa in mind of a sheep with a sore throat. 'Never live it down, what?'

'I'm sure Melissa isn't after any *personal* reminiscences,' said Madeleine primly.

'Of course not. She's quite capable of inventing the spicy bits for herself, *haahaahaa*!'

'I promise you, I won't compromise you in any way,' said Melissa solemnly. She put down her cup and saucer and drew a notebook from her handbag. 'It's just general background information I'm after. I've jotted down a few questions—'

On leaving Tanners Cottage, Melissa crossed the road and made for Ash Close, a development of four houses built a few years previously on a piece of land that was once part of the garden of a neighbouring property. The application for planning consent had met with considerable opposition from certain local residents, notably the Fords, who claimed that the value of their genuine Queen Anne property would be adversely affected by the proximity of such modern monstrosities. Once the houses were a *fait accompli*, however, they had not – as might have been expected – treated the incomers with hostility. On the contrary, they had been most hospitable and welcoming, inviting them to drinks parties and showing as much interest in their private affairs as they did in those of everyone else in the village. Indeed, the consensus among the other inhabitants of Upper Benbury was that they were not altogether displeased at the opportunity to observe the comings and goings of four additional families.

The new houses were built in a semicircle round a green and the one occupied by Harriet Yorke and her husband Ted, a director of a manufacturing company in Gloucester, faced directly towards Tanners Cottage. Although she did not glance back after saying goodbye to the Fords, Melissa had no doubt that they had her under observation as she walked up to the Yorkes' front door and rang the bell. There was no reply, but as she was about to give up and head for home, a red Fiat turned out of the lane and pulled up on the drive beside her.

'Oh Melissa!' Harriet exclaimed as she got out of the car. 'I'm so glad to see you. Something rather upsetting has happened and I'd be grateful for someone to talk to about it. Do come in.' Normally confident and self-possessed, she appeared anxious, almost agitated. As soon as they were inside the house she turned to Melissa and asked, 'Have you seen the picture in the *Gazette*? The one of Hannah Rose – the girl who was murdered?'

'The Fords drew my attention to it. They confirm it's the girl who came to their door selling lace . . . or "peddling some rubbish or other", as Madeleine so charmingly put it. That's why I came over to have a word with you . . . I remembered your mentioning you'd bought something from a gipsy who called at your house. Was it Hannah?'

'Yes, it was. She came to me first . . . at least, before she went to the Fords. I don't know how many houses she'd already been to. Melissa, it was such a shock to see that picture. I feel awful . . . just think, I may have been one of the last people to see her alive.'

'That's enough to shake anyone . . . anyone with normal feelings, that is,' agreed Melissa.

While she was speaking, Harriet was hurriedly shedding her outdoor things and almost throwing them into a cupboard in the hall. Her smooth forehead was creased in a frown; she peered into a mirror on the inside of the door and combed back her mane of reddish-gold hair with hands that moved jerkily, as if they were only just under control. Making an obvious effort to pull herself together she said, 'Do forgive me, Melissa . . . shall I take your jacket? Would you like some coffee, or are you in a dash to get home?'

'I'm not in any particular dash, but I've just had coffee with Madeleine and Dudley, thanks.'

'A sherry, then?'

'That would be lovely . . . it would help to take away the taste of the Fords.' Melissa pulled a face. 'I called round to pick Madeleine's brains about her years as an army nurse, but immediately the subject of the murder came up and I had to listen to her whingeing about how *unpleasant* it was for them to be involved in such a distasteful affair. She doesn't see the point of Dudley telling the police he saw the girl when they had no idea where the *creature*, as she called her, went next. Talk about passing by on the other side—'

'That's Madeleine all over,' said Harriet scornfully. 'She'll happily poke and pry into everyone else's business so long as she doesn't get her own hands mucky. Dudley's just as bad.'

'You're right. He had the cheek to ask me not to mention it to anyone in case the "old gossips" in the village spread it around and their name gets into the papers.'

'Old gossips? He's a fine one to talk! Now, let's have this drink.' Harriet led Melissa into the sitting-room, which – in striking contrast to the Fords' – was prettily furnished in a bright, modern style with simple but skilfully crafted furniture, a few original modern paintings on the walls and flowering plants in hand-thrown pottery containers on the window-sill. She opened a corner cupboard and took out two sherry glasses. 'Sweet or dry?'

'Dry, please.'

As the two settled in armchairs with generous measures of Tio Pepe, Melissa asked, 'How did you get on at the dentist's?'

'Oh fine. It was just for a check-up . . . no problems.'

'Good. So, tell me what happened when Hannah called on you.'

Harriet fingered the stem of her glass and thought for a moment before replying. 'She rang the bell one evening at about half-past five,' she said slowly. 'I was in the kitchen, starting to prepare the supper. I opened the door and there was this girl toting a hold-all and saying, "Will you buy some lace from a Romany gipsy, kind lady?" I was on the point of sending her away; I don't normally buy things at the door, but she was only a little thing, thin and rather tired-looking, and her hold-all seemed too heavy for her.' Harriet's eyes filmed over at the memory and she brushed them with the back of her hand. 'So I took pity on her and let her show me her stuff.'

'I believe you bought something?'

'Yes, some little mats. She said she'd made them herself, but whether that was true or not I've no idea. I thought they'd come in for a Christmas present.'

'Could I see them?'

'Of course.' Harriet left the room and returned a minute or two later with a plastic bag containing half a dozen circles of lace a few inches across.

Melissa examined them for a moment and then said, 'She almost certainly did make them herself – the police found lace-making equipment in her room at the hotel. I recognise the pattern, too . . . there's a picture of a mat like these in the *Gazette*.'

'Yes, I noticed it while I was reading the paper in the dentist's waiting-room. I didn't realise the pattern was the same . . . as a matter of fact, I went upstairs and put them away as soon as the girl left and then went back to my cooking. This is the first time I've looked at them since that afternoon.'

'Which afternoon was this, by the way?'

Harriet looked troubled. 'I've been trying to work it out . . . it was either Monday or Tuesday last week, but I can't remember which. I'd forgotten all about it until I read about the murder, and even then it didn't occur to me that there was any connection.'

'You mentioned that Hannah went to the Fords' after she came to you. Did you see where she went after that?'

'I'm afraid not.'

'So what exactly did you see?'

'I saw the girl cross the road and go up to the Fords' front gate just as Dudley was driving out. I saw him wind down the window to speak to her . . . I couldn't hear what he said, of course . . . and then he drove away. She stood and stared after the car for a moment and I got the impression that he hadn't been exactly polite to her.'

'That figures!' said Melissa with a grimace.

'After that, I drew the curtains and came back downstairs.'

'So you've no idea which way she went after leaving the Fords' house?'

Harriet shook her head. 'None at all, I'm afraid. On the

face of it, I'm not going to be able to give the police much help, am I?'

'Don't you believe it,' Melissa assured her. 'Every tiny scrap of evidence is important. Miss Brightwell said she called on her, but I don't know what time, or what other houses she went to. That's something for the police to check. I take it you haven't been in touch with them yet?'

'Not yet. I did think about going straight to the station after leaving the dentist, but seeing that picture gave me such a shock, I decided to come home and give myself a chance to calm down and get things straight in my mind first. I'm so grateful to you for coming in . . . I feel better already.'

'Good!' Melissa raised her glass in acknowledgement. 'It's just occurred to me,' she went on. 'Hannah was living at a hotel near Stow. That's quite a long way from here – I wonder how she was planning to get back.'

'Isn't there a bus to Stow from Dartley Pike at a little after six?'

'So there is. She was probably aiming to catch it . . . unless—'

'Unless what?'

'Unless there was someone waiting nearby with a car.' Melissa recounted Gloria's story of what her Stanley had seen. 'There's a strong possibility that when Hannah left her family some months ago she went abroad with a long-distance truck driver. The man she was seen with might have been him.'

'Yes, I caught that on the TV news last night. I wonder if he knows what's happened to her,' said Harriet thoughtfully. 'If he's away a lot, he might not have seen the papers. What a shock for him when he finds out!'

'That's a point. So far, the police have no idea who or where he is.' Melissa put down her glass and stood up. 'Thank you very much for the drink. If you're feeling okay now, I ought to get back and do some work.'

'I'm fine now, thanks. As soon as you've gone, I'll call the police and tell them what little I know.'

On her way home, Melissa found herself thinking about the man in the Golden Bell, the man who had given her a come-hither wink, who had turned lascivious eyes on the barmaid . . . and who had just returned home after a week's absence. She recalled how something in the newspaper he was reading appeared to bring about an abrupt change of mood, and how shortly afterwards she had glimpsed him – she was positive now that it was the same man – leaning on a gate and staring moodily at the ground. It set her wondering.

Chapter Thirteen

It was almost midday by the time Melissa reached home. She found Gloria bustling about the kitchen, giving a final polish to the sink and draining-board before hanging up the teacloth and stowing away her cleaning materials and equipment. As always, after her weekly three-hour stint, the place shone; as always, Melissa was generous in her praise and was rewarded by the pleasure that glowed in the beaming, rosy face. There were times when she found herself wishing that she too could derive so much enjoyment from simple household tasks, instead of having to earn her living as a mystery writer constantly driven to spinning ever more complex plots.

As she took her money and put on her jacket, Gloria said, 'I were listening to Cotswold Sound earlier on an' they said lots of people was calling the police to say they seen that gippo girl. "A number of sightings" they said.'

'I wonder if any of the calls came from round here. It seems she was in the village one day last week.'

Gloria's eyes saucered. 'In Upper Benbury? No kiddin'!'

'She was selling lace, like she was in the pub where your Stanley saw her. She called on several people ... Miss Brightwell, Mrs Yorke—' Melissa was on the point of adding, 'and Major and Mrs Ford', but remembered her promise just in time. Not that she had a great deal of sympathy for Madeleine's purely selfish reasons for wishing to avoid publicity. It would probably get around anyway; since at least one person had seen Hannah go up to their house it was likely that others had done so as well. Keeping a secret in a village was well-nigh impossible. Still, a promise was a promise and to tell Gloria anything was as good as putting it on the Internet, as her next words confirmed.

'Where else did she go?' Without waiting for a reply, she went on, 'I'll ask around among my ladies. Coo, wait till I tells my Stanley he ain't the only one what's got something to report!' Her mobile face clouded as she added, 'None of them said nothin' to me, though, so maybe they never saw her after all.'

She looked so crestfallen that Melissa hastened to console her. 'They might have done, but thought nothing of it at the time,' she pointed out. 'There's always someone coming round selling something these days . . . you know, frozen foods, double glazing . . . if Hannah did call on them they probably said, "Not today, thank you," and forgot all about her the minute she'd gone. But once they saw last night's *Gazette* – and Mrs Yorke said it was on the late TV news as well – you said just now the police have reported several sightings.'

'S'pose so,' Gloria admitted, without enthusiasm. It was plain that she felt cheated at not having had the chance to speculate with some of her "ladies" on the possible significance of a gipsy girl's presence in Upper Benbury. 'Just the same,' she added with a hint of resentment, '*someone* might have told me—'

'Oh come on,' Melissa coaxed. 'Did your Stanley say anything to you about the gipsy girl in the pub at the time it happened?' Reluctantly, Gloria shook her head. 'Well, there you are then. It simply didn't seem important . . . but I'll bet plenty of people will remember her now and be talking about it. Oh, by the way, that man your Stanley saw with the girl . . . the one in the car park . . . will you ask him if it was a youngish man, say in his mid-thirties, well set up, might have been wearing a leather jacket?'

'You reckon you know who he were?' Gloria's expression brightened and her eyes sparkled at the prospect of a titbit that no one else had yet had a chance to nibble.

'It's only a hunch. I was in a pub yesterday evening and I noticed a man reading the *Gazette*. He'd been quite cheerful up to then, chatting up the barmaid and so on.' Melissa decided not to mention the pass he'd made at her.

'And then what?' Gloria asked eagerly.

'He suddenly got up and left, and I thought he looked put out about something . . . maybe something he'd seen in the paper.'

'Oooh!' Gloria clapped a hand to her mouth as her fertile imagination set to work. 'I'll bet it were that picture! D'you s'pose he's the murderer? But I thought someone'd been arrested already . . . two other gippos, weren't it?'

'That's right, but it's just possible he's the man she ran away with. If he is, the police would like to talk to him.' Momentarily, Melissa considered confiding her fears for the man's safety, but decided against it. Apart from the fact that it would take too long to explain the complexities of the situation, she had already resolved to make some discreet inquiries of her own. The fewer people who knew about her continuing interest in the case, the less chance there was of it reaching the ears of Ken Harris and Matt Waters.

'My, innit exciting!' Gloria exclaimed, her pique completely forgotten in the light of this new information. 'My Stanley comes home for his dinner at one o'clock . . . I'll ask him then an' let you know.'

'I wouldn't make too much of it . . . it might have been something quite different that upset the man I noticed.'

'You mean, if his team lost or he backed a loser? Nah!' It was plain from her tone that Gloria was reluctant to consider such mundane possibilities. 'I reckons it were more than that.' She appeared to be about to enlarge on this assertion when her eyes fell on Melissa's kitchen clock. 'My, look at the time! I

131

must fly, or we won't get no dinner.' She grabbed her handbag and made for the door. 'See you next week!' And she left the house in a swirl of pungent scent and tossing blond curls.

After she had gone, Melissa fetched cheese and salad from the fridge and made herself a sandwich. As she ate, she switched her mind back to the scene in the Golden Bell the previous evening. She had no doubt that something in the evening paper had had an effect on the man she had been covertly observing, but whether it was Hannah's picture or something totally irrelevant it was impossible to say. The picture was on the centre page – that much she knew for certain – but she had no way of telling which page the man had been looking at when his mood suddenly changed. All she knew was that he had tossed the newspaper on the bar with a perfunctory word of thanks and left with barely a glance at the woman with whom he'd been happily flirting not ten minutes before. The more she thought about it, the more worth while it seemed to probe a little deeper.

She dismissed out of hand the notion of mentioning it to Matt, who would accuse her of letting an over-heated imagination run away with her and as likely as not mention it to Ken, who would then get all officious and tell her to stop meddling in things that didn't concern her. But Bruce Ingram would undoubtedly be interested . . . and highly miffed if she were to pursue a new line of enquiry without putting him in the picture. She picked up the phone and called his office number.

'Hi,' he said when he answered. 'I was just on my way out. What news?'

'Nothing definite . . . just a hunch.' Briefly, she gave him the details. 'I'm thinking of going back to the Golden Bell to see if anyone there knows this guy and I wondered if you—'

'Sorry,' he interrupted with evident regret. 'I'd love to join you, but I've got to interview a council official about a suspect planning consent . . . something about alterations to a listed cowshed.'

Melissa made no attempt to hide her exasperation. 'Of course, drop the donkey for a listed cowshed any day . . . I *quite* understand.'

'Yeah, well you know how it is,' said Bruce apologetically. 'Someone complains because Joe Bloggs has been refused permission to paint his front door a different colour while some wealthy landowner has got away with diverting a footpath. My editor thinks it could be the thin end of the wedge – corruption in the Town Hall and all that. She's particularly anxious for me to follow it up because I have a reputation for—'

'I know, Bloodhound Bruce, the getter of results!' Melissa interrupted, impatient at the note of self-satisfaction that was creeping into his voice. 'Okay, leave it to me.'

'You will let me know if you turn up anything interesting?'

'Of course, if you're available, but supposing you're still out discussing cowsheds when I call? I suppose I could leave a message with a colleague,' she added mischievously, knowing that to let someone else in on what he regarded as 'his' story would be the last thing he wanted.

'No, don't do that!' He sounded so alarmed at the prospect that she almost burst out laughing. 'Tell you what,' he went on urgently, 'call me on my mobile if you come across anything interesting and I can maybe join you later.'

'Okay.'

Melissa was just about to leave the house when the phone rang. Gloria was on the line. There was no mistaking her disappointment in what she had to report. 'I asked my Stanley about that bloke what he saw with the girl, but he weren't nothing like what you said . . . quite a lot older, he thought, and dressed different . . . he never saw his face, but it definitely weren't a young man.'

'Oh well, thanks anyway. Just the same, it could be important. You will make sure he tells the police, won't you?'

'Oh, sure,' said Gloria resignedly. 'He promised to do
that.'

It was gone half-past one when Melissa reached the Golden
Bell and the car park was two-thirds full. The place appeared
to be a popular lunch-time venue for business people; as she
made for the entrance to the saloon bar a couple of smartly
dressed young men carrying briefcases emerged, one with
a mobile phone clamped between ear and shoulder while
juggling with a bunch of keys as he strode towards his car.

Inside, there was an appetising smell of food, a subdued
clatter of cutlery and the inevitable background of piped
music. On the off-chance that one of the customers might be
the man she was looking for, Melissa glanced quickly round
the tables, but there was no one there that she recognised.
A few were in pairs, but the majority seemed to be on their
own, almost all preoccupied with their own affairs. Some
were studying papers, others stabbed the keys of their
personal organisers with one hand while forking food into
their mouths with the other. A man and a woman in earnest
conversation, both formally clad in dark suits, stood at the
bar with drinks in their hands. They spoke in low voices,
their heads close together and their expressions serious and
intense. At Melissa's approach they picked up their drinks and
moved away. They might have been high-powered executives
discussing some highly confidential business deal . . . or lovers
snatching a few stolen moments together.

There was no sign of the woman who had been serving
there the previous evening. Instead, a jovial-looking man of
about sixty with thinning hair and a wispy beard, temporarily
unoccupied with customers, was rinsing glasses at a sink
beneath the counter and drying them carefully before stowing
them on a rack above his head. On seeing Melissa, he laid

down his cloth, gave her a pleasant smile and said, 'What can I get you?'

She ordered a white wine spritzer and perched on one of a line of tall stools ranged along the bar. While the man poured her drink she said, 'There was a lady serving when I was in here yesterday evening . . . is she working today, by any chance? A blonde lady with a nice smile—'

The man gave a nod of recognition as he set her drink in front of her and took the money. 'Ah, that'll be Rosie. She's popped out the back for a minute. Can I help you?'

'I wanted to ask her about a man who was here at the same time. I had a feeling I'd seen him somewhere before, but I couldn't think where. I wondered if he was a regular.'

'Could be. What did he look like?'

'Mid-thirties, well set up, wearing a brown leather jacket that looked expensive—'

The barman gave a knowing grin. 'Give you the eye, did he?'

'Er, well—' Melissa was momentarily taken aback. 'I was with a friend . . . I was going to have a word with this chap, only he got up and left in rather a hurry before I had the chance.'

The barman held a glass up to the light and squinted through it before placing it in the rack. Behind him, a door opened and a woman appeared. 'That's the lady I saw last night,' said Melissa eagerly. 'Excuse me, is your name Rosie?'

The woman nodded. 'That's right,' she replied with a smile of recognition. 'I remember you. You came in yesterday evening with a gentleman.'

'The lady wants to ask you about a customer who was here at the same time,' said the barman. 'Sounds as if it could be Rocky Wilkins.' He put down the cloth and moved away to take an order.

'He was sitting over there, reading a newspaper,' Melissa

said, nodding towards the fireplace. 'In his mid-thirties, well-dressed, very attractive. Is he an actor or a TV presenter or something? His face was awfully familiar.'

Rosie gave a wheezy laugh, displaying lipstick-stained teeth. 'That's our Rocky!' she said. 'Got what it takes, hasn't he? I tell him he should be in show business and he laps it up.'

Melissa pretended to look disappointed. 'So he isn't anyone famous?' Rosie shook her head. 'That's funny. I could have sworn I'd seen him before.'

'You could well have done. Rocky gets around . . . in more ways than one.' Rosie gave a sly wink as she picked up the cloth and continued with the barman's abandoned task.

'You mean, he's a rep of some sort?'

'Nothing so classy as that. Not that he wouldn't be good at it, mind, specially if the customers were female.' The notion set Rosie chuckling again.

'So what does he do?'

'Drives a truck . . . one of those big artics. Goes all over Europe, he does . . . sometimes he's away for a couple of weeks at a time. No telling what he gets up to when his wife's not around to keep an eye on him.'

The words sent the adrenalin racing through Melissa's system. She tried to sound casual as she asked, 'Does he live round here?'

'A couple of hundred yards or so up the lane opposite.' Rosie gestured with her cloth. 'I know that 'cos me and the guv'nor had to practically carry him home one night,' she confided. 'Legless, he was. We propped him against the truck while we got his wife to open up and help us get him inside.'

'I'll bet they had a few words the next day, when he'd sobered up.'

'From the look of her, they'd had more than words before he

left the house.' Rosie's manner became suddenly serious. She leaned forward, rested her forearms on the bar and lowered her voice, 'Between you and me, there's more than one side to our Rocky. He's a charmer all right . . . chats up any bit of skirt that catches his eye, me included. I kid him along 'cos it's good for trade, see – him being a regular – but I wouldn't get involved with him if he won the lottery and offered to share it.'

'You reckon he could turn nasty?'

'It's only guesswork on my part, but I put him down as one that wouldn't take no for an answer. Don't get me wrong, I don't know anything definite against the fellow. For all I know, his wife did get her black eye walking into a door, but you never can tell. Not that he's ever made any trouble in here . . . in fact, when Julie's with him, he doesn't so much as look at another woman. In a way it doesn't add up, but there it is.'

'Never pays to go by appearances, does it?' Melissa remarked, helping herself to an olive from a dish on the bar and privately wondering how the woman would react if she knew the real motive behind her questions.

A customer approached with an order and Rosie moved away. Melissa, by this time bursting with suppressed excitement, finished her drink, said 'Goodbye,' and slipped out. She crossed the road and followed the direction Rosie had indicated. The lane curved away to the right for a short distance and then straightened out. A little further on was a row of houses; opposite them, in what appeared to be a lay-by, a couple of cars were parked and beyond them was the tall outline of the tractor unit of an articulated truck. She stood for a moment, trying to decide what to do next. Then she remembered her promise to keep Bruce in the picture. There was a payphone in the entrance lobby of the pub and she hurried back there, put in a coin and tapped out the number of his mobile phone, hoping that she wouldn't catch him at an awkward moment. As it happened, he was on his way back to his office to deliver his story; his reaction on hearing what she had discovered was both predictable and gratifying.

'You're brilliant, Mel!' he exclaimed. 'Where exactly are you?'

'A few hundred yards from Rocky Wilkins' house. He lives up the lane opposite the Golden Bell and his truck's parked outside. He's not in the pub, so the chances are he's at home.'

'And you're planning to pay him a visit?'

'Sure, why not? Even if it's a false alarm and he isn't the man Hannah ran off with, there's no harm done.'

'Can't it wait till I'm free to come with you? It'd make a brilliant story . . . intrepid lady novelist and journalist from local paper track down vital witness in murder hunt—'

'And while we're waiting for a convenient time to call on him together, Rocky gets into his truck and heads for a destination unknown,' Melissa interrupted. 'Or worse still, Hannah's people get to him before we do. If I can find him, so can they.'

'You've got a point there,' Bruce admitted.

'All we want to know is, is he or isn't he the man who took Hannah Rose to Eastern Europe? If he is, he needs to be warned as soon as possible of the danger he's in.'

'Hmm . . . okay then, go ahead, but promise to keep me posted.' It was clear from Bruce's tone that the danger to Rocky Wilkins from a possible revenge attack from Hannah's relatives was only marginally more important than getting a scoop for the *Gazette*.

'Don't worry, I'll call you the minute I know anything.'

'Thanks.' The reception became distorted; above the crackle on the line she heard him say, 'Touching base now. Call me here if there's any news.'

*   *   *

The minute he set foot in the newsroom, Bruce Ingram was aware of an atmosphere of suppressed excitement which meant one thing: a big story was about to break.

'What's going on?' he asked.

'Word's just come in from the nick,' said Alec Trimble, one of the other reporters. 'The two scrap-metal dealers in the freezer case have been released without charge.'

'No kidding! Any details?'

'Not yet. You were at the earlier briefings . . . how would you say the inquiry's been going?'

'DCI Holloway was playing it close to his chest as usual, but it's pretty clear he was having a hard time building up a case against those two. He was granted one extension . . . maybe there wasn't enough evidence to justify another. I'll bet he's sick as a dog!' Bruce rubbed his hands in glee at the thought, remembering his own short career in the police and the ambitious detective's seeming delight in humiliating his juniors.

'So where does he go from here, I wonder?' said Alec.

Bruce frowned. 'Dunno. Carry on with the house-to-house in the hope of tracing the girl's movements, I suppose.'

'I wonder if the police are any nearer finding the bloke she ran off with. If he had nothing to hide, you'd think he'd have come forward by now.' Alec toyed absent-mindedly with a paperweight on Bruce's desk. 'Y'know,' he went on thoughtfully, 'he could be the killer . . . I've always had my doubts about him.'

'Hells' teeth!' Bruce jumped to his feet.

'Now what?'

'Here!' Bruce slammed his cassette recorder down in front of a startled trainee journalist who was studying a page mock-up on an adjacent desk. 'You can type, can't you? Transcribe that interview for me. Then have a go at writing the story. I'll look it over when I get back.' He grabbed his jacket from a nearby peg and made for the door. 'If the boss asks for me,' he said to Alec over his shoulder, 'tell her I'm on my way to the Golden Bell at Carston and I'll call in later.'

Chapter Fourteen

The sun had been shining earlier, but now the sky was overcast and a stiff breeze had sprung up, sweeping across the open fields that surrounded the village of Carston and sending fallen leaves careering in all directions. Shivering a little as she stepped outside, Melissa put on her gloves, turned up the collar of her coat, recrossed the road and set off to find the Wilkins' house. She had walked only a few yards when a woman cyclist appeared round the bend in the lane, pedalling with her shoulders hunched over the handlebars and her gaze fixed straight ahead. As she passed, Melissa caught a brief glimpse of pale, drawn features framed in a head scarf and eyes watery and reddened by the wind.

She was trying to decide which of the row of cottages might be the one where Rocky Wilkins lived when the problem was solved by the man himself emerging from the one at the far end, crossing the road and climbing into the cab of the tractor. Alarmed at the thought that he might be about to drive off, she hurried forward, but almost immediately he jumped down again with a briefcase in his hand, slamming the door behind him with a violent movement that suggested he was not in the best of tempers. He headed back to the house without appearing to notice Melissa and was halfway up the path to his front door by the time she reached the gate.

'Mr Wilkins!' she called.

He pulled up, swung round and glared. 'Who wants to know?'

'My name's Melissa Craig.' She pushed open the gate and walked towards him; as she drew near, his expression relaxed into a smile which, had she been an impressionable twenty-year-old instead of a mature woman enjoying a perfectly satisfactory love-life, would have set her heart thumping. As it was, she merely said in a brisk, businesslike voice, 'I'd like a word with you if you've got a moment.'

'An . . . ny time! Come along in!' The words fairly throbbed with a seductive intensity that was so plainly the result of constant practice as to be almost comical. With a slight bow and a gesture of invitation, he stood aside while she stepped past him into the tiny entrance hall. He closed the door behind her with no sign of the ill-temper she had witnessed a few moments earlier. There was something in the controlled, deliberate movement and the click of the latch that struck her as vaguely menacing. It gave her a feeling of being locked in and for a moment she found herself wishing she had agreed to wait until Bruce was free to come with her. Still, she was here now. She resolved to be as brief as possible, say what she had come to say and leave.

Rocky put the briefcase down at the foot of the stairs and, with another devastating smile accompanied by a further bow and gesture, ushered her into a small but comfortably furnished sitting-room where a log fire burned in an iron grate. He put a hand under her elbow, guided her towards one of a pair of armchairs placed on either side of the fire and said, 'Sit down, make yourself comfortable.'

A trifle hesitantly, Melissa complied. 'I won't keep you long,' she began.

'No need to rush!' He settled in the other armchair, nonchalantly crossed his legs and sat studying her with such undisguised admiration that she began to feel uneasy. To avoid his gaze, she glanced around the room. There was a pleasant hint of lavender polish in the air and the general impression was of order and an almost aggressive cleanliness.

The fitted carpet was spotless, the curtains were artistically draped and held back with matching ties, the furniture had a waxy sheen, the windows and the looking-glass above the mantelpiece sparkled and the graduated row of copper jugs on the hearth shone like miniature suns.

'Cosy, innit?' he said, as if reading her thoughts. On the face of it, it was an innocuous remark, the comment of a man proud of his home, but he managed to infuse the word 'cosy' with a disturbingly sexual overtone. He spoke with a local accent, but his voice had a throaty, sensual quality that sounded put on, as if he was trying to give an impression of Humphrey Bogart. She guessed it was part of his seduction technique and decided it was time to get things back on track.

'Very cosy,' she agreed, adding pointedly, 'and your wife keeps it beautifully.'

Mention of his wife did not appear to cause him the slightest embarrassment. 'Yeah, Julie likes to see things just so,' he said carelessly. He might, Melissa thought, have been talking about a housekeeper. 'She's just gone to work, so there's no need to worry,' he added with a suggestive leer.

'Worry? What should I be worried about?'

This was getting trickier by the minute. It had not occurred to her, in her excitement at having found him, that he might jump to the conclusion that she was following up his unspoken invitation of the previous evening. She looked back at him warily, sizing him up. He was sturdily built, with powerful-looking hands and wrists. If he started to get physical, things could turn very nasty. 'Look,' she said hastily, 'don't get the wrong idea. I'm not—'

'Oh, come on!' he said, his bold eyes devouring hers, 'I know exactly why you're here. I saw you in the Bell the other night and I read the message. I could see you fancied me and—'

'No, really,' she protested. 'You've got it all wrong . . . just let me explain—'

'It's mutual,' he continued, as if she hadn't spoken. 'No need to be shy.' With a sudden movement that took her completely by surprise, he stood up, bent down and grabbed one of her hands, hauling her to her feet. 'We'll have a great time together, you and I!'

'Now, just a minute!' She made an effort to pull away from him, but he held her against his chest in a bear-hug, making it difficult to breathe. She put both hands on his upper arms in an effort to break free, but it was like trying to push over two oak posts set in concrete. 'Pack it in, will you!' she gasped.

'Why? It's what you came for, innit?' His face moved closer to hers and she leaned back as far as the iron grip would allow.

'No it isn't. I came to warn you—'

'Oh yeah, what of? Been caught fiddling me tacho, have I? Pull the other one!' He put a hand behind her head, his open mouth reaching for hers. Thankful that she was wearing her Dr Martens, Melissa aimed two vicious kicks at his shins.

Both found their target. Rocky gave an agonised yelp and slackened his grip just enough for her to wriggle free. His face contorted as he bent down to massage the bruises. Like many bullies, he appeared to have a low pain threshold. 'Spiteful bitch, you'll be sorry for that!' he snarled.

'You asked for it!' Melissa panted. She tried to dodge past him and make a dash for it while he was preoccupied with his injuries, but he was too quick for her. 'Not so fast, gorgeous!' he snarled, seizing her by one arm. 'I'll teach you to play games with me!' He swung her round and aimed a blow at her with his free hand. She ducked to avoid it and her eye fell on a heavy brass doorstop. She grabbed it and swung it wildly at random, catching him a blow on the side of the head as he made a further lunge at her. With a startled grunt, he staggered backwards, tripped over a coffee table, fell to the floor and lay there groaning, apparently half-dazed, with blood oozing from a cut above one eye.

Melissa was about to turn and flee the house while she had the chance, but the possibility that she had done him a serious injury made her hesitate. While she was considering whether she should call an ambulance, he rolled on to his side and propped himself up on one elbow. He put a hand to his face and then took it away, staring bemusedly first at the blood and then at Melissa. 'Christ, what hit me?' he muttered.

Relieved that he did not appear seriously hurt, Melissa allowed herself a little smirk of triumph. She held up the doorstop which – somewhat to her surprise – was still in her hand. 'This!' she said, brandishing it in front of him, 'and I'll use it again if you give me any more trouble!'

He raised an arm in a gesture of surrender. 'Okay, okay, so I got the wrong idea. Put that away, for God's sake.' He dabbed again at the cut on his face, which was now bleeding more freely. 'Look, get me a towel or something, will you? Julie'll give me hell if I make a mess on the carpet.'

Cautiously, still keeping an eye on him, Melissa put down her impromptu weapon. 'Where will I find one?' she asked.

'Try the door at the end of the passage.'

The door led to the kitchen, which had the same air of having just been spring-cleaned as the sitting-room. Melissa found some clean tea-cloths in a drawer, snatched one and hurried back to find Rocky in a sitting position on the floor, leaning against an armchair and wearing an expression of mortal suffering. He took the cloth and dabbed gingerly at the cut, then scrambled to his feet and stumbled towards the mantelpiece to peer into the mirror. 'Hope this don't leave a scar!' he mumbled.

'I doubt if it'll spoil your fatal beauty, if that's what's worrying you,' she retorted. 'And just for the record, it's nothing to what's likely to happen to you if Hannah Rose's menfolk get their hands on you.'

Rocky stiffened; in the mirror, Melissa saw his mouth fall

open and his eyes bulge. 'What the hell do you know about Hannah Rose?' he gasped.

'Quite a lot,' Melissa said quietly. She was aware that reaction was bound to follow the shock of the attempted assault, but for the moment she felt ice-cool and in total control. 'You took her with you on a run to Eastern Europe last year, didn't you?'

Rocky turned round to face her, shaking his head like a swimmer trying to clear water from his ears and running a hand through his thick, carefully styled hair. 'Christ! I need a drink!' he said pathetically. He limped over to the sideboard, pausing on the way to massage his shins. He took out a bottle of whisky and a glass, poured a measure, tossed it back and poured another. As an afterthought, he waved the bottle in Melissa's direction. In his consternation over this new turn of events, he seemed to have lost all animosity towards her.

'Want one?' he asked.

'No thanks.'

'So what's all this about Hannah?'

'You know she's been murdered?'

At the word 'murdered' a subtle change came over Rocky. His eyes narrowed and his jaw set in a hard, pugnacious line. He lowered his head and glared at Melissa like an animal driven into a corner. 'What's that to me?' he demanded. 'You suggesting I did it?'

'No, of course not,' she said hastily. 'Two men have already been arrested, but that's not going to satisfy Hannah's relations. They blame you for her death because you took her away from the protection of her family. It's your blood they'll be after . . . that's why I came here. I tried to tell you, to warn you—'

'Yeah, yeah, so you said.' His expression took on a cunning, shifty quality that set the hairs rising on the back of Melissa's neck. Until this moment, she had never even considered the possibility that he, and not the two men in custody, might be Hannah's killer. Now, she was not so sure. Fighting back a threatened wave of panic, she backed slowly towards the door.

'That's all I wanted to say. Just keep your eyes open for any sign of strangers who might be taking an interest in you. I've explained to the police and they—'

Mention of the police was a mistake. Shouting obscenities, Rocky charged. Melissa fled from the room and dashed across the hall, but before she could reach the front door he caught up with her and grabbed her round the waist. She screamed and he clapped a hand over her mouth. She sank her teeth into his thumb and with another oath he shifted his grip to her throat, squeezing so hard that she could barely draw breath. She lashed out backwards with one heel and jabbed her elbows as hard as she could into his stomach. He gave a gasp of pain and slackened his grip just enough for her to tear his hands an inch or two away from her throat. She let out another, half-strangled scream and reached frantically for the latch. Her fingers closed over it and she managed to drag the door open a fraction, but Rocky's hand came over her shoulder and pushed it to. As it was on the point of closing there was a thud as something heavy landed against it from outside, forcing it ajar. A man's booted foot appeared in the gap.

'What the hell—?' Rocky began.

'Police!' shouted the owner of the foot. 'Open up!'

The pressure on the inside of the door was abruptly released and it flew open. At the same instant, Rocky let go of Melissa. A man in jeans and an anorak stumbled across the threshold and cannoned into her. The head-to-head collision threw her sideways and she staggered back against the wall with her hands over her face, half stunned, bewildered and fighting for breath. She was dimly aware of shouts, grunts and gasps, the sound of a heavy fall and a slamming of doors, followed by silence. She lowered her hands and saw her deliverer rising unsteadily from the floor. Gingerly massaging his jaw, he turned to face her.

'You okay, Mel?' he asked, with a semblance of a grin.

'Bruce! How in the world did you get here?'

'Never mind that now . . . I've got to catch that bastard . . . he went out the back—' Somewhere close at hand, a car started and drove off at high speed. 'That's him, he's getting away!' Bruce rushed outside, but was back a moment later, stabbing at the buttons on his mobile phone. 'Police? This is an emergency. A woman has been attacked in number eight, Farm Villas, Carston. Assailant Rocky Wilkins, believed involved in the disappearance last year of murder victim Hannah Rose, escaped in a dark blue BMW—'

Melissa listened in astonishment as he reeled off the details. When the call was finished she said weakly, 'Would you mind explaining exactly—?' She was unable to finish; the reaction she had anticipated during the scrimmage overtook her and she began shaking violently.

Bruce put an arm round her shoulders, his face full of concern. 'Mel, what is it? Are you hurt?'

'No, not really,' she said through chattering teeth, 'just scared out of my wits.' She leaned against him for a few moments, taking deep breaths, fighting off the threat of nausea. When she was steadier she said, 'I couldn't believe what was happening . . . all I did was try to warn him about Hannah's people, but he thought I—'

'Fancied him?' said Bruce. 'Yeah, I guessed as much.'

'You did?'

'Had a chat with Rosie in the Golden Bell. She thinks I'm your boyfriend, you've been bowled over by some sexy bloke you met there and I'm trying to win you back. Very sympathetic, she was . . . said I might find you here.'

Melissa jerked away from him. 'You mean you told her I'd fallen for that oaf?'

Bruce laughed aloud at her air of indignation. 'Not in so

many words,' he assured her. 'Not my fault if she misread the situation, is it?'

'Of all the cheek!'

'Did the trick, though, didn't it? Now, I think you could use a coffee before the police get here.' He led her into the kitchen and bustled about, filling the electric kettle and poking into cupboards for what he needed while Melissa sat in a chair and attempted to sort her jumbled thoughts into some kind of order.

'The last time I spoke to you, you'd just got back to your office and I said I'd call you there if I had any news,' she said. 'The next thing, you turn up here like the proverbial knight in shining armour to save me from a fate worse than death.'

Bruce paused in the act of spooning instant coffee into a china mug decorated with poppies. 'It could be a lot more serious than that.'

'What?'

'The two men the police were holding have been released without charge. The news came through just as I got back to the office and one of my colleagues reckons the truck driver who took Hannah away is the one who killed her – he's thought so all along. I couldn't be sure Rocky was the man, but I daren't take a chance so I dropped everything . . . and here I am.'

He put a steaming mug of coffee on the table in front of her and she picked it up and sipped it gratefully. 'Mm, I needed that,' she said. After a moment a thought struck her. 'I believe your colleague could be right,' she said slowly. 'About Rocky being the killer, I mean.'

'What makes you say that?'

'He took a bit of persuading that I wasn't after his body, but once he got the message he quietened down. Then I said my piece about Hannah's relations being out for his blood. He seemed disturbed by the fact that I knew of his association with her and might think he'd killed her, but I assured him that wasn't the case . . . and then I started to say I'd warned the police of the possibility of an attack on him and he didn't even let me finish . . . he just went berserk.'

'When you mentioned the police?'

'That's right.'

'And when I tried to shoulder my way through the door he tried to hold it shut until I pretended I was from the police. Then he let go and made a bolt for it. I tried to grab him, but he caught me off balance and clocked me one.' Bruce fingered his jaw and winced at the recollection. 'Yes, it figures. I wonder if he's been picked up yet?' He lifted his head at the sound of an approaching car. It pulled up sharply just outside; moments later there was a hammering at the front door. 'That'll be the Bill,' he said, and went out into the hall. He was back almost immediately, accompanied by a young woman police constable and a stony-faced Detective Chief Inspector Holloway.

Chapter Fifteen

'**M**rs Craig,' said DCI Holloway. There was no need for him to add, 'And what have you been up to this time?' – his demeanour and tone of voice said it for him. He gave Bruce a hostile glance. 'I'll talk to you later, Ingram,' he said curtly. 'I don't conduct interviews in front of the press.'

'I'm here as a material witness—' Bruce began, but Holloway made a dismissive gesture.

'Later,' he repeated.

Bruce flushed and drew in a quick breath; for a moment, Melissa thought he was going to make an angry retort, but with an obvious effort he controlled himself and said, 'All right, Mr Holloway, I'll wait in the next room . . . but please bear in mind that Mrs Craig is still shaken after a very frightening experience.'

'So I understand. I also know that Mrs Craig is a very resourceful and resilient lady.' This time, there was a hint of grudging admiration in the detective's voice.

Melissa gave Bruce a quick, reassuring smile. 'I'll be fine, thanks,' she said.

Reluctantly, the reporter withdrew. When the door closed behind him, DCI Holloway sat down opposite Melissa while the young policewoman found a stool and perched, pen and notebook at the ready, alongside a Formica-covered work surface running the length of a bank of storage units with moulded doors in limed oak. The kitchen, like the sitting-room, was small but fitted out to show-room standards with top-quality equipment including a built-in oven, hob and dish-washer. It crossed Melissa's mind that the business of a long-haul truck driver must be extremely lucrative.

'If there's anything you'd prefer to say privately to WPC Savage—' Holloway began and Melissa felt her momentary annoyance at his dismissal of Bruce softening at this unexpected show of delicacy on his part.

'No, it's quite all right,' she said. 'It wasn't so much a case of attempted rape, although I daresay it would have come to that if I hadn't managed to fight him off . . . and no doubt he'd claim I encouraged him—'

Holloway's sandy eyebrows shot up. 'Perhaps you'd like to clarify that last remark?' he said stiffly.

'I . . . it's not easy to explain.' Melissa found herself floundering. With hindsight, her tactics seemed slightly ridiculous. Yet the fact was, they had produced results. It was up to her to make them sound plausible.

'I noticed Wilkins . . . I didn't know who he was at the time . . . when I was in the Golden Bell last night, having a drink with . . . a friend.' For the moment, she decided to keep Matt Waters' name out of it. 'There was something about him that interested me . . . he was almost the exact embodiment of a character for a novel I'm thinking of writing.' She broke off as she caught the detective's eye and read in it a hint of slightly scornful condescension. 'I know this must sound odd to anyone who isn't a writer—'

'Please continue,' he said, in a voice totally lacking in expression.

'He was reading a newspaper and I was making a mental note of his features and the clothes he was wearing and so on,' Melissa continued, increasingly aware of how eccentric she must sound to her unimaginative listener, 'and suddenly he looked up and saw me watching him. He gave me a sort of come-hither look . . . so I turned away immediately,' she added hastily, seeing the eyebrows at work again. 'And then my friend came back with our drinks and I forgot about it for the time being.'

'For the time being,' Holloway repeated, as if the words held some inner significance. 'But I assume you decided later on that this "character" as you call him was worth a little further investigation . . . in the interests of research for your novel.' His tone carried a resigned acceptance of the universal truth that there is no limit to the oddities of human behaviour.

'No, it wasn't that.' As concisely as possible, Melissa described the sequence of events in the pub: Rocky's cheerful demeanour when she first noticed him: the reference during his conversation with Rosie to his recent absence from home, suggesting – with hindsight – that he might be a long-haul truck driver: his subsequent abrupt departure in apparent ill-humour. That morning, the E-FIT picture of Hannah in the centre pages of the previous day's *Gazette* made her wonder if that was what brought about his sudden change of mood. 'It was then that I decided to try and find out if he was the man Hannah Rose had run away with,' she finished.

'And at this point, you got in touch with a representative of the press.' This time Holloway's tone was accusatory. 'It didn't occur to you, I suppose, to come to us with the information?'

'It wasn't information as such . . . it was only a very long shot, and in any case, it wasn't as if the man was a suspect. I simply wanted to find out if he had been involved with Hannah Rose and if so warn him to be on his guard against a possible attack from her family. I was – and still am – seriously afraid that they will do everything in their power to find the man who took her away from them, and punish him according to their own code.'

'Yes, I understand you have been at pains to impress that opinion on Sergeant Waters.' It was impossible to deduce from Holloway's tone whether or not he took her fears seriously.

'The fact is – as you know – that I have had contact with the murdered girl's aunt . . . and I also happen to know something about Romany customs.'

Holloway made an impatient gesture. 'Quite so. Let's get back to the point, shall we? How did you come to be here, and exactly what happened after you arrived?'

'I made some inquiries at the Golden Bell.' Without risking further ill-concealed derision by revealing details of her conversation with Rosie, Melissa described briefly how she had intercepted Rocky outside his house, how he had misinterpreted her motive in approaching him, and the outcome of the brief struggle that took place as a result. 'I was scared at first that I'd done him a serious injury,' she confessed, 'but he seemed more concerned about possible damage to his looks.'

There was a stifled titter from WPC Savage that earned her a scathing glance from her superior officer. He turned back to Melissa. 'And then what happened?'

Shuddering slightly at the recollection, gingerly fingering her neck where Rocky had gripped her, Melissa described the truck driver's reaction to her warning. 'He as good as admitted that he knew Hannah, although he insisted he didn't kill her. He was obviously uneasy to think I knew about his connection with her, but his attitude wasn't threatening until I mentioned I'd spoken to the police.'

'About your speculation concerning possible danger to whoever had taken the girl away?'

'I never had the chance to tell him that. The word "police" was enough to make him lose his rag and attack me. If Bruce . . . Mr Ingram . . . hadn't turned up when he did, I really think he might have killed me. As it was, he let go of me, took a swipe at Mr Ingram and made a bolt for it.'

'I see.' Holloway thought for a moment before saying, 'Thank you Mrs Craig, I think that'll be all for now. If you'll be kind enough to call in at Headquarters some time – say tomorrow – to sign your statement?'

'Yes, of course.'

'I'll see Ingram now. I suggest you go home and rest.' For the second time since the start of the interview, he dropped his official manner and revealed a human face. 'Or maybe,' he added with a hint of a smile, 'you'll want to do some work on your novel, now that you've come across this interesting character.'

Melissa found herself smiling in return. 'I might just do that,' she agreed.

As she stood up, WPC Savage said, 'Will you be all right on your own?'

It was the first time she had spoken. Holloway gave her a sharp look, which softened to a nod of approval. 'Good point. Perhaps Mrs Craig would like to wait until you're free to accompany her?'

Melissa shook her head. 'That's kind of you, but I'll be okay. My car's parked at the pub; I'm sure Mr Ingram will drive me back there when you've finished talking to him.'

'As you wish.' Holloway's formal demeanour returned. 'Audrey, tell him to come in, will you?'

'My God, what an officious, self-opinionated sod that man is!' Bruce muttered angrily as the front door of the Wilkins' house closed behind them.

Melissa gave him a sympathetic glance. 'Did he give you a hard time?'

'Anyone listening would have thought I was a suspect instead of a witness trying to help. He didn't even give me credit when I gave him the registration number of Wilkins' car.'

'Good heavens, how did you manage to get that?'

'Made a mental note of it as I arrived. Habit, I suppose . . . I had no particular reason to think it was his.' Bruce took Melissa by the arm. 'How are you feeling now?'

'Fine, thanks. If you wouldn't mind giving me a lift back to the pub, I'll collect my car and go home.'

'Sure.'

They had almost reached the gate when they heard the sound of the front door of the adjoining house opening. A voice called out, 'Excuse me, what's going on?' and they turned to see a young woman in outdoor clothes with a baby tucked under one arm. They waited while she hurried up the path to her own gate and said, 'Are you the police? Has something happened to Julie?' There was a note of anxiety in her voice as she looked from one to the other.

'No, we're not . . . the police are—' Melissa began, but Bruce cut her short by asking, 'Do you mean your next-door neighbour?'

'Yes. When I came home from my walk and saw the police car—' The woman broke off, eyeing them doubtfully. She was on the plump side, with a round, homely face framed in a tumble of dark, straggling curls that blew across her face in the chilly breeze. 'Who are you, then?' she asked.

'My name's Bruce Ingram from the *Gazette* and this is my colleague, Mrs Craig.' Bruce dived into a pocket and produced his card while Melissa, dumbfounded by his effrontery, looked on in amazement. 'I wonder, can you spare a few minutes, Mrs . . . er?'

'Lister . . . Penny Lister.' She scrutinised the card before handing it back. 'What do you want to know?'

Bruce glanced down at the infant, which was beginning to grizzle and squirm in its mother's arms. 'Pretty baby,' he said. He put out a hand and the grizzling stopped as one tiny fist closed over his forefinger and large eyes regarded him with curiosity. Not for the first time in their acquaintance, Melissa saw mistrust melt away under the effect of his disarming smile. 'Don't think he . . . or is it she? . . . likes being out here in this cold wind,' he went on, with an air of almost fatherly concern.

'She. Her name's Kirsty.' Penny jiggled the baby against her shoulder, patting its back and crooning in its ear. 'You're right,

156

it is cold out here . . . I'd just taken her outdoor things off when I saw you and I felt I just had to—' She broke off and turned back towards her own front door, saying, 'Perhaps you'd better come in for a moment.'

'Thank you.'

By now completely won over, Penny led the way up the path. As they followed, Melissa hissed in Bruce's ear, 'Since when have I been on the staff of the *Gazette*?'

'I did it to hide your real identity,' he whispered back. 'Think of ex-DCI Harris's reaction if he heard about this little show!'

'Oh Lord!' Melissa clapped a hand to her mouth. 'He'd go ape!'

'Exactly.' Bruce gave her a sideways grin. 'See how considerate I am.'

Penny ushered them in and closed the front door. The hall was a mirror image of the one in the adjoining house, with the staircase to the left and the front room to the right. There was an old-fashioned hall-stand behind the door, the pegs hung with an assortment of jackets, coats and caps and the lower part a clutter of boots, gloves and shoes. Penny led them into the front room and deposited Kirsty on a woollen blanket spread on the floor, where she lay contentedly kicking her plump legs and blowing bubbles at the ceiling while her mother slipped off her shabby duffel coat and threw it over the back of a chair. 'You'll have to excuse the clutter,' she said, scooping up an armful of toys and small garments from a couch with sagging cushions to make room for them to sit down. 'I'm not such a good housewife as Julie.'

'Julie? Would that be Mrs Wilkins?' asked Bruce, who had already produced a notebook.

'That's right.' Penny glanced from him to Melissa and back again. The look of anxiety returned. 'Before I answer any of your questions you must tell me . . . is she all right?'

'So far as I know,' said Bruce. 'She isn't at home at the

moment . . . but what makes you think she might not be all right?'

'Last night they – she and Rocky – had a most fearful row. They were shouting at one another . . . the noise was terrible, it woke Kirsty . . . and at one point I heard a thump and a scream and I wondered if he was knocking her about again.'

'Again? Does he make a habit of it?'

'No, I wouldn't say that. Most of the time they seem okay, but she has to watch her step and now and again he gets mad and lashes out at her. I wouldn't stand for it myself, but she's so besotted with him she just takes it . . . or she has done up to now. When I saw the police car, I wondered if she'd decided enough was enough and was going to charge him.'

'No, I understand Mrs Wilkins is at work as usual,' said Melissa. 'In fact, I think I met her on the way here . . . does she ride a bicycle?'

'That's right. She works in the deli at the superstore outside Stowbridge. She uses the car sometimes, but she usually cycles to work.'

'Have you any idea what they were rowing about last night?'

'I couldn't hear what they were saying, but I do know she's very jealous of him . . . doesn't like him so much as looking at another woman, especially if she's pretty. Most of the time he behaves himself when he's at home, but there's no saying what he gets up to when he's away. She doesn't worry about me, though,' Penny added with a slightly rueful smile. 'He's got a roving eye all right, but I'm not his type . . . he likes them sexy and glamorous.'

'You have a lovely personality, and that counts for far more than glamour,' said Bruce gallantly. Penny's smile of pleasure transformed her face. Despite her undistinguished features, shabby clothes and slightly dishevelled appearance there was something warm and appealing about her. Her skin was clear and her brown eyes wide and candid. 'So you and Julie are friends?' Bruce went on. 'Does she confide in you?'

'She never says a word against Rocky, if that's what you mean. She's very proud of him . . . shows off all the things he brings back from his trips . . . and the photographs he takes while he's away. Some of them are ever so good . . . he's turned the attic into a darkroom and he develops them himself.'

Bruce was scribbling in his notebook. 'That's an interesting hobby,' he remarked casually. 'What sort of pictures does he take?' There was a gleam in his eye that Melissa instantly recognised, but Penny took the question at its face value.

'Views of places in foreign parts mostly,' she said. 'Good as pictures in travel brochures, some of them.'

'People?'

'Sometimes. He did a series of shots of the gipsies at the Stow Horse Fair last year.'

It was confirmation, if any were needed, that Melissa's hunch had been correct. 'Was there a shot of a girl making lace?' she asked.

Penny's forehead puckered in a frown and she shook her head. 'I don't remember seeing one,' she said. 'I daresay he does take pictures of girls, but I doubt if he shows them to Julie.' Her expression became suddenly keen and alert. 'That girl whose body was found in a freezer . . . she was a gipsy, wasn't she? Do you suppose Rocky knew her? Maybe that was what he and Julie were rowing about last night.' She put a hand to her mouth at the thought of the possible implication. 'You don't suppose he killed her, do you?'

Bruce put the book in his pocket and stood up. 'I'm afraid we can't help you there. The fact is, Mrs Craig and I came to talk to Rocky about his job. We're putting together a feature about long-haul truck drivers for the *Gazette*.' His candid gaze never wavered as he told the barefaced lie. 'It seems, however, that the police also want to talk to him . . . we'd just started our interview when they arrived and he left in rather a hurry. I don't suppose you've any idea where he might be heading?'

'No, none at all. Look, don't you think Julie should know about this? If Rocky's in some sort of trouble—'

'What time does she finish work?'

'I'm not sure . . . not before six, I wouldn't think.' As she spoke, there was a ring at the bell. She went to the window and peered out. 'It's a policewoman,' she said, looking apprehensive.

'I expect Chief Inspector Holloway will want to ask you a few questions, just in case you can help him with his inquiries, but there's nothing for you to worry about,' said Bruce reassuringly. 'Come along Melissa . . . we'd better be going. Goodbye, and thank you so much for your time, Mrs Lister.'

They stepped past a surprised-looking WPC Savage and Bruce took Melissa's arm. 'You quite all right now?' he asked.

'Yes, fine.'

'Right, let's get moving.' He hurried her to his car, which was parked a few yards away.

'What's the rush?' she asked as she buckled her seat belt.

'We're going to have a chat with Julie Wilkins before the police get to her.'

'Why?'

Bruce drove a few yards until he reached a field entrance, slammed the car into reverse and executed a rapid three-point turn. 'I want to try and find out a bit more about Rocky's picture gallery before Prune-Face hears about it,' he said as he headed back towards the main road at a speed that had Melissa clinging to the edge of her seat.

'I don't understand,' Melissa began. 'Why do we—?'

'Your tussle with Rocky has blunted your detective instincts,' Bruce told her cheerfully as he set the car hurtling along the winding road to Stowbridge as if it was a race track. 'That photo of Hannah . . . the one you saw in Rachel's caravan?

With any luck there's a copy – or at least, the negative – still in the house.'

'Of course!' Melissa mentally kicked herself for not having thought of it herself. 'I didn't think of that. But I don't see what you hope to—'

'If I could get my hands on it before the police do,' Bruce began. The prospect excited him so much that he took a sharp bend too fast, making the car rock alarmingly on its suspension.

Melissa reached for the grab handle. 'If you carry on driving like this, the police will be getting their hands on you!' she told him through clenched teeth. 'Anyway, you're kidding yourself. Julie won't have seen any of Rocky's girlie pictures . . . you heard what Penny said.'

'She might be willing to have a rummage round when she hears what he's been up to this afternoon—'

'And I suppose you plan to have Hannah on the front page of the *Gazette* while DCI Holloway is still plodding through statements from Rocky's neighbours?'

'Why not? We'd only want to borrow it for an hour or two, until we can get one of the girls in the newsroom to run it through the scanner.'

'You'll never get away with it. Even if Julie falls for whatever cock and bull story you plan to tell her, the police are bound to be keeping a watch on the house in case Rocky comes back. As soon as she appears, they'll pounce on her.'

'You're probably right, but it's worth a try.' They were approaching the entrance to the superstore and Bruce at last slowed to a reasonable speed. He turned into the car park, found a space and cut the engine. 'I'm going to see if I can have a word with her. Are you coming with me, or are you going to wait here?'

'Neither,' said Melissa. 'You please yourself, but I've had more than enough excitement for one day, thank you. I'm going to take a cab back to the Golden Bell, pick up my car and go straight home.' She unbuckled her seat belt and got out.

Bruce looked disappointed but resigned. 'Just as you like. I'll call you later, after I've had a chat with Julie.'

'I doubt if you'll have the chance to do even that.' Melissa indicated with a jerk of her head a police car that she had just spotted turning into the car park. A uniformed officer got out and hurried towards the store entrance. 'Looks as if your favourite DCI has radioed for a patrol to pick her up.'

'Shit!' said Bruce. 'If I could have had just five minutes with her first—'

Melissa got back into the car. 'Well, it's an ill wind,' she said. 'You can drive me back to the pub instead and save me the taxi fare.'

Chapter Sixteen

That morning, after a restless night, Julie had woken up with a sense of foreboding in her brain and a dull ache behind her eyes. Rocky was still asleep; very cautiously, so as not to wake him, she rolled over and propped herself up on one elbow to look at him. Her throat tightened with love for him. If he was in some sort of trouble, no matter what it was, she would protect him with her dying breath. He was so attractive, with his tanned features and crisply curling hair, like the heroes on the covers of the romantic novels one of the girls at the superstore brought in to read during meal breaks. Julie herself wasn't much given to reading and she wasn't interested in story-book affairs. She had her man and in any case, looking after him when he was at home and keeping the house the way she wanted it took up most of her time.

Rocky grunted and stirred slightly as she slid out of bed but he did not wake, even when she gave an involuntary cry from the pain of her bruised ribs. She put on her dressing-gown and slippers, crept out of the bedroom and went to the bathroom. She peered at her face in the mirror; her eyes were still puffy from crying and her cheeks were pallid except for the mark where he had struck her. Last time it happened she had blamed it on a collision with a cupboard door she had carelessly left open. She would have to think of a different explanation this time. It wasn't a very bad bruise; if she could let her hair hang loose round her face no one would even notice, but working in a food department where the hygiene rules were strict and caps had to be worn, that wasn't possible. Still, she told herself as she crept downstairs to make a cup of tea, it was only once in a while and it was always because she had done something Rocky had told her not to do. It was her own fault really. She had so much to be thankful for; dozens of women would give their ears for a husband as attractive as Rocky. He was generous too . . . he brought her lovely presents back from his trips and they had a beautiful home.

After drinking her tea she went back upstairs to have a wash and get dressed. Rocky was still sound asleep; she'd have to wait a while before she could start hoovering or running the washing machine. He'd give her a shout when he was ready for her to start cooking his breakfast. Except on the days when he had to get up early to start work, he hated to be disturbed until he'd had his sleep out. So she ate her cereal and toast without listening to her favourite radio programme and then did some quiet jobs around the house.

As she worked, the picture of the gipsy girl kept coming back into her mind. It was easy, of course, to understand why Rocky hadn't shown it to her. It was because he knew how jealous she was. If she didn't get so up-tight every time there was a pretty woman around, there'd have been no need for him to keep the photo hidden; she'd have known about it all along and there wouldn't have been that terrible scene. It was her own fault, really. As for burning the photo and the negative . . . well, they'd agreed it was the obvious thing to do, hadn't they? Otherwise there'd have been the risk of it getting out that he'd known someone who'd gone and got herself murdered. Like Rocky had said, it would be bad for business. A man in his position couldn't afford to get mixed up with a police inquiry about someone whose picture he just happened to have taken, along with lots of others of horses and gipsy caravans, all those months ago.

It was gone ten o'clock when Rocky awoke and shouted

down for a cup of tea. When she brought it he told her to wait while he drank it, then made her take her knickers off and get back into bed. Having his weight on top of her was painful because of her sore ribs, but it was only for a minute or two and she didn't complain out of relief that he was in a good mood and never said a word about last night. While he was eating his breakfast he chatted quite cheerfully about this and that before settling down to watch the telly while she tidied the kitchen, did the washing, cleaned the bathroom and bedroom and prepared the vegetables for their evening meal. By the time she had finished he was ready for lunch, which they ate together off trays in the sitting-room while watching their favourite game show. Her shift at the superstore started at half-past two; at ten past she kissed Rocky goodbye, got out her bicycle and set off for work.

A couple of hours later she was having her tea break in the staff canteen when she received a message to say that she was wanted in the manager's office. She was aware of enquiring eyes following her as she left; one or two of the girls had given her funny looks when she explained about missing her footing as she got out of the bath and hitting her face against the wash-basin, but it never entered her head that there might be a connection between this summons and the events of the previous evening. The sight of a uniformed policeman standing beside the manager's desk came as such a shock that she put a hand to her mouth to stifle a gasp of fright.

'Ah, Mrs Wilkins,' said the manager, 'this is PC Hobson and he'd like a word with you in private. I have to pop out for a few minutes so you can talk in here if you like.'

When he had gone, the officer cleared his throat, consulted a notebook and said, 'Are you the wife of Mr Petroc Wilkins who lives at number eight, Farm Villas, Carston?'

'Yes, of course.' Julie hardly recognised her own voice, it

sounded so thin and strained. 'Please, what's wrong? Has something happened to my husband?'

'Not so far as I know, Madam. It appears there has been an incident at your house and as your husband isn't available, Chief Inspector Holloway would be obliged if you could spare a short time to help him with his inquiries.'

Julie stared at him in horror. 'An incident? Do you mean someone's broken in?' She had a sudden, nightmare vision of her beautiful, orderly home pillaged and desecrated by intruders.

The officer's face was expressionless as he replied, 'I'm afraid I haven't any more information at the moment, but no doubt Mr Holloway will explain. It shouldn't take long . . . I'll drive you to your house and bring you back after you've spoken to him. Your boss has given permission,' he added, as Julie hesitated.

'All right,' she said in a shaky whisper. The feeling of apprehension that she had felt on waking came flooding back and she began to tremble. 'I'll go and get my coat.'

The officer nodded. 'I'll wait for you by the staff entrance.'

The drive took less than ten minutes but to Julie, desperate to find out what was going on, it seemed interminable. When they reached the house she saw that Rocky's car was missing, but another police car was parked outside and one or two curious neighbours were standing a short distance away, staring and whispering amongst themselves. She ignored them, scrambling out of the patrol car before PC Hobson had switched off the ignition and running up to the front door with her key in her hand, only to have it opened from inside by yet another uniformed officer, this time a woman.

'Mrs Wilkins? I'm WPC Audrey Savage.'

'What is it?' Julie panted. 'What's happened?'

She glanced round the hall; everything seemed as usual except for a rug that appeared to have been kicked to one side. Instinctively, she bent to put it to rights, but the policewoman gently restrained her, saying, 'Please don't touch anything for the moment.'

'Did someone break in? Is there much damage?'

'If you would just come in here, Chief Inspector Holloway would like to ask you a few questions.'

Julie found herself being ushered into her own front-room; she looked wildly about her, ignoring for the moment the man wearing a raincoat over a grey suit who rose from the settee as she entered. A coffee table had been overturned, some of her precious ornaments lay on the floor, chairs had been pushed to one side and . . . horror of horrors . . . there was a patch of blood on the carpet. She let out a scream.

'Rocky's been hurt? Is it bad? Have they taken him to hospital?'

'Sit down, Madam, and try not to alarm yourself.' The man indicated a chair; mechanically, Julie obeyed. 'So far as I know,' he went on, 'your husband hasn't been seriously hurt, but we don't know where he is and we hope you'll be able to help us. It appears he left home in rather a hurry. Have you any idea where he might have gone?'

In her confusion, Julie barely understood a word. She stared dumbly at the detective; he had sandy hair and pale eyes, and like the officer sent to fetch her from work, his expression gave nothing away. Her agitated gaze moved back to the stain on the carpet; it seemed to be spreading before her eyes and she had a sudden urge to fetch water, huge quantities of water, to wash it away. If only she could do that, perhaps this would all turn out to be nothing but a hideous, fantastic dream—

'Mrs Wilkins?' The detective's voice brought her back to reality. He repeated his question and she shook her head.

'He never said he was going out,' she whispered.

'I don't imagine this was a planned departure,' said Holloway drily. 'The fact is, we were called to the house by a member of the public who reported that an assault had taken place here.'

'An assault? Are you saying someone attacked Rocky?'

'Not exactly.' The detective's mouth curled in a faint, sardonic smile. Then his manner abruptly changed and he leaned forward, fixing Julie with a penetrating stare. 'Has your husband ever mentioned a young woman called Hannah Rose?'

It was the question Julie had been dreading. Deep down, despite her frantic efforts to banish the thought, she had known from the beginning that there was some connection between this living nightmare and Rocky's relationship with the dead girl. But he had sworn that he was not her killer; she believed him and had vowed to protect him. She swallowed hard, steeling herself to keep calm, to think carefully before she spoke so as not to say anything that might give him away. After a moment, she said, trying to sound natural, 'Do you mean the girl they found in the freezer?'

'That's right.'

'Well, of course, we've talked about her. I mean, everyone's been talking about it, haven't they? Such a dreadful thing to happen.'

'We have reason to believe that your husband knew her—'

'No!' This time, Julie almost shouted. 'He never!'

'—and that he took her with him on one of his trips to Eastern Europe,' Holloway continued as if she had not spoken. 'We also have information suggesting that her relatives hold him responsible for her death and are planning to carry out a revenge attack on him.'

'Are you saying Rocky's been kidnapped?' Julie felt her self-control snapping; she sprang from her chair and clutched at Holloway, half hysterical with fear. 'What will they do to him? You must find him . . . why aren't you out looking for him?'

'Please, Mrs Wilkins, try to keep calm and answer the Chief Inspector's questions.' It was the policewoman speaking now;

her hand was on Julie's shoulder, gently pressing her back into her chair. Her voice was soothing and reassuring.

Julie sank back and burst into tears. 'Don't let them hurt Rocky,' she begged.

'We have no reason to believe that these people have actually found your husband.' The detective's voice was brisk, almost abrasive. 'In fact,' he went on, 'our informant called on him today with the intention of warning him to be on his guard against such an attack. Unfortunately, he seems to have misread the lady's intentions and she was forced to defend herself. With that.' Holloway indicated the brass cat that Rocky had proudly brought home from one of his trips. 'I wouldn't worry too much about the injury,' he went on drily. 'Cuts to the head usually bleed quite freely and it didn't prevent him from making a quick getaway the minute the lady told him she had mentioned her fears to the police.'

It was all getting too complicated. Julie covered her face with her hands. 'I don't understand,' she whispered. 'Why would he run away? He hasn't anything to hide.'

'That remains to be seen. We have the registration number of his car and my officers are on the look-out for him. No doubt he'll be picked up soon and brought in for questioning; meanwhile I'd like your permission to search this house. Of course, if you object, I can easily obtain a warrant—'

And so the nightmare continued.

At five o'clock, as the world of Julie Wilkins was being dismantled before her eyes, Melissa Craig drove her car into the garage, locked it and trudged wearily towards her front door. She had just reached it when a cheery voice behind her called, 'Yoohoo!' and she turned to see Iris, clad in a baggy sweater and corduroy trousers, scrambling over the stile from the field opposite the cottages.

'Been blackberrying,' she announced, indicating the basket

of glossy fruit in her hand. 'Fancied a crumble for supper. Plenty of apples there.' She waved a hand in the general direction of the laden tree in her garden. 'How about coming to share?'

Melissa hesitated. It would be an enormous relief to unload the day's adventures into a sympathetic ear. She would almost certainly receive a scolding for yet again poking her nose into police business and putting herself at risk, but one thing Iris could be relied on to do was to treat anything she was told as confidential. The same could not, however, be said of Iris's fiancé. On the contrary, his regard for both Melissa and Ken was such that he would feel duty bound – as he would see it, in the interests of her safety – to say something about this latest escapade.

'Well, what about it?' said Iris impatiently. 'Ken's away, isn't he?'

'Yes, till tomorrow. What about Jack?'

'In London, seeing lawyers about the house in France. Staying overnight.'

'Then . . . yes, I'd love to come.'

'Fine. About six-thirty.'

'Lovely. That gives me time for a good long soak. I'm all in.'

'It shows.' Iris gave Melissa a searching look. 'Been up to something you don't want Sir to know about?'

'You don't miss much, do you?'

Iris gave a sardonic cackle. 'Can't wait to hear about it.' She fished her latchkey from her pocket and let herself into her cottage. Thankfully, Melissa did the same.

Before going upstairs to run her bath, she checked her answering machine for messages. There was one, from Ken Harris. 'Just to let you know the job's going okay,' he said. 'It should be tied up in the morning and I hope to be back in the office by about three o'clock tomorrow. I'll be round in the evening about six.'

'Oh will you?' she muttered. It would be lovely to see him again, of course, but it would also be nice if now and then he were to add something like, 'if that's okay with you.'

'We're not cohabiting yet, *Sir*,' she informed the machine as she stabbed the reset button. 'You're taking a little too much for granted these days.'

Supper with Iris was the usual demonstration that vegetarian food, prepared by a genuine enthusiast, could be as delicious as anything containing meat. When she had finished her portion of blackberry and apple crumble, Melissa sat back with a sigh of contentment, the day's adventures temporarily forgotten. 'Iris, that was a superb meal,' she declared.

'More?' Iris gestured with the serving spoon.

'Thanks, but I couldn't manage another scrap.'

'Glad you enjoyed it. When are you going to convert your ex-copper to healthy living?'

Melissa gave a resigned chuckle. 'Not a hope. I did learn something the other day that'll gladden your heart, though.'

'Oh?'

'Joe Martin – my agent. He's gone on a fitness spree . . . joined a health club and forsworn red meat.'

'Good for him. Always knew he had good sense.' Iris gave Melissa a keen glance, her grey eyes serious. 'Seen him lately?'

'Not for a while. We need to have a talk soon about what I'm going to do next. I've made up my mind that the book I'm working on now will be the last Nathan Latimer novel.'

'Going to kill off the great detective? Surely not!'

'No, just give him honourable retirement. I want to do something different.'

'How does Ken feel about it?'

'Ken? I don't discuss my books with him . . . except to check police procedure and that sort of thing. He doesn't even read them,' Melissa added, a shade wistfully.

Iris said nothing. She began stacking plates and the two of

them cleared the table. They settled in front of the sitting-room fire with mugs of coffee, Melissa in an armchair and Iris in her favourite position, cross-legged on the rug with Binkie blissfully purring on her lap.

'Right,' said Iris. 'Going to tell how you came by those marks?' She gave Melissa a quizzical glance. 'Have to think of something good to tell Ken.'

Melissa fingered her neck where Rocky had gripped her. The same problem had exercised her mind while she was having her bath. 'I'll say a beginner at a self-defence class got carried away and grabbed me too hard,' she said.

'What self-defence class? You don't go to one.'

'I'm thinking of enrolling tomorrow.'

'He'll never wear it.'

Melissa gave a deep sigh. It was true; there was going to be another clash between her and Ken that, like so many others, would end in stalemate.

'So what really happened?'

Iris listened in silence while Melissa recounted the chain of events that had taken her to number eight, Farm Villas, Carston and her near-fatal encounter with the man she believed to be the truck driver who had taken Hannah Rose away from her family. 'It didn't enter my head that he might be the killer,' she finished, 'but even if he isn't, he's certainly got something to hide. I wonder if he's been picked up yet.'

'Let's find out.' Iris rose from the floor in a characteristically athletic movement and switched on the radio.

They were just in time to catch the announcer on the local news bulletin saying, 'Here is an item which has just come in. This afternoon, a woman was subjected to a serious assault in a house at Carston. Shortly afterwards, a man believed to be long-distance lorry driver Petroc 'Rocky' Wilkins fled from the house and drove away in a dark blue BMW. A man who attempted to detain him was also attacked and slightly injured. Police are anxious to question Wilkins in connection with this and other serious matters and are appealing to members of the public to report any sightings of the man or the car. They stress that he has a history of violence and should not be approached.'

After giving the registration number of the BMW, the announcer read the closing headlines. Iris leaned forward and switched off the set. 'Let's hope they nab him soon,' she said.

Chapter Seventeen

Somewhat to her surprise, Melissa awoke on Thursday morning from a peaceful and unbroken night's sleep. She got up and went downstairs to brew a pot of tea; while waiting for the kettle to boil, she scrutinised her neck in the hall mirror and was relieved to find that the bruises made by Rocky's fingers had already begun to fade. The weather was still too warm for high-necked sweaters, but a scarf worn as an accessory with a shirt and her hair allowed to hang loose round her face for a day or two should be sufficient to conceal those tell-tale marks. Provided, of course, that there was no question of removing the camouflage in Ken's presence; she would have to avoid love-making for a day or two. That would be no bad thing – it wouldn't do him any harm to be reminded that she wasn't there for the taking whenever he pleased.

This train of thought led to the recollection that she had promised to let him know by Saturday whether she was ready to agree to his proposal for the two of them to set up house together after having her and Iris's cottages knocked into one. Saturday was only two days away and she was no nearer coming to a decision. Without warning, after many years when she had hardly given a thought to the father who had cast her out at the time of her greatest need, one of his many-times-repeated maxims echoed in her head: 'When in doubt, don't,' he used to say. To a rebellious teenager this had always seemed nothing but an excuse to avoid risking the slightest inconvenience or disturbance to himself. Once she had plucked up the courage to tell him so, quoting '*He who hesitates is lost*' and '*Faint heart never won fair lady*' back at him, and been banished to bed without supper for her pains. But as she grew older she learned that it was not always wise to ignore persistent doubts.

She knew in her heart that Iris had been right in saying that Ken Harris would not wait for ever for a commitment from her, and that to lose him altogether would leave a void that would be hard to fill. On the other side of the equation was the undeniable fact that in recent months his attitude towards her had become steadily more possessive and claustrophobic. He was fond of reminding her that he was motivated only by love and consideration for her safety and welfare, just as her father had claimed to be. Once again her thoughts flew back to her childhood frustrations, her mother's gentle assurances that, '*He loves you really, darling, he's only thinking of your own good,*' and her own tearful, angry response, '*No he's not, he's just thinking of his own convenience.*' What her father had wanted was a docile, dutiful daughter who would stay at home and share with her mother the domestic role which he considered appropriate for all women. The day that she informed him of her intention to enter university after leaving school, the angry scene that followed and her refusal to back down, stood out in her memory as the first victory in her long and sometimes bitter fight for independence. So far she had firmly resisted any attempt to deprive her of that independence; now she had to decide whether the time had come for at least a partial surrender.

The whistle of the boiling kettle jerked her mind back to the present. While waiting for her tea to brew she opened the kitchen window and leaned out, savouring the freshness of the morning air. After an unsettled spell, the weather had turned mild again, but everywhere there were unmistakable signs of autumn. A fine mist lay over the valley like a damp veil, shrouding the trees and hedgerows and filtering much of the warmth from the early sun. Pearls of dew glistened on the grass and clung to the lacy network of spiders' webs that festooned the hawthorn hedge.

She closed the window, shivering slightly although not from cold. The comparison with lace brought back to mind the tragic fate of Hannah Rose. As she poured out her tea and sat at the table drinking it, unanswered questions began lining up in her head like the checklists she made a habit of preparing when unravelling the intricacies of her plots. At the top of the list was the obvious one: Did Rocky Wilkins kill Hannah? There was no doubt that he had known her and it now seemed certain that he had taken the photograph that stood on the chest of drawers in Rachel's caravan and processed it himself in his attic darkroom. Was that evidence still there, and was it indeed a murderer's guilt that made him panic at the mention of the police? Had the police searched the darkroom and if so, what had they found there? Did they even know of its existence? It was unlikely that they had questioned Penny, and from what Penny had said about Julie Wilkins, she was far too devoted a wife to volunteer any information that might endanger her husband.

At this point, Melissa found herself faced with a problem: Should she, when making her formal statement in a few hours' time, include the information that she and Bruce had gleaned from Julie's concerned neighbour? Common sense – and conscience – insisted that she should, but she found herself hesitating. Bruce urgently wanted a copy of that picture in order to claim a scoop for his newspaper, so he would quite possibly 'forget' to mention Rocky's hobby or the existence of the darkroom until he had done his level best to get his hands on it. If in the meantime she, Melissa, reported their conversation with Penny Lister in full, it would earn Bruce the blackest of black marks from DCI Holloway and possibly make him *persona non grata* at future press briefings. Since

Bruce was an old friend, she decided to have a word with him first. It was a little after eight o'clock; hoping to catch him before he left for work, she called his home number.

'That's a nice thought, Mel, and I appreciate it,' he said when she explained the reason for her call. 'Actually, I was going to give you a bell . . . I thought you'd be interested to know what I turned up yesterday evening.'

'Yesterday evening? Where?'

'In Carston. I went to see Penny.'

'Hoping that Julie Wilkins would have poured her troubles into her friend's sympathetic ear and you'd get a story?' Instead of a joking response to what was intended as a good-natured taunt, there was silence at the other end of the line. A trifle impatiently, Melissa said, 'Well, had she?'

'As it happens, yes,' said Bruce, 'but that wasn't my reason for the visit.'

'No?'

'No. You were probably still too shaken up after your struggle with Rocky to take much notice of your surroundings while we were talking to Penny, but it was obvious to me that she was having a hard time, coping with that kid on her own . . . I mean, there was no man around.'

'How did you figure that out?'

'No men's clothing on the hall stand, no men's boots or shoes, no man in any of the photos. The furniture was pretty shabby and her and the kid's clothes looked as if they'd come from jumble sales . . . I had the impression that life was a bit of a struggle for Penny and it seemed to me she deserved something better and . . . well . . . to cut a long story short, I bought a cuddly toy for Kirsty and some flowers and chocs for Penny and took them round.'

'That was kind of you.'

'Mel, you wouldn't believe how touched she was, how grateful. Anyone would have thought I was there to tell her she'd won the lottery. As I guessed, she's all on her own

– the kid's father dumped her when she told him she was pregnant and her parents are dead—'

'Poor girl.' There had been times during Melissa's long acquaintance with Bruce when he had shown himself to be as hard-headed as any other journalist on the track of a story, but she also knew him to be capable at times of great kindness and humanity. This, she sensed, was one of those times. It occurred to her how similar Penny's situation was to her own when Simon was a baby, yet at the same time, how different. At least her dead lover's parents had looked after her and given her and her child a home, even though her own had rejected her.

'Anyway,' Bruce went on, 'we got talking . . . and then of course the subject of the rumpus next door came up. As we guessed, the patrol car that turned up at the superstore had been sent by Holloway to pick up Julie and bring her home. Then he asked her a lot of questions about Rocky that she couldn't answer.'

'Couldn't or wouldn't?'

'Some and some, by the sound of it.'

'Did they find Hannah's picture?'

'Possibly. Not the one you saw in Rachel's caravan, though.'

'There were others of her?'

'That has yet to be established.' There was a tantalising pause; evidently, Bruce had something sensational up his sleeve and was determined to milk it for maximum effect.

'Oh, do get on with it!' Melissa said impatiently. 'Did the police search the house? What did they find?'

'They searched the house all right . . . and they found the darkroom in the attic. They brought down a quantity of photographs; some were in albums that had been stored openly on shelves. They'd also broken into a locked cupboard and found—' Bruce paused on a note of rising intonation, a sure sign that he was about to release his bombshell. Melissa mentally allowed him a count of five and was on the point of giving him a further prompt – in somewhat more energetic terms than before – when he continued, in an uncharacteristically serious voice, '—more photographs, the kind that no nice person would want to look at.'

This was something entirely unexpected and it took a few seconds to sink in. 'You mean, hard porn?' she said, almost in disbelief.

'Very hard, so I understand. It seems that Rocky has some seriously original ideas about accessories and camera angles.'

'You mean, he took the pics himself?'

'Maybe not all of them. Apparently he features in some.'

'Good Lord! Did Julie see them?'

'A few, for identification purposes I suppose. Penny says the poor woman's distraught at the knowledge of what her wonderman has been up to. She was prepared to lie through her teeth for him – after they saw the E-FIT of Hannah in the *Gazette* the two of them destroyed the last copy of a picture that Rocky had taken of her and the negative as well.'

'Would that be the one I saw in Rachel's caravan, d'you think?'

'I imagine so. He'd hardly have let her see any of the other sort.'

'He can't be very bright, keeping all that obscene material in the house for his wife to find.'

'She'd been forbidden – under threat of violence, Penny says – to go near the studio, but she disobeyed once because some of the people where she works jokingly suggested he might be hiding girlie pictures up there. And the only one she found was a perfectly innocent one of a gipsy. Ironic, isn't it? I reckon he's been making a fortune selling the dirty ones to perverts like himself. You can tell from the way their place is furnished that there's plenty of money sloshing around . . . more than you'd expect your average truckie to bring in.'

'Yes, that did occur to me, but I didn't give it that much

thought. Has Julie told the police about the photo they destroyed?'

'She most definitely has not. In fact, she's regretting now having blurted it out to Penny . . . even though she feels nothing but revulsion over the pornography, she's convinced herself Rocky's innocent of the murder and she'll do all she can to protect him.'

'So Penny, like a good friend, reveals all to the press instead.' Melissa felt her sympathy evaporating in the face of this apparent act of betrayal. 'Hoping you'd make it worth her while, I suppose.'

'I didn't go there to get a story, nothing was said about money and I promised her that everything she told me is off the record,' said Bruce quietly.

He sounded hurt rather than offended and Melissa was quick to apologise. 'But surely,' she added, 'the police should be told about the destruction of the photograph?'

'What proof is there that it really was of Hannah? It's only hearsay, not evidence. Even if Julie was prepared to make a formal statement about it, she'd only be incriminating herself.'

'Mm, you're probably right. Bruce, you hinted a moment ago that some of the other pictures might be of Hannah as well?'

'Not having seen any of them, I can't say for sure, but they might be. The police may be able to identify her in some of them. If they can't, it'll be difficult to prove that Rocky was involved with her.'

'Not even if Julie decides to shop him?'

'He'd simply deny it . . . claim she was trying to drop him in it by way of revenge.'

'True. Well, Bruce, thanks for bringing me up to date. Bad luck about missing your scoop over the photo.'

'I think maybe I've got something better than a scoop.' And he rang off, leaving Melissa to speculate on this somewhat cryptic remark.

*   *   *

Yesterday, while still in a state of shock, Melissa had paid little attention to WPC Audrey Savage's appearance. Now, sitting opposite her in an interview room at police headquarters, she saw that the young officer had curly blond hair, freckles and an engaging smile that revealed small, even teeth. 'I take it you'll be pressing charges?' she said as Melissa, having read over her statement, signed it and handed it back. 'When we catch him, that is.'

'To be frank, I'd rather not.' Visions of appearances in court, titillating reports in the tabloids and stormy scenes with Ken Harris flashed through her head. 'You've surely got enough on him already, without my four penn'orth.'

The young officer's eyes grew suddenly keen and questioning. 'What do you mean by that?'

Realising that she had been on the point of revealing how much she knew about Rocky's unusual hobby, Melissa said hastily, 'I took it for granted that he's in the frame for Hannah Rose's murder. From the way he reacted when I mentioned her name, it was obvious that he knew her and he's almost certainly the man she ran off with. I suspected it all along . . . I told Sergeant Waters—'

Audrey nodded. 'So I understand. All we need now is evidence,' she added wryly. 'And of course, Wilkins himself.'

'I take it he's not been spotted yet?'

'Not that I've heard.'

'What about Hannah? Have the house-to-house inquiries turned up any more sightings?'

'Yes, several, but all earlier in the day, nothing after she called on Major and Mrs Ford.'

'Theirs is the last house at their end of the village,' Melissa pointed out. 'If she was heading back to catch the bus on the main road, there'd be nowhere else for her to call.'

'Yes, that's just the trouble,' Audrey sighed. 'We're hoping some passing motorist may have seen her.'

'Or given her a lift.'

'Exactly.' The two women exchanged glances. Each knew what the other was thinking.

Melissa stood up to leave. 'Well, with DCI Holloway on his track, I'm sure his days of freedom are numbered,' she remarked with exaggerated solemnity, and Audrey replied, 'Oh, undoubtedly they are,' with an earnestness that belied the merry twinkle in her eyes. It was clear to them both as they shook hands that they were at one in their assessment of the officer in question.

'You're sure you're quite recovered after your ordeal?' said Audrey. 'We can arrange for you to see a victim support counsellor if you're suffering any after-effects.'

'No, I'm fine, thanks. I take my support from thinking of Rocky's sore head and shins . . . to say nothing of his wounded vanity,' Melissa grinned. 'I hope you get him soon,' she added, becoming serious. 'He's a thoroughly nasty piece of work.'

'Oh, we'll get him, never fear.'

When Melissa reached home, Iris was at her front door, on the point of poking something through the letter-box. Spotting the car, she marched towards it, waving an envelope. 'Glad I caught you,' she said. 'Easier to explain than a note. Going to London to meet Jack . . . something about the house . . . won't be back till tomorrow.'

'Oh, right. You want me to feed Binkie?'

'Please. Gloria's supposed to come this afternoon to do extra cleaning. You'll be here to let her in?'

'Yes, no problem.'

'Good. Spare key in there.' Iris thrust the envelope through the driver's window into Melissa's hand. 'Must fly. Taxi due in ten minutes.' With a hasty wave, she scuttled indoors.

A short time later, Melissa heard the crunch of wheels on the drive and glanced out of her sitting-room window to see her friend, clad in a shapeless tweed coat with a leather pouch slung over one shoulder, handing a battered suitcase to a taxi driver, who stowed it in the boot while Iris scrambled inelegantly into the passenger seat and slammed the door. Melissa stood watching as the car disappeared and then went into the kitchen to fill the kettle for a cup of coffee. Her thoughts were gloomy. In a few weeks' time there would be a removal van at the door and Iris would leave Elder Cottage for good. She felt a surge of envy for her friend, so confident that she had made the right decision, so positive about her future with Jack. Then she gave herself a shake.

'Stop feeling sorry for yourself,' she said aloud as she made her coffee. As she did so, she heard the sound of an approaching car. Thinking that it might be Iris returning for something she had forgotten, she went to the front door. But it was not the taxi that drew up outside, but a Ford Sierra that had seen better days. The driver got out and came towards her. It was Rachel.

Chapter Eighteen

Rachel's features were drawn and there were dark rings under her eyes. As she approached the door of Hawthorn Cottage her scarlet shawl began slipping from her shoulders and she dragged it awkwardly back into place with hands that shook.

'Mrs Melissa,' she said in a voice that sounded harsh and unsteady, 'Please, I must speak to you.'

'Of course . . . come in.' Melissa led her unexpected visitor into the kitchen. 'Sit down. I've just made coffee. Would you like some?'

'Thank you.'

Melissa filled a second mug and put it on the table alongside a jug of milk, a bowl of sugar and an open packet of ginger nuts. Rachel helped herself to milk but declined the sugar and the biscuits with a shake of the head. She raised the mug to her mouth, gripping it with both hands as if in an effort to steady them. After a few hesitant sips she put it down and stared into the contents as if she saw something fearful in their depths.

There was a long silence. At last, Melissa said, 'Rachel, what's the matter?'

The reply came in a low, tremulous whisper. 'I am afraid!'

'Afraid of what?'

'Of what my man and his brethren are planning to do.' Rachel broke off, her mouth working, and put one hand over her eyes. 'I cannot sleep,' she continued, her voice barely audible. 'I lie awake in fear . . . if they carry out their vow, they will bring great trouble on our people.'

'What vow is that?'

'They have found him . . . and they mean to—' Once again, emotion stemmed the flow of words, but the gipsy had said enough to confirm Melissa's own fears.

'You're talking about the man Hannah ran away with, aren't you?' she said.

Rachel raised her head, plainly startled by the question. Her eyes seemed to burn with the same fierce, angry light as on her previous visit. 'The man who brought about her death,' she corrected harshly. Her expression altered to one of suspicion as she asked, 'Has someone spoken to you of this already?'

'I have read about the customs of your people, and I feared something of the kind,' Melissa said. 'But Rachel, your menfolk must realise that there is nothing to prove that the man you are speaking of is the one who actually killed her. The police are doing all they can, but—'

'The police!' Rachel's voice rang with scorn. 'What is it to them that a gipsy has died?'

'I assure you, they're taking the case very seriously . . . sooner or later Hannah's killer will be found and punished.'

'We *know* who he is,' Rachel declared. She leaned forward and spoke in a voice that throbbed with a blend of fear and anger. 'Listen, and I will tell you. After Hannah's body was found, ever since that day, there has been much secret talk among the men, but we women were told nothing. Yesterday we knew something had happened . . . there had been news, but still we were kept in ignorance. In the evening they left the camp and when they returned we saw there had been a fight – they had bleeding knuckles and one had a cut over his eye.'

Melissa had a sickening vision of Rocky being seized and dragged away to some remote hiding place, there to be mercilessly beaten by men on the fringe of society whose one thought was of revenge. He was strong, he would have put up a fight – the injury to one of the gipsies would seem to prove that – but he would have been heavily outnumbered. She swallowed hard, but said nothing and waited.

After a moment, Rachel continued, 'Straight away they held a *kris* . . . a council meeting. Only the men are allowed to be present at such meetings, but we were curious . . . and afraid.' Her voice died away on the last word and she lapsed into a brooding silence that seemed to last for a long time, staring at her coffee but making no move to drink it.

In an attempt to bring her out of her reverie, Melissa said hesitantly, 'You said there had been a fight. What was it about?'

'Oh, that was nothing.' Rachel's dismissive gesture indicated that to return to camp with a few bruises after an evening out was a regular event, something Melissa was quite prepared to believe. At least, it was now clear that Rocky had not, as she first thought, been involved. 'But a *kris* is something rare,' Rachel went on, 'called only when there is a matter of importance to discuss, so I and my sisters followed the men in secret. We hid ourselves and listened. Most of the time they spoke one at a time in low voices and we could make nothing of what they were saying, but when they gave their verdict, they spoke as one man.'

Pin-pricks of apprehension crept along Melissa's spine as she asked, 'What verdict?'

'Our leader, our *Rai*, said, "So we are all agreed. He must be punished," and together they repeated the words. And this can mean only one thing – they will do this man some harm and bring ill fortune on us all. Mrs Melissa, you must help me stop them!'

'I? What can I do?' Melissa had listened to the story with growing alarm. With Rocky's exposure and flight, and the belief that the police had the investigation into Hannah's murder well in hand, she had mentally written herself out of the affair. Now, it seemed, Fate was doing its best to suck her back into an even more dangerous scenario.

'Warn him!' Rachel's tone was beseeching. 'Warn this man of the danger he is in.' She reached across the table and clutched Melissa's arm. 'I cannot do it . . . if it became known that I had betrayed my own kin, I would become an outcast. I trust you, even though you are a *gadgy*. All I ask is that you go to see this man and tell him what I have told you. I will give you his name, tell you where he lives—'

It was time to put an end to this crazy charade. Melissa put her own hand over the gipsy's and gave it an encouraging squeeze. 'Listen, Rachel, there's nothing for you to worry about, truly. The man is known to the police and he has already been warned of the danger he is in.'

Astonishment made Rachel's huge eyes appear even larger. 'How is this possible?'

It was too long and complicated a story to repeat. All Melissa said was, 'I have friends in the police, and I learn things from them. They too are looking for this man, but he is in hiding . . . he was gone when they came to question him, but I'm sure he'll soon be found. Please Rachel,' she went on earnestly, as the gipsy shook her head in disbelief, 'Trust me, I'm telling you the truth. Your people must leave it to the law to bring him to justice. Go back and tell them that.'

'I shall tell them nothing.' Rachel's tone was bitter. 'They must not know of this visit. I am a mere woman who knows nothing, understands nothing.' She looked down at her mug of coffee and almost absent-mindedly raised it to her lips.

Melissa reached out to take it from her. 'That must be cold. Let me make you some fresh . . . or I can warm it up in the microwave.'

'It doesn't matter. I must go now. I took the car without asking leave and I must return before it is missed.' Rachel swallowed a mouthful of the tepid coffee, then hastily put down the mug and got to her feet. 'Someone is coming!' she said in alarm. A car was approaching the cottage. It stopped; a door slammed, heavy footsteps crunched on the gravel and the doorbell sounded.

'I'm not expecting anyone,' Melissa muttered uneasily. She glanced at Rachel, who had turned a sickly yellow and stood looking wildly around her, clutching her shawl around her body as if trying to hide within its folds.

'Wait here, I'll go and see who it is.' Melissa tried to sound calm, but her own heart was thumping at the possibility that men from the Romany camp had followed Rachel and were about to cause an ugly scene. Before opening the door, she peered through the sitting-room curtains to check who was outside, thinking that all she could do if the worst came to the worst was bolt the door, lock every window and summon the police. To her immense relief she recognised Ken Harris's car. 'It's all right, it's someone I know,' she called over her shoulder, and went to let him in.

It was clear that he was not in the best of moods. Instead of entering, he turned and gestured with a scowl at Rachel's dilapidated Ford. 'Where did that heap of junk come from?' he demanded.

Melissa's hackles rose. 'It belongs to a friend of mine who's just leaving,' she said curtly.

'I didn't know you had friends who don't pay their car tax!' he grunted. 'I'll have something to say to him about that.'

'You'll do nothing of the kind, you're not a policeman now. And it's not a him, it's—' Melissa broke off as Rachel emerged from the kitchen. She appeared only marginally less scared than a moment ago when she feared that her own menfolk had arrived to mete out their own brand of punishment to a disobedient wife.

'Goodbye Mrs Melissa, and thank you,' she whispered.

'It's been nice seeing you, Rachel, and please remember what I told you.'

'I will.' Rachel's eyes rolled as she sidled nervously past Ken, whose bulk all but filled the narrow passage. He glared down at her, but said nothing. Melissa, with less ceremony, brushed him aside and escorted her visitor to the door.

Rachel stepped outside, took a couple of steps towards her car and then turned to say in a low voice, 'Take heed of my earlier warning.' In response to Melissa's questioning look, she added, 'Cleave to the one who truly loves you.' Without waiting for a response, she strode away.

Melissa watched her get into her car. She was on the point of following her to ask what she meant by her cryptic pronouncement, but stopped when she heard Ken's voice behind her, irritably demanding to know what all that was about. Reluctantly, she closed the front door and faced him. His expression was set and angry. 'She's that gipsy woman you got mixed up with before, isn't she?' he barked, without giving her a chance to speak. 'I thought I told you to keep away from those villains.'

Melissa glared at him. 'What business is it of yours who I invite into my own home?' she retorted. 'And what are you doing here anyway? Your message said you wouldn't be in the office until three . . . I wasn't expecting you until this evening.'

'I got back early and found a message to call Matt Waters. He told me what you've been up to.' His tone was accusing, almost hectoring as he followed her into the kitchen. 'The minute my back's turned—'

'So that's it . . . my bodyguard has been telling tales!' Melissa swung round and faced him across the table, on which still lay the detritus of the interrupted coffee break: the two mugs, one still half-full, the jug of milk, the sugar, the packet of biscuits and a scattering of crumbs. Mechanically, she began clearing it away.

Ken frowned. 'Bodyguard?' he repeated. 'What are you talking about?'

'Don't pretend you didn't brief Matt to keep an eye on me while you were away. I tackled him about it and he didn't deny it.'

'So what? I was only thinking of your safety. You went and put yourself at risk once before, getting mixed up with that lot, and now it seems you've done it again . . . and worse. I think that's proved that I was right.'

'It's proved nothing of the kind. I warned Matt – and I asked him to be sure to pass the warning on to DCI Holloway – that whoever took Hannah Rose away from her people might very well be at risk of some kind of tribal retribution.' She was on the point of adding, 'And as it happens, I've just learned *I* was right,' but refrained. That would lead to further questions, meaning she would have to repeat what she had just been told. That might lead to a police raid on the Romany camp, which could land Rachel in serious trouble with her menfolk. Rocky himself had been warned, the police already knew of the danger and it was up to them to protect him once they found him.

So all she said was, 'By a fluke, I found out who the man was and since no one appeared to be taking my warning seriously I decided to go and see him myself . . . but presumably you know all this. I suppose Matt saw my statement and decided to lodge a formal complaint about me.'

'There's no need for sarcasm,' said Ken in a quieter tone. 'I asked him to keep an eye on you, yes, I admit it. It's only because I care about you . . . can't you imagine how I felt when he told me what had happened?'

Melissa felt a twinge of compunction. 'Yes, yes . . . I know, and I'm sorry if I gave you a fright. It's nothing to the fright Rocky gave me,' she added jokingly, but there was no answering smile. 'Look,' she said in what she hoped was the voice of sweet reason, 'I don't want to quarrel with you, so let's not talk about it any more. I'll make you some coffee – I could do with another cup myself.' She filled the kettle, set it to boil and fetched clean mugs. 'As things have turned out, my intervention has brought about a breakthrough in a rather nasty case. All right, it could have gone horribly wrong, but I came out of it unscathed, thanks to Bruce Ingram.'

'Ingram!' Ken almost shouted. 'That's something else we'd better get straight once and for all. Melissa, I absolutely forbid you to have anything more to do with that irresponsible bloody scribbler!'

'You what?' Melissa kept her voice steady with an effort; inwardly she was seething again.

'You heard me!' His face had turned a dull red, he was breathing heavily and his large hands gripped the edge of the table. 'In future, you'll stay clear of Ingram and his hare-brained schemes!'

'And what makes you think you have the right to tell me who I may or may not associate with?'

'If you and I are to have any sort of life together—'

'I have to do as I'm told, is that it?' He did not answer, but his expression remained hostile. 'Well, here's something *you'd* better get straight, Ken Harris. You're not a big-shot police inspector any more and I'm not one of your raw recruits. I'm a grown woman, I've led an independent life and looked after myself and made my own decisions for more years than I care to think about . . . and if throwing in my lot with you means handing you the right to order me about—'

'Mel, please!' He walked round the table and tried to put his arms round her, but she held him off. 'Darling, don't be angry with me . . . I can't bear the idea of your running into danger.'

'You prefer me to sit at home and be a good girl and not speak to strangers, is that it?'

'Now you're being childish. Of course I don't expect you to—'

'Then what do you expect? No, let me tell you.' Melissa could hear herself becoming steadily more wound up; she knew she was putting at risk a relationship that had brought her much happiness, but all she could think of at that moment was the fact that her independence was under threat. 'I think you want to take over my life and be available whenever it suits you, drop everything and come running when you lift your little finger—'

'That's not fair!'

'Isn't it? Let me remind you of the message you left for me yesterday. "I'll be round about six," you said. Not "if that's all right with you," or "let me know if it isn't convenient".'

'I assumed that as I'd been away for three days you'd want to see me.' He managed to appear hurt and huffy at the same time and she knew she had got under his skin.

'Suppose I'd made other arrangements for this evening?' she said quietly.

'Well, have you?'

'No, but that isn't the point. You have absolutely no right to take me for granted.'

'I can see that.' He showed no sign of contrition; rather, he sounded like a man who has suddenly discovered a serious flaw in some expensive object he had been thinking of buying. 'I think I'd better leave you alone for the time being so that you can think things over.'

'That's a very good idea,' she said coldly. Without another word, he turned and left the house.

The kettle that she had set on the Aga set up a fierce hissing as the water boiled. She made coffee, filled one of the two clean mugs and put the other one back in the cupboard. Outside, she heard the sound of Ken's car starting and driving away.

'I'll be thinking things over all right,' she muttered aloud, 'and I suggest you do the same.'

Chapter Nineteen

Melissa took her second mug of coffee upstairs to her study. She placed it carefully on a mat bearing round its rim the legend, *The Grey Goose, Stowbridge* and in the centre a crude representation of a goose in flight. She had picked it up on impulse on leaving the pub with Ken Harris after their first date and it had been in daily use ever since to protect her desk from heat marks. The design was partially obliterated by rings of tea and coffee; more than once she had been on the point of replacing it with something a little more elegant and once she had actually thrown it into the waste bin but later, out of what she recognised was a slightly ridiculous sentimental attachment, retrieved it.

Today, however, she had more pressing problems to consider than the fate of a stained circle of cork. She had promised to give Ken her answer to his proposal – how quaint and old-fashioned that phrase sounded! – by Saturday, the day when Iris also was expecting a decision from her about Elder Cottage. She had just two days to make up her mind about the direction her life was to take in the foreseeable future.

She sat slowly sipping her coffee while abstractedly contemplating the view from her study window. It was the kind of pastoral scene beloved of compilers of guide books to the Cotswolds: a blue sky flecked with white puffballs of cloud, fields dotted with grazing sheep, and dry-stone walls topped with cushions of emerald moss and splashed with grey and yellow lichen. The hawthorn tree that gave her cottage its name was spangled with scarlet berries that shone like fairy lights where they caught the autumn sunshine. Beyond the boundary between the cottages and the neighbouring fields the land dipped steeply for a short distance, levelled out beside the stream that ran along the valley bottom and then sloped gently upwards to a clump of woodland on the crest of the hill. There was an air of permanence about the familiar landscape that seemed to accentuate the present turbulence in her own life.

The telephone rang and she automatically reached out to answer, but stopped with her hand on the receiver, telling herself that it might be Ken, conciliatory, apologetic and wanting after all to see her that evening. A week, even a couple of days ago, it would have been the thing she most wanted to hear, but some inner voice warned her that the relationship was at crisis point and she needed space and solitude to analyse her own feelings. So she waited until the answering machine cut in and delivered its pre-recorded greeting and request for a message. To her intense relief it was not Ken on the line, but Joe Martin. She stopped the tape and picked up the receiver.

'Joe, I'm here . . . just couldn't get to the phone in time,' she lied, mentally registering surprise and some concern at the pleasure she could hear in her own voice.

'Mel! I'm off to catch a plane for Stockholm in half an hour, but I thought I'd try and catch you before leaving . . . you mentioned you wanted us to meet for a talk some time soon.'

'That's right. Joe, I need some guidance about where I'm going from here. I think I already mentioned that *Drop Dead!* will be the last Nathan Latimer book, for a while at any rate. I've been playing with one or two ideas—'

'Yes, you did say something about it, but I wasn't sure if you were serious. What's the problem? Is the old boy having a mid-life crisis?'

'No, but I think maybe I am.'

That wasn't what she had intended to say. It had slipped out on an unexpected wave of emotion, as if her anger and hurt after the stormy scene with Ken had up to that moment been held in check by some kind of mental barricade that had suddenly given way. The last thing she wanted was to involve Joe; for one thing, he had been in love with her himself for so long that he could hardly be expected to take a dispassionate view of the situation.

She was trembling, and she realised to her dismay that she was close to tears. Joe must have sensed it, for he said, 'Mel, what's the matter? Has something happened?'

'Yes, but it's all right now.' At least she had the perfect explanation ready to hand, without having to lie or pre-varicate. She took a deep breath, determined not to break down and make a fool of herself. 'I had a bit of a skirmish yesterday with a man who turned out to be a rather nasty type of crook.'

'Good heavens! What happened?'

'I'd rather not go into details now. You'll quite likely read about it in the papers in a day or two . . . although you'll no doubt be sorry to hear I've been promised my name won't be mentioned so there'll be no publicity.' She felt her poise and her sense of humour come back with a rush on spotting a chance to tease him about his well-known relish for anything with the potential to boost sales of his authors' books.

'Never mind that – are you all right?' His concern was unexpectedly heart-warming and she felt herself breathing more easily as she assured him that she was fine. 'Look,' he went on, 'I can easily reschedule the Stockholm meeting if you'd like me to come down. Just say the word and I'll—'

'Joe, that's really sweet of you, but there's no need. I do want to talk to you, though. One day next week?' She reached for her desk diary and flipped it open, picturing him doing the same at the other end of the wire.

'How about Tuesday?' he suggested after a brief interlude of page-rustling. 'I'll catch an early train . . . we could have lunch at that pub you were telling me about. What's it called, the Golden Bell?'

'No thanks, anywhere but there!' she said hastily. 'Tuesday would be fine,' she went on quickly to forestall the obvious question, 'but I think I'd rather meet you in town. It's ages since my last trip to London . . . I could do a bit of shopping.'

'Great. Why not stay overnight? We could have dinner and maybe do a show—'

'That sounds wonderful.'

'I'll get you booked into a hotel.'

'Thanks Joe, I'm really looking forward to it.'

'Me too. Must go now or I'll miss my flight. Bye.'

He rang off, leaving Melissa somewhat bemusedly asking herself how it was that her mood could have changed so suddenly. She was still wondering when the phone rang again. This time she answered without hesitation; when Bruce came on the line in his usual breezy fashion she could not keep the laughter out of her voice as she returned his greeting.

'What's the joke?' he asked.

'I've been forbidden to talk to you,' she replied.

'You what?'

'You're an irresponsible scribbler who puts me at risk with your hare-brained schemes.'

'Oh, I get it . . . your ex-copper has heard about yesterday and is not best pleased.'

'Right first time.'

'I see. Do want me to hang up and never darken your doors again?'

'What do you think?'

'I can understand his concern, but he can't know you very well if he imagines you'd take that sort of instruction lying down.'

'Exactly. Bruce, it so happens I was going to call you later on. Guess who came to see me this morning? Apart from old Bossy-Boots, that is.'

'No time for guessing games. I've an urgent appointment in ten minutes, but I thought you'd like to know there have been some interesting developments in the Rocky Wilkins saga.'

'Have there? Do tell!'

'Not now. Why don't we meet for a drink this evening and exchange news?'

'Sure. Where?'

'Do you know the Lamb and Shearling, at the back of Northgate?'

'No, but I think I've heard of it. How do I get there?' Part of her mind went off at a tangent; the name rang a bell. She was certain there had been a recent reference to it, or something like it, but in what connection?

'It's just round the corner from the *Gazette* offices,' Bruce was saying. 'I suggest you pick me up here – you can use the office car park. Say about six?'

'Right. See you then.'

Melissa put down the phone and somewhat reluctantly settled down to begin work on the final draft of *Drop Dead!* Somewhat to her surprise, the task went smoothly; there were no further interruptions and it was not until she began to feel hungry and realised that it was almost two o'clock that she put the script aside and went downstairs for a belated lunch. She had just finished her cheese omelette when Gloria arrived. Her toffee-brown eyes were rolling with merriment and her voice was shaking with barely controlled laughter as she announced that she had come for Iris's key.

'What's the joke?' Melissa asked as she handed it over.

'Ooh, Mrs Craig, it were so funny! I were in the shop just now and we was all talking about that feller in the BMW what they just caught—'

'Have they caught him? I hadn't heard.' Presumably that was the development that Bruce was so excited about.

'It were on the one o'clock news. And there were something about people ringing the police to say they saw the same sort of car in a lay-by on the Stow road the night that gipsy disappeared.'

'That's interesting.' Melissa recalled how she and Harriet Yorke had speculated about Hannah's possible movements after leaving the Fords' cottage. 'But I don't think it's particularly funny,' she added reproachfully, as Gloria still appeared to have trouble containing her mirth.

'Course it ain't, but listen . . . Mrs Ford were in the shop as well . . . and Mrs Foster said to her, "Your husband's got a car like that, hasn't he? I hope he's got a good alibi," . . . an' everyone laughed 'cept her . . . you should have seen the old girl's face . . . it were like she'd swallowed a whole bottle of vinegar! "Do you imagine my husband would associate with *that* sort of person?" she says.' The story had been punctuated throughout with barely suppressed giggles; at the end, Gloria gave up the unequal struggle and collapsed into uproarious laughter. 'She took it so serious, you wouldn't believe,' she finished, pulling a paper tissue from her pocket to wipe her streaming eyes.

'Well, you could hardly expect her to see the funny side of a crack like that,' Melissa pointed out with a sympathetic chuckle. Poor Madeleine, she thought; she never did have a sense of humour.

'Tell you what, though,' said Gloria when she was once more capable of coherent speech. 'You remembers what I told you about that time my Stanley were leavin' the pub and saw the girl getting into a car with a feller? He reckons that were a BMW.' Her face grew suddenly serious. 'Wonder if it were the same one?'

'I shouldn't think so . . . there's quite a few of them about. Besides, you said she was with an older man.'

'So I did. Maybe it were Major Ford!' There was another minor explosion.

'I hope you won't go repeating that suggestion in the shop,' said Melissa, with mock severity.

'Course not,' Gloria assured her. 'That's the trouble with that Mrs Foster, she's a terrible gossip,' she added with a total absence of self-awareness. 'Well, I must get on with Miss Ash's windows. I'll drop the key back when I've finished.'

'Just a minute,' said Melissa. 'That pub where your Stanley saw Hannah . . . what did you say it was called?'

'Can't remember exactly . . . the Lamb an' Something—'

'Would it be the Lamb and Shearling?'

'Thassright. Funny name, innit? What's a shearling?'

'It's a young sheep that's just been shorn.'

'Ah!' Gloria paused for a moment to digest this nugget of information before heading for the front door of Elder Cottage.

The saloon bar of the Lamb and Shearling was unexpectedly crowded, mostly with young people of both sexes, a few of whom Melissa recognised from her occasional visits to the office of the *Gloucester Gazette*. Bruce led her to a table and went to the bar to order their drinks, pausing once or twice on the way to exchange remarks with someone she assumed to be a colleague.

'I gather this is the *Gazette* staff's favourite watering-hole,' she commented when he returned with her glass of orange juice, a pint of bitter for himself and two packets of crisps.

'That's right. It's handy for a recap of the day's news over a quick noggin before heading home. They do quite decent lunch-time food as well.' Bruce drank deeply from his glass before setting it down and exhaling with a sigh of satisfaction.

'So what's new in the Wilkins case?' Melissa asked. 'I know he's been picked up,' she added. 'It was on the lunch-time news – Gloria told me. She also said something about a BMW having been spotted in a lay-by on the Stow road the evening before Hannah was missed from her room at the hotel.'

'Yes, that came out at this morning's briefing. The police aren't sure there's a connection, but they're appealing to the driver to come forward so that he can be eliminated, the usual stuff. There have been other sightings too. It seems the public have been spotting dark-coloured BMWs all over the place.'

'I know. We've even got one in Upper Benbury – Dudley Ford's recently acquired one and Madeleine was having her leg pulled about it in the shop this morning. She was not amused.' Melissa drank some of her orange juice and began wrestling open her packet of crisps. 'Going back to the car in the lay-by, if it does turn out to be Rocky's, that puts him squarely in the frame for Hannah's murder, doesn't it?'

'Sure does.'

'Is that the interesting new development you were hinting at this morning?'

'No, there's something else. One other item that was given out at the briefing was about a disturbance last night at the travellers' camp on the Cirencester road.'

'The one where those two men were arrested for questioning about Hannah's murder?'

'And later released without charge.'

Melissa, remembering Rachel's reference to her menfolk having been involved in a fight, felt an inward buzz of excitement. 'So what happened?' she asked.

'The occupants of a nearby house heard a rumpus going on and reported it. It was all over by the time the police arrived, but it seems some outsiders turned up at the camp and started a fight. They left a few cuts and bruises by way of souvenirs, but as you can imagine, no one was going to press charges. Officially the incident is being treated as some sort of quarrel between rival gangs.'

'But you reckon there's a connection with Hannah's murder?'

'The question was raised as to whether it was a case of her people deciding to take the law into their own hands after two men they believed to be guilty were released. The police refused to comment.'

'Is that what you think?'

'I don't believe it's quite that straightforward. If it had been a serious attempt at a punishment beating, the injuries would have been a lot more serious.'

'So they would,' Melissa agreed. 'On both sides,' she added meaningly.

Bruce gave her a keen look. 'I think you've been holding out on me. You mentioned on the phone you'd had a visitor.'

'I wanted to hear your story first. Yes, Rachel came to see me this morning.' As accurately as she could, Melissa repeated everything the gipsy had told her. 'I can only guess what happened when the Romanys invaded the travellers' camp,' she went on while Bruce digested the information along with the remainder of his crisps. 'Probably they set off with the idea of settling the score there and then, but the fact that subsequently they were overheard to say, "*He must be punished*" – as if they were speaking of just one man – suggests to me a) that the travellers managed to convince them that they really were innocent of Hannah's murder and b) that they were able to give them vital information about her killer . . . her presumed killer, I should say.'

'You mean Rocky?'

'Who else? Remember what Rachel said the first time she came to see me: *The blame for her death lies at his door*. He's the one they're after. I don't think Rachel would be too bothered if all they intended was to give him a thrashing, but I think she's afraid they'll do him serious, maybe permanent, harm.'

'How would the travellers have known who he was?'

'Maybe Hannah herself told them. They admitted knowing the girl; two of them had sex with her.'

'You could well be right,' said Bruce thoughtfully. 'Have you reported Rachel's visit to the Bill?'

Melissa shook her head. 'It wouldn't have added to what they already knew and would only have led to trouble for her. She was terrified of her husband finding out she'd been to see me. I told her that the police are well aware of the probable threat to Rocky's safety and that reassured her. Now he's in custody, there's even less point in saying anything.'

'Yes, I see what you mean. Well, that seems to be that.' He finished his drink and stood up. 'Would you like another – or more crisps?'

'Thanks – no more crisps, but I wouldn't mind another juice.'

'Right.' He took their empty glasses and went to order refills. The crowd had thinned; more people were leaving than arriving, but as she sat idly watching, Melissa noticed a well-set-up elderly man who entered from the street, nodded a greeting to the couple behind the bar and made for a door in the far corner. He was followed almost immediately by two more men of similar age and appearance, and as Bruce returned with the drinks he found his way momentarily blocked by a further group of three heading in the same direction. A solitary figure in tweeds brought up the rear and made straight for the bar.

'Good heavens!' Melissa exclaimed as Bruce settled back into his seat, 'there's Major Ford!'

Bruce paused in the act of raising his glass and glanced over his shoulder. 'The former owner of the notorious freezer?' he said in a low voice. 'So it is!'

'Whatever can he be doing here?' she said curiously, as the Major greeted the barman in his customary penetrating voice and handed him an envelope with the instruction to check that it was all in order. He then produced a pocket diary and proceeded to recite a list of dates while the man made notes in a well-thumbed book with a pencil attached by a string which he took from a shelf behind him. 'Oh, I get it,' she whispered, 'it's the regular get-together with some of his ex-army pals. Madeleine calls it his geriatric play-group.'

A sudden thought struck her. She put down her drink and went across to intercept the Major as, having completed his business, he too headed for the door in the corner. 'Good evening, Dudley,' she said. 'Can you spare a moment?'

He appeared startled at seeing her, but quickly recovered, removed his tweed cap and gave his customary polite bow. 'Mrs Craig . . . Melissa! Fancy seeing you here!' His slightly bloodshot eyes flickered in an upward direction. 'Just on my way to a get-together with the old army pals,' he explained. 'Our good ladies give us a pass to attend, *haahaahaa*!' His unmelodious laughter echoed round the bar, causing heads to turn. 'So what can I do for you?'

'Is this where you always hold your meetings?'

'For the past couple of years, yes. Used to go to the Crown but the landlord jacked up the rent.'

'I don't suppose you happened to be here the night that gipsy girl came in, trying to sell her lace?'

The Major made a great to-do about returning the diary to his inside breast-pocket before saying gruffly, 'When would that have been?'

'Ah, that I can't tell you . . . quite a few weeks ago, possibly longer. Stanley Parkin was here at the time and he thinks he saw her in the car park later on with a man, but he's a bit vague as to when it was. It occurred to me that you or one of your members might have seen her as you were leaving.'

'Can't say I did. Can't speak for the others, of course. Has Parkin reported it?'

'Gloria said he was going to.'

'Better leave it to the boys in blue to follow up, then.' He broke off to exchange greetings with two more of his colleagues, assuring them that he would be 'with them in a jiffy'. Outside, the cathedral bell struck the hour; he checked his watch and said, 'Have to ask you to excuse me, our meeting's due to start,' raised his cap once more and hurried away.

'It was a long shot, but I thought it was worth asking him,' Melissa said after explaining to Bruce her reason for questioning the Major.

'Can't see that it would help much if any of them did see her, not after all this time,' he commented. 'Unless, of course, it would help to identify the man she drove off with.'

They finished their drinks and got up to leave, reaching the door just as a group of four men were about to enter. They were all similarly dressed in casual, slightly shabby clothes; three appeared to be in their late teens or early twenties but the fourth was an older, strikingly handsome man with a swarthy complexion and straight black hair. They stood aside to allow Melissa and Bruce to pass but received their polite thanks in unsmiling silence.

'They don't look too happy,' Melissa commented.

'Come to drown their sorrows after a bad day at the races, maybe,' Bruce suggested with a grin as they crossed the pub car park to a footpath that served as a short cut back to the *Gazette* offices. He glanced at his watch. 'I must be on my way . . . I promised to look after Kirsty so that Penny can go to a social evening at Carston Village Hall. She hardly ever goes out because she can't afford to pay a baby-sitter.'

Melissa was on the point of making a teasing response, but a glance at Bruce's expression told her that his concern for the young single mother and her child was utterly sincere. From the time when she first knew him she had been struck by the contrast between his dogged determination in pursuit of a story and his blend of idealism with an active social conscience. It set him apart from the popular conception of a hard-nosed newshound.

'That's really nice of you, I'm sure she'll appreciate it,' she said warmly.

'Have you any plans for the evening?'

Melissa pulled a face. 'No. I was supposed to be seeing Ken Harris, but after this morning's dust-up—' She gave a slightly bitter laugh before adding, 'It won't exactly help things along if I tell him about this meeting.'

'Are you planning to?'

'If he asks. He's got to get it into his head that I'm not going to let him choose my friends for me.'

'If you want my advice—' Bruce began.

'Yes?' she said as he broke off and looked uncomfortable.

'Nothing,' he said. He took her car key from her and unlocked the Golf, keeping his face averted.

'Are you trying to tell me something?' she persisted.

'No, really.' He held the driver's door open while she got in and then handed her the key. 'Forget I said anything . . . it's none of my business.'

'Well anyway, thanks for the drink.'

'My pleasure. If anything else interesting breaks, I'll let you know.'

'Please do.'

She waited while he got into his own car and drove off, then followed at a slower speed, trying to imagine what he had been about to say.

Chapter Twenty

After parting from Bruce, Melissa set off for home. It was still only half-past seven and the evening stretched ahead, bleak, empty and uninviting. To eat a solitary dinner in front of the television was a depressing prospect. Almost without thinking, she took the road into Cheltenham, parked the Golf on Imperial Square and headed for a restaurant on the Promenade where she occasionally had lunch when in town. On the way she passed the converted Regency building where Harris Investigations occupied a small suite of offices. The downstairs rooms were in darkness but lights were burning on the top floor. Melissa stared up at the uncurtained windows and felt a tightness in her throat. If things had gone according to plan, she and Ken would probably at this moment be having a drink together, consulting a menu, catching up on events of the past few days. Instead, he was working late and she was standing out here on her own because the evening had been ruined for both of them on account of a stupid quarrel. *It was his fault for being so dictatorial*, her inner voice reminded her, but common sense responded, *Yes, but we've got to have it out sooner or later and there's no time like the present*. On impulse, she changed direction, crossed the road, mounted the short flight of steps leading to the entrance and grasped the handle of the outer door, which normally stood open. It was closed and locked.

Momentarily disconcerted, she hesitated. Perhaps after all Ken wasn't there. Maybe Tricia, his young assistant, had forgotten to switch off the light ... or possibly he was in the habit of leaving it on overnight as a security measure. She was on the point of going away when she spotted the bank of name-plates and associated bell-pushes set into the outer stonework. She pressed the one marked Harris Investigations, thinking how odd it was, considering the number of times she had called in to see Ken during working hours, that she had never noticed it before.

Through a temporary lull in the traffic she could hear the distant ringing of the bell. If Ken was there, he was probably at his desk, absorbed in writing a report. She pictured him raising his head in surprise at the unexpected sound. He would wonder who could be calling out of hours, whether it was a genuine visitor or a group of yobbos fooling about. He might wait to hear if the summons was repeated before taking any action.

She rang again. After a few seconds the light in the inner porch came on and moments later she heard the sound of footsteps descending the stairs and crossing the hall. She had a sudden misgiving; it might not be Ken at all, but a cleaner or caretaker who would doubtless not be best pleased at being dragged down four flights of stairs on a fool's errand. She began to wish she had never thought of the idea. Then a key turned in the outer door, it swung open and he was standing there, looking disgruntled, a little suspicious ... and very tired.

For a moment he stared at her without speaking. Then he said, 'Come in,' and she stepped inside while he relocked the door and followed her up to his office. 'I was on my way to get something to eat when I saw your light,' she explained.

'I stayed on to write a report. Too many interruptions during office hours.'

'I'm sorry, I'll leave if you like.'

'No, that's okay, I'm just about done.' He began gathering

papers together and pushing them into a folder. 'I haven't eaten yet either . . . mind if I join you?'

'Please do. You're sure you've finished? I don't mind waiting if—'

'It's no problem. I'll check it over in the morning before I give it to Tricia to put together.'

She kept her eyes on him during the conversation, but he hardly looked at her. Normally, he would have expressed pleasure at seeing her and given her a kiss or at least a hug, but this evening he made no attempt at physical contact. So she stood by the door and waited while he put the report in a filing cabinet, closed the drawer, picked up a bunch of keys from his desk and switched out the lights before locking up. They descended the stairs and left the building in silence. Ken secured the outer door and they headed towards the town centre, still without speaking.

After a few moments he asked in a voice that held a hint of weariness, 'Where would you like to eat?'

'I was going to the Brasserie.'

'That suits me.'

They had a drink in the bar while waiting for a table. He said, 'So what brought you into Cheltenham this evening?'

'I was on my way home from Gloucester. I was feeling hungry but I couldn't face the thought of cooking a meal.' She drank a mouthful of her non-alcoholic cocktail, helped herself to an olive from a glass dish on the bar and said, 'To save you the trouble of asking, I was in Gloucester having a drink with Bruce Ingram.' She met his gaze squarely as she spoke and saw the heavy features set like a freeze-frame in a TV commercial.

'I see,' he said stiffly.

'I don't think you do. It wasn't anything so childish as an act of defiance after your outburst this morning . . . it so happened that he called me to say he had something interesting to tell me and we arranged to meet for a chat before he went off to keep another appointment.'

'And what was this interesting something that made you—' Ken broke off abruptly and picked up the menu, having evidently thought better of what he had been about to say.

Melissa cocked an eyebrow and finished the question for him. 'Defy your orders?'

'There's no need to put it like that. It wasn't intended as an order—'

'Oh, but it was. You "absolutely forbade me" – your words – to have anything to do with Bruce.'

He gave a deep, rumbling sigh and ran his fingers through his crisp grey hair. 'Should've put it more diplomatically, I suppose.'

'You shouldn't have said it at all.'

'Mel, we have to get this sorted.' He reached out and touched her gently on the hand. 'But not now, we're both tired. Let's call a truce for this evening. Now, what do you want as a starter?'

After their meal, Ken walked Melissa back to her car, kissed her affectionately but without passion and waited while she settled into the driver's seat, buckled her safety belt and wound down the window saying, 'Good night, and thanks for the dinner.'

'My pleasure. I'll give you a call tomorrow.'

'Sure.' She turned the key in the ignition; there was a tired whirring sound from the starter motor, then silence. She cursed and tried again with the same result. 'Oh hell, what do I do now?'

'I've got some jump leads in my car. Wait here while I go and get them. And keep your doors locked till I get back,' he added. 'There are some rum characters about at this time of night. Shan't be long.'

Well now, aren't you glad he's with you? It was that

exasperating inner voice again. *What would you do if you were on your own?*

'Call the AA, of course,' she said aloud, beating her hands impatiently on the steering wheel. 'And then go into the Queen's and order coffee and wait there until they arrive.' She pressed the button to switch on the radio, realised it was pointless and switched it off again. The minutes ticked past. A group of noisy youths came round the corner by the Town Hall and headed in her direction, jostling one another off the pavement into the road and yelling abuse at the drivers of passing cars who hooted as they were forced to swerve round them. Their drunken shouts and raucous laughter echoed incongruously round the elegant square with its carefully tended gardens. Melissa peered uneasily along the road that Ken had taken, wishing he would hurry up.

The next moment his Rover slid into the space beside her. Thankfully, she released the bonnet catch on the Golf and held the torch he handed her while he connected the jump leads. 'Right, start her up,' he commanded. She turned the key; magically, the engine fired. 'Keep it running for a minute or two before you switch on your lights,' he said. 'I'll follow you home in case you have any more trouble.'

'Really, there's no need, it sounds perfectly healthy now,' she protested, but she knew she was wasting her breath. As usual, he had taken command. It was comforting, but at the same time infuriating. The drunken shouts came nearer and there was a crash of broken glass, followed by the wail of a siren. 'Come on, let's get out of here,' said Ken and for once Melissa obeyed without question.

At first, the drive back was uneventful. There was no moon but the sky was clear, the air was still and the roads were comparatively quiet. The Golf purred along as if it had never given any trouble in its life. Glancing from time to time in her rear-view mirror, Melissa saw the Rover's headlights a steady hundred yards or so behind her. From time to time another car would pull out, overtake them both and rush ahead on full beam, carving its way through the darkness until its rear lights dwindled into tiny red pinpoints before vanishing altogether in the distance.

The turning from the main road to Upper Benbury was narrow and twisty. It wound downhill for half a mile and then crossed a short stretch of common land before climbing into the village. Melissa drove with her usual caution, prepared to pull on to the verge at the first sign of headlights coming from the opposite direction, but there were none. Once she had to brake sharply as a badger lumbered across in front of her before disappearing under the hedgerow; from then on she crept along in second gear in case some other creature should stray into her path. Ken was still behind, keeping a little closer now that they had left the highway. She wound down her window, enjoying the cool freshness of the night air. An owl hooted and from somewhere not far away the nocturnal peace was shattered by a thin, agonised shriek as a predator, probably a fox, claimed its prey.

Suddenly there were other sounds as well, man-made: a crash of breaking glass followed by a shout of alarm. Melissa's first thought, that a nearby house was being burgled, was swiftly followed by the realisation that the nearest dwelling was a quarter of a mile away. Whatever the cause of the commotion, it was close at hand. Her heart began thumping with apprehension and she slowed down still further as she approached the final bend at the bottom of the hill, then did an emergency stop on seeing the road ahead blocked by two cars.

The events that followed were to live on in her memory for a long time. The car nearest to her, which was slewed across the road, was surrounded by a group of men, two of whom were in the act of dragging the furiously protesting driver from his seat and propelling him roughly towards the vehicle in front. In a moment of bewildered horror, Melissa recognised Major Dudley Ford.

'Lock your doors and call 999!' It was Ken Harris, who had leapt out of his car and thrust his mobile phone through her open window as he went charging past with a heavy flashlight in his hand and shouting, 'Police, stop!'

By this time the abductors had almost reached the car in front with their prisoner. One was holding a rear door open; another had leapt into the driver's seat and was revving the engine. In a matter of seconds, the gang would escape; with their victim's own car blocking the road, pursuit would be impossible. Ignoring Ken's instruction to remain where she was, Melissa grabbed her heavy metal steering-wheel lock from the passenger foot-well and hared after him, shouting directions into the phone as she ran.

At the sound of the challenge the men wavered, then redoubled their efforts. They had almost succeeded; several yards still separated them from their pursuers when there came an unexpected intervention. A posse of youths, whom Melissa immediately recognised as members of the Woodbridge family, emerged from a clump of trees and came rushing down the steep bank with Curly, their mongrel terrier, racing ahead of them. Terrifying drama degenerated into pure farce; like a troop of cavalry arriving in the nick of time they waded into the mêlée, shouting and laying about them with heavy sticks while Curly pranced around, barking furiously and snapping indiscriminately at ankles. Within seconds, almost without putting up a fight, the would-be kidnappers piled into their car and fled, leaving their dazed victim in the middle of the road.

Melissa raced forward and caught him by the arm. 'Dudley, are you hurt?' she asked.

'Hurt? No, not at all,' the Major assured her.

'Any idea who they were?' asked Ken.

'Absolutely none.' The Major took a handkerchief from his

pocket and wiped his brow with a shaking hand. 'They were following close behind me . . . much too close . . . and then they went tearing past, flashing their lights. I thought I'd seen the last of them, but after I turned into the lane, there they were, blocking the road in front of me and I had to do an emergency stop.'

'Sounds like a classic case of road rage,' Ken said grimly. 'Have you any idea what you'd done to upset them?'

'Of course not,' said the Major huffily. 'I told you, I don't know the blighters from Adam. I was simply driving along, minding my own business.'

'So what happened next?'

'They all got out of their car and headed in my direction. I could see they were out for trouble so I locked my doors and tried to reverse away from them, but unfortunately I misjudged it and went up the bank. Then they broke the window and dragged me out.'

'Did they say anything?' Ken asked.

'Something about teaching me a lesson I wouldn't forget. Disgraceful behaviour!' he finished, his indignation rising as he recovered his nerve. 'I don't know what the world's coming to. In my young days hooligans like that would have had a good thrashing!'

It was a sentiment Melissa had heard many times. For once, she was inclined to agree with him.

'Now, as for these young heroes—' He turned to his deliverers, who were listening open-mouthed as he described the adventure. 'Thanks lads, that was a jolly good show! Here, let me give you a little something.' He beckoned them to the edge of the road and pulled out his wallet, took out several banknotes and handed them over while saying something in a low voice. The brothers exchanged glances and then responded with vigorous nods, gratified smiles and a chorus of thanks before disappearing into the shadows.

The Major put away his wallet and rejoined Ken and

Melissa. 'Well, that's that,' he said. 'Not much wrong with this country when it can produce splendid lads like that, eh? So, all's well that ends well, what?'

'Not entirely,' said Ken.

'Eh?'

'Those people must be caught. I don't suppose you got the number of their car?'

'I'm afraid not.'

'But you could give the police a description?'

'Not a very good one, I'm afraid. It's dark, and anyway my eyesight's not what it was. Look, we'd better not stay here, cluttering up the road.' He went over to his car, switched on the interior light and began brushing away fragments of the broken window. Considering his age and the ordeal he had just been through, he had so far displayed an astonishing degree of self-possession, due no doubt to his military training and experience. His praise for his three young rescuers had been like something out of a war-time propaganda film, although Melissa found his distribution of largesse somewhat out of character as neither he nor his wife was renowned for generosity. She was surprised, too, at his lack of interest in establishing his attackers' identity. His face was in shadow, making it impossible to read his expression, but she sensed that he was anxious to leave the scene as soon as possible to avoid any more questions.

'You're sure you're okay to drive?' she asked.

'Of course I am,' he insisted. 'No need to fuss. And I'd be grateful if you'd say nothing to Madeleine about this. She'll only worry, and she's not terribly well.'

'So how are you going to account for the damage to the window?' This time it was Ken Harris, standing beside the car with an elbow on the roof while holding his mobile phone to his ear.

'What? Oh, I'll tell her it was down to some young vandals

in the pub car park. I'm relying on your discretion,' he added to Melissa.

Meanwhile, Ken was giving directions on the phone. 'Half a mile beyond the pub, turn right,' he commanded whoever was on the other end. 'The police will be here in a couple of minutes,' he informed the Major. 'They'll want to ask you a few questions . . . if you'd rather speak to them here, I'll keep you company until they arrive.'

'No need, I assure you.'

'You never know, those villains might come back. Perhaps it would be better if you were to wait as well, Melissa. The more witnesses, the better.' At that moment, his gaze fell on the crook-lock which she was still clutching. 'Good God, woman!' he exclaimed in horror, 'what were you planning to do with that?'

'Clobber one of them, I suppose, if they wouldn't let Dudley go,' she said sheepishly.

'Well, put it out of sight before the police arrive and nick you for carrying an offensive weapon,' he ordered and for the second time that evening she meekly did as she was told.

'Look,' the Major pleaded, 'there's no need for you to stay. There's not much chance of catching those ruffians, is there? I really don't see the point of taking it any further.'

'That's up to you, sir,' said Ken stiffly. At that moment, the wail of a siren and a flashing blue light signalled the arrival of a patrol car. 'Here come the police. You tell them what you like, but I shall be giving them my own account of this very nasty incident and no doubt Mrs Craig will do the same.'

Chapter Twenty-one

'**R**um business, that,' said Ken.

'The sort of thing you read about in the paper, but never think is going to happen to people you know,' Melissa agreed.

'Quite. Got to hand it to the Major, though . . . he's a tough old warrior. I've seen people half his age go to pieces after an ordeal like that.' Ken spooned sugar into the mug of hot tea that Melissa had just handed him and stirred it vigorously. 'From what I know of him, though, I'd have expected him to want the police to move heaven and earth to catch the villains,' he added thoughtfully. 'Still, if his wife is unwell, I can understand him not wanting to upset her. What's wrong with her, by the way? When we went to that ghastly party of theirs a while back, she gave me the impression of being as strong as an ox.'

'As far as I know, she is. There didn't seem to be anything wrong with her yesterday. Dudley's the one with health problems . . . he has to take medication for high blood pressure and he suffers from angina. I just hope he doesn't keel over from delayed reaction to the shock.'

'He should be seen by a doctor after all that excitement.'

'Well, you heard what he said. At least, Madeleine will know what to do if there's a problem – she used to be an army nurse.'

'In which case, she's had plenty of experience in dealing with crises.'

Ken lapsed into silence while he drank his tea and Melissa, covertly watching him, could imagine what was going on in his mind. Like her, he would be wondering whether there was more than concern for his wife's peace of mind behind Dudley Ford's reluctance to pursue the matter further.

After the officers in the patrol car had noted and passed on to their control room the somewhat sketchy details of his attackers' appearance that he had managed to recall, together with Ken and Melissa's account of what they had witnessed, the three cars had driven the short distance back to the village in convoy. Despite his protests, Ken had insisted on waiting until the old man was safely indoors before following Melissa back to Hawthorn Cottage, where they were now sitting in the kitchen discussing the evening's events. It had not been her intention to invite him in and the half of her brain that was not engaged on an attempt to make sense of what had happened was trying to think of a stratagem to get rid of him without a confrontation. At the moment, however, he too appeared preoccupied with the extraordinary sequence of events the pair of them had just witnessed. Despite being retired from the police force, his interest in any unusual case was as strong as ever.

'It's probably a face-saving device,' she said. 'He wouldn't want it to be known that he'd been rescued from a man-handling by a bunch of village lads . . . he'd feel a bit of a wally if that got around.'

Privately, she did not believe that it was anything of the kind. On the face of it, Major Ford's account of his ordeal made sense . . . but for one detail. His attackers had obviously known which route he would take after they had passed him on the main road because they had been lying in wait for him. She glanced across the table at Ken, who was frowning into his empty mug, still deep in thought. She could not believe that this point had escaped him and she guessed that the reason he had not mentioned it was to avoid giving her any excuse to probe more deeply into the episode – or, as he would have described it, 'poke her nose into what was none of her business'. She certainly had no intention of referring to it herself until she had more time to think . . . and to talk to Dudley Ford. She recalled the moment when she had tackled him in the bar of the Lamb and Shearling about the possibility of his having seen Hannah Rose there. On reflection, it occurred to her that he had taken an unusually long time over the simple act of returning his wallet to his pocket, almost as if he was not entirely at ease over her enquiry. Neither had he shown any particular interest in it; in fact, for a man with such a passion for law and order and the bringing of criminals to justice, his reaction had been strangely lukewarm. It was out of character, as was the way he had dished out banknotes to youths whom he would normally, given the hour and the circumstances, have suspected of being up to no good. A reward for heroism or an inducement to them to keep their mouths shut?

To her relief, Ken glanced at the clock, stood up and reached for his jacket, saying, 'You must be tired, Mel. I'll go home now, but I'll give you a call tomorrow.' At the door, he took her face between his hands and kissed her gently on the mouth. He drew a quick breath as if about to say more, but changed his mind and got into his car, which he had already turned and left pointing towards the road. She waited while he started the engine, slid quietly into gear and drove away before closing and bolting the door and returning to the kitchen. She put their tea mugs into the dish-washer, rinsed out the teapot and put it away before going upstairs to bed. Her brain was seething; she lay awake for a long time, reconstructing every detail of the night's events, trying to recall the faces of the four men entering the pub as she and Bruce were leaving, thinking over Rachel's warning and her own confident reassurances . . . and asking herself whether she had made a dreadful mistake. An altogether new scenario was forming in her mind; if it was anywhere near the truth, then Dudley Ford's claim that he had no idea of his attackers' identity was suspect. Moreover, it would mean he was still in serious danger. She fell asleep trying to figure out a way of warning him without betraying him to his wife.

In the event, the problem was solved for her. She awoke early after a restless night and took a shower to clear her head before going to her study to work on the script of *Drop Dead!* At half-past seven the phone rang. The caller was Dudley Ford; he spoke hurriedly and his voice was low and slightly muffled, as if he had a hand cupped over the mouthpiece.

'Melissa? I apologise for ringing at this hour . . . I know you're an early riser and I thought—'

Sensing that he was anxious to say what he had to say as quickly as possible and without Madeleine's knowledge, she skipped the preliminaries and said, 'What is it, Dudley?'

'I wonder, could I call in for a word this morning? There's something I want to—'

'Is it about last night?' she enquired as he seemed uncertain how to finish.

Either he did not hear, or he deliberately avoided the question. 'If I were to pop round in an hour or so, when I come to the shop to collect the papers—'

'Yes, of course.'

'Thank you . . . I won't stay long . . . thank you very much.'

After he had hung up, Melissa tried to return to her task, but concentration was impossible. The book was almost ready for submission to the publisher; as with all her novels, she had meticulously edited it chapter by chapter and the final run-through was little more than a safety precaution. Normally, her mind would already be clearly focused on a new plot; instead, for the past few weeks, she had found herself with half a dozen random ideas churning around in her head, each with as much direction and purpose as driftwood tossed around by rushing water. It was an uncomfortable, unfamiliar feeling that had been insidiously creeping up on her over recent months. She had been trying to reassure herself that once the current book was finished, the problem would be resolved and all would become clear, but it simply hadn't happened. This must be the dreaded phenomenon known as writer's block, something she had never experienced since writing her first book. She forgot all about Dudley Ford and sat staring in front of her with a sense of rising panic. Then her eye fell on the calendar, on which her trip to London the following Tuesday was noted in red, and she felt comforted. Joe would help her to get back on track. He was such a rock, full of common sense and quiet wisdom.

She was startled out of her reverie by a ring at the doorbell. She glanced at the clock on her desk; almost an hour had slipped past since Dudley's phone call. With an effort, she switched her mind back to the present and went downstairs to find him standing on the doorstep with Sinbad panting beside him. In contrast to his normally brisk, self-confident manner, he was wearing a hangdog expression that gave him an uncanny resemblance to his pet. In different circumstances, Melissa would have found it difficult not to laugh at the notion, but as it was, it merely increased her concern for him. His cheeks sagged and his skin had an unhealthy pallor; he seemed to have aged several years overnight.

'Come in, Dudley,' she said, trying not to show her anxiety over his appearance. 'Would you like some coffee?'

'Thank you.' He followed her into the kitchen and sat down at the table while Sinbad waddled over to inspect the blanket beside the Aga where Binkie often slept when Iris was away. He sniffed around eagerly for a few seconds, growling softly as if challenging the invisible cat to emerge from its folds before retreating in evident disappointment and flopping on to the floor at his master's feet. 'Good boy, stay!' the Major commanded unnecessarily. He murmured a further polite 'Thank you' as Melissa handed him a mug of coffee and sat for several seconds without speaking while vigorously stirring it despite having declined both milk and sugar.

Melissa broke the silence by asking, 'Was Madeleine very upset about the damage to the car?'

He shook his head. 'Haven't told her,' he said. 'She was having a bath when I got home. She'll have to know sooner or later, of course.' He fiddled with the handle of his coffee-mug and nervously chewed the ends of his bristly white moustache before adding, 'There's no need for her to know anything else. No need at all. You do understand that, don't you, Melissa?'

'You made it very clear last night that you wanted the whole thing hushed up,' she replied. 'Is that why you're here – to make sure I don't say anything that might rouse Madeleine's suspicions?' She paused for a moment to give him a chance to respond, but he only looked at her with growing unease. Thinking to give him a lead-in to what she was certain was on his mind, she said, 'Those men who attacked you last night . . . they looked like gipsies.' Still he remained silent. She drew a deep breath and took the bull by the horns. 'Were they relations of Hannah Rose? You did know her, didn't you?'

The last vestige of colour drained from Dudley Ford's haggard cheeks and he bowed his head. 'Yes, I knew her,' he admitted. Almost unconsciously, she felt, he had emphasised the word 'knew' as if admitting that he was using it in its old-fashioned sense of carnal knowledge. 'Those men,' he went on, 'I'd seen them before . . . at least, I saw two of them only yesterday morning. I happened to be at the front gate putting the dustbin out when they drove past very slowly as if they were looking for something. When they saw me, they turned their faces away and drove off. It struck me as suspicious and I took the number of their car and circulated it to the Neighbourhood Watch Committee, just as a precaution.'

'You're absolutely sure they were among the gang who attacked you?'

'Oh yes, and you're quite right, they are members of Hannah's family. They must have been watching me . . . following me. They think I killed her and I suspect they were going to kill me in revenge. But how do you know all this?'

'Some weeks ago Hannah was seen getting into a car of the same make as yours outside the Lamb and Shearling. There was a man with her, described as elderly. Was that you?'

He gave a heavy sigh. 'Yes,' he whispered.

'And I saw four men who looked like gipsies entering the pub shortly after you arrived. I couldn't be sure they were the ones who attacked you – not sure enough to pick them out in an identity parade, that is – but there doesn't seem much doubt.'

'I suppose they waited for me to leave and then followed me. If only I'd spotted them in time, maybe none of this would have happened.'

'They'd have waited for a chance to try again. Dudley, why in the world didn't you tell the police that you recognised them?' Even as she asked the question, Melissa guessed what the answer would be.

'Don't you see . . . it would all have to come out . . . Madeleine would know about it . . . my relationship with Hannah . . . everything!' He shut his eyes and hid his head in his hands, no longer the swaggering, arrogant retired army officer, but a foolish old man caught in a trap as old as time.

'Then why are you telling me?' Melissa persisted.

He spread his arms in a gesture of helplessness. 'I need your advice . . . don't you see, these people know where I live and of course you're right, they'll try again. I need protection . . . you have friends in the police and you know how they handle these things. Is there any way I can ask for their help without all this getting back to Madeleine?'

'To be absolutely frank, Dudley, I don't think there is. Once you tell them what you've just told me—'

'I know, I know!' he groaned. 'I had a very strong motive

and the poor girl's body was found in my old freezer, but I didn't kill her and they can't possibly prove that I did.'

'Just the same, you're bound to be a prime suspect, unless in the meantime they can find enough evidence to charge someone else. And even then, there's no guarantee that Madeleine wouldn't find out one way or another. If you really want my advice, Dudley, it's a risk you have to take, otherwise you'll be looking over your shoulder for the rest of your life.'

'I know,' he repeated. 'I've been an utter fool. It all happened so . . . naturally. She was outside the pub one night after one of our meetings. I left a bit later than the others . . . I had some business to attend to . . . and there she was, crying her eyes out, saying someone had stolen her purse and she had no money to get home.'

'"Home" being the Crossed Keys near Stow, I suppose?'

'That's right. She was working there as a chambermaid and selling lace to make a little extra. I don't know what came over me . . . I could have given her money, but instead I found myself offering her a lift. She was so young and pretty and vulnerable . . . I couldn't just leave her there on her own at that time of night, with possibly undesirable characters hanging around.'

'That was nice of you,' Melissa said gently. The man might have acted like a gullible fool, but she could only admire him for his old-fashioned chivalry.

'I was never one to leave a defenceless woman unprotected,' he said with a flash of his familiar, exaggerated gallantry. 'On the way she told me how she'd run away from her family with a truck driver who'd promised to take her to Hungary, where her people originally came from.'

'Rocky Wilkins,' Melissa interposed.

He looked at her in surprise. 'You know about that?'

'Yes, and so do the police. He was picked up yesterday. I understand he'll be facing a number of charges.'

'Do they think he killed Hannah?'

'He's certainly a suspect, but it's early days yet. Look, I'm sorry I interrupted. Please go on.'

'Yes, well, this fellow – Wilkins, you say his name is? – was supposed to bring her back, but she said he abandoned her there and it took her weeks to find someone else to give her a lift back to England, by which time her family had moved on. She found this job in Stow and was waiting for them to show up for the horse fair so that she could rejoin them. When we got near the hotel, she asked me to pull off the road a short distance away . . . she said she didn't want anyone to see her arrive in a car and start asking questions. She offered me some of her lace by way of thanks, but I wouldn't take it because of Madeleine . . . she'd have wanted to know where it came from. Then Hannah said it was against Romany custom to accept a favour from – some word she used that I took to mean a non-Romany – without giving something in return.'

'*Gadgy?*'

'That's right. You know about their customs?'

'A little. I can't say I've ever heard of that one,' said Melissa drily. 'So she offered to repay you in kind, I suppose?'

He nodded. His ashen cheeks turned a dull red and he began fiddling with Sinbad's lead, which was lying across his lap. Evidently taking this as a sign that it was time to be moving on, the dog stirred, whined and began hoisting itself to its feet, but flopped back on to its belly on receiving the muttered command, 'Sit!'

There was a long silence. Melissa offered more coffee, which Dudley refused with a shake of the head. Eventually, she said, 'I get the picture . . . there's no need to say any more. Just one question: exactly what happened on the evening Hannah called at your cottage selling lace?'

'I was furious with her . . . I thought for a minute she'd come on purpose to make trouble, but she denied it, said it was pure chance . . . she had no idea where I lived. Then she said something like, "But you wouldn't like your wife to know about us, would you?" and she had a sly look that told me straight away that she was after more money to keep her mouth shut.'

'You'd paid her before, I take it?'

'Oh yes . . . I gave her something every time we—' Once again, he flushed scarlet and hung his head.

'Did you give her money this time . . . when she called at your house?'

'No. I was too angry . . . I told her to clear off and I'd see her later. I assumed she'd be catching the six o'clock bus back to Stow and I told her I'd wait for her in a lay-by near the bus stop.'

'Ah, so it was your car that was there,' said Melissa half to herself, wondering whether this new piece of the jigsaw would put Rocky in the clear as far as the murder was concerned.

Dudley looked at her in horror. 'I was seen?' he faltered. 'By someone in the village?'

'Not as far as I know. It was mentioned on the radio that Rocky drove off in a BMW and I heard that several people have reported seeing one parked on the Stow road that evening.'

'Oh, dear God, what have I got myself into? If it's all going to come out anyway, perhaps I should tell Madeleine after all . . . make a clean breast of the whole thing.'

'It doesn't look as if there's much chance of keeping it from her, does it?' Dudley shook his head in evident despair. Melissa waited a moment, then said, 'I take it Hannah never showed up?'

'No. I was there well before the bus came, but there was no sign of her. I supposed she'd gone on to more houses, trying to sell her damned lace, and was planning to catch a later one. I couldn't sit there indefinitely and I assumed I'd see her as usual after our next club meeting.'

'So Monday afternoon was the last time you saw her?'

'Yes.' He raised his head and looked her directly in the eye.

'I swear before God that I didn't kill her. You do believe me, don't you?'

'Yes Dudley, I believe you.'

With the air of a man who has come to a decision, the Major got to his feet and straightened his bowed shoulders. 'Melissa,' he said and this time his voice was firm and strong. 'I apologise for burdening you with my troubles. It's been a great help talking to you.'

'I'm glad.'

'And you do understand, all this is in the strictest confidence?'

'Of course.'

At the door, he held out his hand. 'Thank you for giving up your time to listen to me.' For the first time in their acquaintance, he spoke with a quiet dignity that was entirely without affectation. 'I see now what I have to do,' he went on. 'I've got myself into this pickle and I must take the consequences like a man.'

He set off along the track, walking slowly but with a firm tread and an upright bearing, the dog trailing at his heels. Melissa watched until they were out of sight before she went inside and closed the door.

Chapter Twenty-two

After Dudley Ford's departure, Melissa went back to her study and tried to resume work on the draft of *Drop Dead!*, but in a very short time her attention began wandering. She found herself trying to foresee the probable course of events that would flow from the confession Dudley intended to make to his wife, and to imagine how the proud, conventional Madelcine would receive it. Ever ready to disparage someone who fell short of her own loudly-expressed standards of probity and morality, what would be her reaction to the knowledge of how far below those standards her own husband had fallen? Would it come as a devastating shock ... or was it possible that she had already detected something in his recent behaviour that had aroused her suspicions? She was a shrewd, intelligent woman and she had been married to Dudley for many years. Did the beautifully made-up, carefully controlled features conceal a knowledge that she would have died rather than reveal to the world? One could never be certain what lay below the surface of an apparently rock-solid relationship. Accepting the futility of further speculation, Melissa forced her mind back to the task in hand.

It was not long, however, before her concentration was broken by another, more disquieting thought. By jumping to the conclusion that Rocky Wilkins was the man on whom the Romanys were seeking revenge, she had not only put the unfortunate Major's life in danger, she had also given a false reassurance to Rachel. The fact that she had spoken and acted in good faith would count for nothing with the gipsy; once the police raided the Romany camp and made their arrests – as they undoubtedly would once they knew the whole story of Ford's relationship with Hannah Rose – she was certain to feel betrayed. Melissa's imagination, over-active as usual, conjured up a vision of Rachel turning up on her doorstep, dark eyes smouldering with fury at the treachery of the *gadgy* she had misguidedly trusted, a virago seeking revenge. She might even threaten violence, carry a concealed dagger or – less lethal but, in Melissa's present over-wrought state of mind, none the less disturbing – call down some ancient Romany curse on her head. At this point, common sense took charge, prompting her to clap her hands to her forehead and exclaim aloud, 'Now you're being melodramatic and ridiculous!' From then on, she applied herself to her reading with renewed determination until an awareness that it was after twelve o'clock and she was feeling hungry turned her thoughts to lunch.

She had just transferred a portion of soup from the freezer to the microwave when she heard an approaching car. A hasty peek from the sitting-room window revealed Iris alighting from a taxi. Catching sight of Melissa, she signalled 'See you in a minute' before paying off the driver, dumping her suitcase inside her own porch and then striding purposefully towards the door of Hawthorn Cottage. Melissa hurried to let her in.

'Guess what!' she said, almost before the door had closed behind her. 'Dudley Ford's in intensive care in Stowbridge Hospital. Suspected heart attack.'

'Good heavens! When?'

'About half-past nine. In the shop for his morning paper. Here's yours, by the way.' Iris thrust a copy of *The Times* into Melissa's hands.

'Thanks, I'd forgotten all about it. How bad is Dudley?'

'Not sure. Still partly conscious when the ambulance came.

Someone sent for Madeleine and she went with him. No news since.'

'I can't say I'm surprised. He didn't look at all well when he called here this morning.'

Iris's brow lifted. 'How did that happen?'

Without realising what she was doing, Melissa prevaricated. 'Why do you ask?'

'Mrs Foster said he was much later than usual. Madeleine wanted to know why.' Iris gave Melissa a keen glance. 'You know something.' It was a statement, not a question.

'Yes, I do . . . quite a lot,' Melissa admitted. 'Some of it was told to me in the strictest confidence.'

Iris's grey eyes gleamed with curiosity. 'You know me. Soul of discretion.'

Through the open kitchen door they heard the ping of the microwave. 'That's my lunch-time soup,' said Melissa. 'Why not come and have some with me – I've got plenty for two. Carrot and coriander in vegetable stock,' she added, forestalling the inevitable question from her fiercely vegetarian friend.

'Thanks, I will.'

In the kitchen Binkie, who had remained skulking in the garden until he had seen his canine enemy leave the premises, was happily dozing in his accustomed place beside the Aga. He opened one eye as the two women entered and was greeted with a cry of joy by Iris, who scooped him into her arms, sat down with him on her lap and crooned over him while Melissa, studiously ignoring this outpouring of affection, took a further portion of soup from the freezer and put it to thaw and reheat. She got out crockery, glasses and cutlery and cut slices from a loaf of olive bread, part of a selection of Italian-style loaves that Mrs Foster, in an attempt to 'go foreign', had recently begun stocking.

'So what's it all about?' asked Iris, still vigorously caressing Binkie's soft fur.

'It's a job to know where to begin, it's all getting so complicated. You remember the two travellers who were arrested in
connection with Hannah's murder and later released without
charge?' Iris nodded. 'It seems Hannah's family had made up
their minds they were guilty anyway and went off to their
camp to dish out a bit of rough justice.'

'The sort of thing you'd expect from that lot.'

'Yes, well, no one knows for sure, but it looks as if the
travellers managed to convince the Romanys that they didn't
kill Hannah and told them exactly where they nicked the
freezer her body was hidden in. They all jumped to the same
conclusion . . . the owner of the freezer must be her killer.'

Iris's hand froze in the region of Binkie's tail; her eyes
rounded and her mouth fell open. 'Dudley?' she exclaimed.
'Don't believe it! Kill a gipsy – why would he do that?'

'Why indeed?' Melissa felt it was fortunate that she was at
that moment engaged in pouring soup into bowls, giving her
the excuse to turn her head away from Iris. She had a feeling
that it would not be long before that astute lady, without
any outside help, would think of a highly believable motive
for such a murder, but she had no intention of betraying
the Major's confidence by feeding in any further direct
information. It would not require a great leap of imagination
for Iris to find the answer to her own question.

For a few moments the friends ate in silence. Presently,
Iris laid down her spoon, drank some mineral water and
said, 'D'you reckon there's anything in it . . . Dudley and
the gipsy?' When Melissa hesitated, she went on, 'Have you
been hearing his confession? Is that what you meant by "in
the strictest confidence"?'

'Well . . . yes.' There was no point in denying it, and at
least she knew Iris would keep it to herself. 'But there's a
lot more to it than that,' Melissa went on. 'Last night, he
had a very narrow escape.' She outlined the attack on the
old soldier which had so nearly succeeded. 'I suspect it was

delayed shock that brought on his heart attack. I wonder if there's any news? Perhaps I ought to give Madeleine a call.'

'Probably still at the hospital.' Iris helped herself to some grapes from the bowl of fruit that Melissa put on the table. 'So, what made him come and see you?' It was plain that she had no intention of being deflected by speculation about the progress of Dudley's illness.

'He was terribly anxious that Madeleine shouldn't know about the attack on him. He thought it would upset her.'

'That all?' The sharp grey eyes were like miniature lasers. Whilst listening to Melissa's account of the previous night's adventure, it was obvious that Iris had been doing some swift thinking. 'Didn't want her to know about his fancy woman, more like it.'

'Well, yes, that too,' Melissa admitted. 'It did occur to me, on reflection, that Dudley had seen Hannah that night in the Lamb and Shearling, but didn't want to admit it for fear of getting involved in more police inquiries. It seemed odd, though, knowing how he's always going on about civic duty and upholding law and order. It set me wondering whether perhaps he was the man Gloria's Stanley saw with Hannah in the pub car park. Stanley's sure to have heard about the Fords from Gloria, but I doubt if he's ever actually set eyes on either of them, so he wouldn't have recognised him – especially as it was dark.'

'And was it Dudley?'

'Yes. He said he offered her a lift because someone had stolen her purse and she had no money to get back to the Crossed Keys.'

'And that's how it started,' Iris mused. 'Poor old Dud. And now he's in the ITU. Wonder if he'll make it.' She ate the last of her grapes and began peeling a banana.

Melissa made coffee and cut slices from a home-made fruit cake. 'I do hope so,' she said with feeling. 'In a way, I feel responsible.'

'How come?'

'As I said, it must have been an almighty shock, being set on by those villains . . . enough to give anyone heart failure. And you see, I might have been able to prevent it. I knew the Romanys were plotting a revenge attack on the man they believed had killed Hannah.'

'Who told you that?'

'Rachel. She came to see me soon after you left yesterday and told me what was being planned. She was terrified of the trouble it would cause and begged me to warn the intended victim. If I'd only known it was Dudley . . . but I was so sure it was Rocky Wilkins. And Rachel's going to be mad at me as well.'

'Now you've lost me,' said Iris as she accepted a slice of cake and a mug of coffee. She listened attentively to the account of Rachel's visit. 'Won't be getting Brownie points from Ken over this lot,' she predicted with a cackle when Melissa had finished.

'You can say that again. He turned up just as Rachel was leaving and we had the mother of all run-ins.'

'Made it up yet?'

'A sort of armed truce. I know what you're thinking,' Melissa added, seeing Iris's knowing expression. 'Today is Friday, and tomorrow's the day I've promised to give both you and Ken a decision.'

'As long as you haven't forgotten.' Iris's voice and expression were deceptively bland, as if she already had a shrewd notion of what that decision was going to be.

'I haven't,' Melissa said a little curtly. Then she asked in a softer tone, 'Tell me about the London trip. Did it go well?'

'Fine. No problems. Got the last of the legal points sorted, Jack's off to France to do the necessary in front of the *notaire* and then the property's ours.'

'That's great. Oh Iris, I do hope it all works out well for you both.'

'Thanks, me too.' Iris stood up. 'Better get home now and do some more sorting out. Gloria show up yesterday, by the way?'

'Oh yes, and she returned your key.' Melissa fetched it from a drawer and handed it over.

At the door, Iris hesitated and said, 'D'you reckon Dudley might have done it?'

'Killed Hannah, you mean?' Melissa shook her head. 'He solemnly swore he didn't and for all his faults, I find it hard to believe he'd harm a woman, even to save his own reputation.'

'So who d'you think did?'

'It could have been Rocky. Maybe Hannah was threatening to tell his wife too . . . and I can certainly believe *him* capable of murder.' Involuntarily, recalling her own recent violent encounter with the man, Melissa put a hand to her throat. 'And then there's the two men the police originally arrested. They haven't yet got enough evidence to charge them, but that doesn't mean they aren't guilty.'

'They convinced the Romanys,' Iris pointed out.

'That's only surmise on my part.'

'Hm, see what you mean. Maybe we'll never know.'

At that moment the telephone rang and Melissa went back to the kitchen, saying over her shoulder, 'This might be news of Dudley. Hang on a minute.' She picked up the handset and said, 'Hello', but at first no one answered. After a couple of seconds she said, 'Hello, is anyone there?' and a faint voice that she barely recognised as Madeleine's said, 'Melissa, is that you?'

'Yes. Oh Madeleine, Iris and I are so worried . . . is there any news?'

There was another pause, during which Melissa could hear unmistakable sounds of a battle against tears. At last, Madeleine quavered, 'Dudley . . . he had a second heart attack . . . he died two hours ago.' Before Melissa could say anything, she rushed on, choking over the words. 'Please . . . I must talk to you . . . could you possibly—?'

'I'll be with you in ten minutes.'

Melissa could not remember ever before having seen Madeleine Ford without her make-up or other than immaculately dressed, and for a moment she barely recognised her in the apparition who opened the front door when she arrived at Tanners Cottage. Her silvery-grey hair, which she normally wore in an elegant knot at the back of her head, had lost its lustre and hung limply around her shoulders. Her greenish eyes, their papery lids pink and swollen and their colourless lashes almost invisible without mascara, seemed to have shrunk to half their normal size, and her skin had a greyish tinge and the slightly puckered texture of a partly deflated balloon. Her mouth was bunched in a despairing attempt at self-control, an attempt that collapsed as Melissa, almost in tears herself, stepped into the hall and embraced her, saying, 'Oh my dear, I'm so sorry . . . so very sorry.'

For several minutes she sobbed on Melissa's shoulder without restraint. When she became calmer, she blew her nose, wiped her eyes and made ineffectual attempts to pat her hair and tweak her clothes into place. 'Please excuse the *déshabillé*,' she said pathetically. Even in her distress, she was careful to give the word its correct French pronunciation. 'I was still in bed when the call came . . . there wasn't time to—' The tears threatened to flow again, but this time she fought them back.

'Can I get you anything?' Melissa said gently. 'Some tea, or maybe a brandy—?'

'I've already had a scotch . . . will you have one with me?'

'Maybe just a small one.'

'Come this way.' As she spoke, Madeleine took a few steps along the passage, swayed and grabbed at the old-fashioned hall-stand. Melissa had a suspicion that the hiccup she uttered at the same time was not entirely the effect of excessive weeping. Her suspicions were confirmed when they reached the sitting-room and she saw on the sideboard an uncorked whisky bottle with an empty tumbler beside it. Madeleine took a second tumbler from a cupboard and slopped whisky into it with an unsteady hand.

'No really, just a small one if you don't mind,' Melissa repeated, dismayed at the size of the drink she was offered. 'If you say so.' Madeleine tipped half the contents of the glass into her own and put both drinks on a tray with a small bottle of soda water. She swayed a little as she picked up the tray and Melissa stepped forward to take it from her, but she gave an impatient toss of her head saying, 'I can manage. You go and sit down.' She set the tray on a low table in front of the hearth, where the remains of the previous day's log fire lay in a cold, ashy heap, waved her guest to an easy chair and lowered herself into another. 'Help yourself to soda. I'm having mine neat.' She raised her glass, gave a mirthless laugh and said, 'Here's to widowhood!'

Melissa diluted her scotch with a generous splash of soda and sipped it slowly, while watching with increasing disquiet as Madeleine tossed hers back and then sat turning the empty glass between her fingers. She had slim, elegant hands with beautifully shaped and varnished nails. They made a bizarre contrast to her neglected face and the rumpled slacks and baggy sweater which were evidently the first garments that came to hand when the news of her husband's collapse reached her. After a moment she hoisted herself out of her chair, saying, 'Haven't you finished your drink yet? I'm ready for another.'

She stumbled against the table and almost fell. Melissa hastily got to her feet and grabbed her by the arm. 'Madeleine, I don't think you should drink any more for the moment. Have you had anything to eat?'

'They offered me something at the hospital, but I couldn't touch it.' Madeleine pressed her lips together and put a hand to her eyes; once more, she appeared on the point of breaking down. She made what was evidently a supreme effort at control and said, 'Dudley and I had a cup of tea in bed first thing. He made it and brought it up . . . and it was his turn to get the breakfast, but he said he was going to collect the paper and walk the dog first. I must have fallen asleep again . . . and then the phone woke me up . . . it was Mrs Foster from the shop, telling me—'

'So you've had no food all day? Shall I make you a sandwich?'

'No thank you . . . I'll have something presently. You're quite right, it's a mistake to drink on an empty stomach.' With a theatrical gesture, Madeleine put the glass on the tray and sank back into her chair. 'There's something I want to tell you,' she said, 'and I'm not sure where to begin.'

Melissa waited, sipping her drink and thinking what a bizarre state of affairs it was that within a single day both husband and wife – the one through guilt and the other from the shock of sudden bereavement – should have been forced to abandon their pretensions and reveal something of their own weaknesses. It was even more strange that circumstances had made her their chosen confidante. *Ah well*, she thought as she waited patiently for Madeleine to collect her thoughts, *at least it helps to put my own problems into perspective*.

At last, Madeleine began to speak. 'Dudley was conscious when we got to the hospital,' she began. 'I had to wait while they worked on him . . . gave him drugs and wired him up to the monitor in the ITU . . . and then they let me see him.' Her manner suddenly came alive as she added, 'I was astonished at all the hi-tech equipment . . . we had nothing like it when I was nursing for the army.' For a moment, professional interest had superseded emotion.

'Was Dudley still conscious?' prompted Melissa after another pause.

'Oh yes, and he was fairly calm . . . the drugs, of course . . . but he was so afraid, poor man . . . he asked me to go to the police and tell them about the people who attacked him last night . . . and why. It came as a shock . . . he never mentioned it at the time, but I understand you and your friend came to his aid.'

'It was very fortunate that we and the Woodbridge boys came along when we did.' Melissa found herself hoping that Madeleine would never learn of her own partial responsibility for that ugly incident.

'Yes, so I understand. Dudley told me he came round to see you this morning. He said he asked for your opinion about what he should do.'

Melissa detected an underlying note of resentment in Madeleine's voice. 'It was only out of concern for you,' she said. 'He knew he should report the attack, but he—'

'Didn't want me to learn of his affair with that little gipsy tart!' Madeleine interrupted with a sneer. Her manner had undergone a dramatic change; her greenish eyes had hardened and her voice had a contemptuous edge as she went on, 'He said he knew it would all have to come out and he wanted me to hear it from him. I had to sit there listening to a sickening, maudlin confession . . . pleas for forgiveness . . . promises to reform . . . and—' Suddenly, she sat bolt upright and leaned forward until her face was inches away from Melissa's. 'He told me nothing I didn't know already . . . nothing! Not just about the gipsy tart, but a dozen stupid little infidelities over the years. Did he really think I didn't know? Until *her*,' she spat out the word, 'I never set eyes on the women . . . at least he had the decency not to get involved with anyone in our own circle, but I always recognised the symptoms . . . the perfume clinging to his clothes, the petty lies, the chocolates and flowers he'd buy me to assuage his pathetic conscience. And all the time he thought he was getting away with it. Men are such fools.' As if exhausted by this outburst, Madeleine sat back and closed her eyes.

'I had no idea . . . I mean, he told me about Hannah, but not—' Melissa floundered in embarrassment. 'There's really no need to say any more—'

'Oh, but there is.'

'Can't it keep until you've had a chance to calm down? You've had a dreadful shock . . . you're traumatised . . . maybe you need counselling—'

'Don't quote all that modern jargon at me!' The transformation was almost complete. The strain and the grief were for the moment cast aside; despite her ravaged face and dishevelled appearance, Madeleine's familiar, imperious manner had returned. She got up from her chair, saying, 'Wait here, I have something to show you.' She strode across the room, showing barely a trace of unsteadiness. At the door she turned and said, 'There is something you can do for me . . . make some strong coffee. I'll have to sober up before—' She left the sentence unfinished and disappeared.

Melissa went to the kitchen. Mechanically, she set about her task, filling the kettle and searching in cupboards for coffee, cafétière, cups and saucers. She found a tin containing digestive biscuits and put several on a plate; despite Madeleine's earlier protests, she might be ready now to have a morsel to eat. And all the time, her brain was seething over the awful possibility that presented itself.

It was no surprise that Madeleine had known about Dudley's relationship with Hannah Rose, but the fact that there had been other – many other – affairs was something that had not occurred to her. Until now, thanks to Madeleine's determination to preserve the façade of her marriage, scandal had been avoided. Her husband, deluding himself that he had managed to conceal his peccadilloes, would have been equally anxious to retain the trust of his neighbours in the village community where the couple saw themselves as respected and influential figures. Dudley in particular liked to think his much-vaunted stand in favour of law and order counted for something. And then, out of the blue, Hannah had arrived on his doorstep and threatened to expose him for the pitiable old roué that he was. It made a powerful motive for murder, yet his impassioned declaration rang in Melissa's ears above the hissing of the kettle: *'I swear before God that I didn't kill her!'* Was that a final, despairing act of deception?

Overhead she could hear movements: footsteps going briskly to and fro, drawers opening and closing, taps running, a toilet being flushed. She brewed the coffee, put everything on a tray and emerged from the kitchen just as Madeleine descended the stairs. The change in her appearance was as striking as that in her manner a few minutes earlier. Her hair was drawn back into the familiar sleek knot, skilfully applied make-up disguised the worst traces of weeping and she had changed into a fashionable navy-blue and white dress and jacket with navy tights and elegant court shoes. She wore a pearl choker and earrings and carried a leather handbag and a pair of gloves in one hand. The other held a plastic supermarket carrier with something bulky inside it.

For a moment, Melissa stood and gaped in astonishment. It was not until Madeleine said, 'Ah, you found everything – well done!' that she pulled herself together and went into the sitting-room. Madeleine followed her and sat down, depositing her belongings on the floor at her feet while Melissa, her thoughts still chaotic, put the tray on the table between them, poured out two cups of coffee and offered the plate of biscuits.

'I feel so ashamed of myself, going to pieces like that,' Madeleine said, taking dainty nibbles from the biscuit between sips from her cup. 'I'm sure I don't need to ask you not to let it go any further.'

'Of course I won't,' Melissa assured her, doing her best to appear normal. 'There's no need to feel ashamed. It was a perfectly natural reaction . . . anyone in your situation would have—'

'My situation!' Madeleine appeared to find the expression amusing. She finished her coffee, put down her cup and saucer and reached for the carrier. 'I told you, didn't I, that I had something to show you? I wonder if you can guess where this came from.' She drew out a bundle, threw aside a quantity of tissue paper wrappings and shook the folds from a scarlet shawl that was almost identical to the one that Rachel wore. 'Exquisite, isn't it?' she murmured, turning it between her fingers. 'Hand-worked, of course, and beautifully done. I buried her shoes and the rest of her clothes in the garden, but I couldn't bring myself to destroy this. It was on the grubby side so I washed it . . . in any case, I had to get rid of the blood.'

Melissa stared at the shawl in horror. Despite the hot coffee, she suddenly felt as cold as ice. Both her tongue and her brain were momentarily paralysed and it was several seconds before she managed to say, in a voice that she hardly recognised as her own, 'Hannah . . . that must have belonged to Hannah!' At last, the final piece of the puzzle had fallen into place. 'You said you'd been covering up for Dudley all these years,' she said slowly, as if she was thinking aloud. 'And he swore before God that he didn't kill her – and he was telling the truth, wasn't he? – so that means—' She broke off, unable for the moment to continue for the constriction in her throat.

'You're quite right – for once in his life, he wasn't lying,' Madeleine agreed.

Melissa found her voice. 'Of course he wasn't,' she said harshly. 'You're the one who's been acting the lie. You killed her, didn't you?'

Madeleine was rolling up the shawl, swathing it in tissue paper and returning it to the carrier. Her eyes met Melissa's with a look of defiance. 'It was an accident,' she said, as if that explained everything.

Chapter Twenty-three

'She says she didn't mean to kill her; it was an accident,' said Melissa.

'D'you reckon it's true?' said Iris.

'Oh yes, it's true all right.'

Having made her extraordinary confession, Madeleine Ford had asked Melissa to drive her to police headquarters, where she demanded, in characteristically imperious fashion, to speak to the officer in charge of the Hannah Rose murder enquiry. In response to the receptionists's courteous request for information, she had brandished her plastic bag and announced that she had important information and new evidence. As soon as DCI Holloway appeared she turned to Melissa with a gracious smile and said, 'Thank you for the lift. You may leave me now, I shall be quite all right.'

Melissa had half expected to hear some oblique and possibly sarcastic reference from the detective to the frequency of her appearances in connection with the case, but although he gave her a long, hard look before escorting his unexpected witness to an interview-room, he gave no sign of recognition. Perhaps he considered her presence on this occasion as irrelevant, in which case it was unlikely to reach the ears of Ken Harris. This thought was swiftly followed by another: *So what if it does?*

She could recall little of the drive home. She had arrived on her friend's doorstep in a state of emotional exhaustion. After hearing her almost incoherent account of Madeleine's confession, Iris insisted on putting her through a series of yoga exercises. She then covered her with a blanket and left her lying on the sitting-room floor in a state of deep relaxation from which she drifted off to sleep. Now, over an hour later, she was seated in a comfortable armchair, sipping appreciatively from the glass of home-made elderberry wine that Iris had just given her. Some minutes ago she had been drowsily aware of sounds from the kitchen suggestive of a meal being prepared, but for the moment Iris was sitting cross-legged on the hearth-rug with Binkie on her lap and a full glass in her hand, demanding to know the whole story.

'It's all pretty sordid,' Melissa began sadly. 'Madeleine must be hurting like hell, but you'd never think so. She was very distressed when I got to the house, but once she'd had a good howl she pulled herself together and when I left her at the nick she was virtually back to normal.'

'Always thought she was the tougher of those two,' Iris commented. 'So what's her version?'

'She says that on the day Hannah called at their house, Dudley was just going out and he waylaid her on the drive and ordered her to leave. There was some altercation between them, enough to rouse Madeleine's suspicions. She was closing the garage door behind Dudley – who, she insists, had no idea she was listening. She couldn't hear everything that was said, but the minute he drove off she invited the girl into the house on the pretext of being interested in what she had to sell, and started questioning her. To use her own words, Hannah was "extremely impertinent" and refused at first to answer, but Madeleine insisted.'

'She was always good at insisting,' Iris interposed with a sardonic cackle.

'Reading between the lines, I'd say the girl took exception to Madeleine's tone and began taunting her with hints about sexual romps in the back of the car. Then she got bolder and threatened to "tell a tale or two" around the neighbourhood if

Madeleine didn't cross her palm with a considerable amount of silver.'

'Blackmail, eh? That wouldn't have pleased her ladyship.'

'It didn't. She lost her rag and slapped Hannah across the face – which would account for the bruising the pathologist found on the body.'

'Then what?'

'The girl started screaming obscenities and went for her like a tigress. She had to fight her off and in the struggle Hannah tripped, fell backwards and hit her head a fearful crack on the corner of the Aga. She lost consciousness immediately; Madeleine swears she did everything she could to revive her, but she soon realised the girl was dead.'

'She never thought of calling a doctor?'

'She claims her army experience taught her to recognise death when she saw it. Besides, she realised right away that if she reported the accident, all sorts of questions would be asked and Dudley's secret life exposed. That prospect seemed unthinkable . . . and there seemed to be the ideal solution to hand. The old freezer Dudley had already arranged for the council people to collect was still in the garage, waiting for the Woodbridge brothers to help manhandle it to the gate. She stripped the body, put it into the freezer, locked it and "lost" the key.'

'Must have been a struggle on her own.'

'Her nursing training would have taught her how to lift patients. She's remarkably fit for her age and being desperate would have given her added strength.'

'But didn't it occur to her that the freezer might be dismantled?'

'Apparently not. She believed it would simply be dumped at a tip along with a hundred others and if by an unlucky chance the body was ever found, it would be virtually impossible to establish where it had come from. She must have had kittens when she realised it had been stolen.'

'And more kittens when it turned up, complete with corpse,' said Iris drily. 'Why strip the body, by the way?'

'To make it look like a sexual attack, I suppose. I was so gobsmacked, I never thought to ask.'

'Kept her wits about her, didn't she?' said Iris scornfully.

'She's been amazingly cool and calculating throughout . . . until now. It's Dudley's death that has broken her.'

'But why confess?' Iris wondered. 'Now the old boy's popped his clogs there's no reason why his fling with Hannah should ever come out—'

'She doesn't care about that, not any more. What's been tormenting her all these years, more even than the knowledge of Dudley's infidelity, is the lie she's had to act, not just to him but to the outside world.'

'All these years? You're saying Hannah wasn't the first?'

'Far from it. There were others – lots of them – but she never let on to Dudley that she knew about them. All she wants now is to clear her own conscience. She was brought up very strictly and telling the truth was something that was dinned into her from babyhood. Now he's dead there's no further need to sacrifice her principles on his behalf. She's prepared to face up to the scandal, even to a prison sentence, rather than keep up the deception any longer.'

'Extraordinary,' Iris muttered into her glass. 'Always thought she was a bit holier than thou . . . but . . . who'd have believed it of Dudley? Not my idea of a sex-pot.'

'Nor mine,' Melissa agreed. The two lapsed into a thoughtful silence, mulling over the events of the past few hours. Iris continued to stroke Binkie with her free hand while Melissa absent-mindedly contemplated the effect of firelight glowing through the deep crimson of elderberry wine. Presently, she said, 'I've just thought of something. When I was talking to the two of them a couple of days ago about Hannah's visit to their house, I happened to ask Madeleine whether she'd seen the girl herself.'

'And she denied it, of course.'

'As far as I can remember, what she actually said was, "I was in the garage . . . Dudley told me about it afterwards". That was perfectly true . . . not the whole truth, of course—'

'Best she could do without telling an actual porky,' said Iris. 'All the same, she must have been forced to tell a good few over the years.'

'And now she wants to wipe the slate clean. I advised her to talk to her solicitor before giving herself up, but she wouldn't hear of it. You know Madeleine . . . once she sets her mind to anything, you can't shift her.'

'Beats me,' said Iris with a shrug.

'You never know what goes on in people's heads, do you?' A bell sounded in the kitchen. Iris gently removed Binkie from her lap and got to her feet with the supple movement that always made Melissa envious. 'Supper's ready. Come and eat.'

On returning home, Melissa checked her answering machine. She found two messages from Ken Harris, the first left at four o'clock – around the time when she was listening in a stunned silence to Madeleine Ford's bizarre confession – and the second three hours later, wanting to know where she was and why she hadn't returned his earlier call. There was also a message from Bruce Ingram, enquiring about the identity of 'that very posh-looking old bird' in whose company he had spotted her at police headquarters.

She was trying to decide whether to respond to either caller right away or wait until the morning when the phone rang. As she half expected, Ken Harris was on the line.

'Where the hell have you been?' he demanded. 'I've been trying to reach you since this afternoon. Is anything wrong?'

'No, nothing. Why do you ask?' She felt like adding, *And why do you have to get so testy if I don't happen to be available the minute you want me?* but refrained. It would only make him even grumpier.

'I wondered where you were. You're not usually out for such a long time. Are you sure everything's all right? You sound strange.'

'I'm perfectly all right, thank you.'

'Aren't you going to tell me where you've been?'

'Not now Ken, I'm tired. Let's leave it till tomorrow.'

'Tomorrow's what I want to talk to you about . . . remember you agreed—'

'Yes, I remember.' *The day of decision. Well, I've made up my mind. I hope I'm doing the right thing, that's all.* Aloud, she said, 'Do you want to come here, or shall we meet out?'

'Perhaps I could come to your place first. We have a lot to discuss.'

'All right. About six?'

'Fine, see you then.' His tone had softened; he sounded cordial, yet somehow vaguely impersonal. He might have been talking to a friend or colleague rather than a lover. Melissa frowned thoughtfully as she replaced the receiver before dialling Bruce's home number.

'Sorry I've been so long getting back to you,' she said. 'I had rather a trying afternoon and Iris has been restoring me with yoga and elderberry wine.'

'Sounds a fascinating form of therapy. So, who was the lady and is there a story in it?'

'There certainly is, and I'll give it you in return for a favour.'

'Consider it done.'

'Thank you. I'm not going to tell you the lady's name, but she claims to have important information and evidence in the Hannah Rose case. It's almost certain to mean that someone will shortly be charged.'

Bruce whistled. 'No kidding! What information and evidence?'

'That I can't tell you, but I'm pretty sure it's authentic.'

'So how did you get involved?'

'She told me her story and then asked me to go with her to police headquarters, so I did.'

'She's a friend of yours, then?'

'I've known her for some time.'

'Quite the diplomat, aren't we? Well, thanks for the tip. I can get this into the early editions . . . ahead of the nationals. Brilliant!'

'By the way, what news of Rocky?'

'Still being questioned in connection with "certain serious matters" – doubtless relating to the merchandise he's been trading in. I understand he had a briefcase full of samples when they picked him up.'

'No wonder he did a runner. How's Julie coping?'

'Pretty well, all things considered. Penny's being very supportive. That girl,' – Bruce's voice acquired a note of tenderness that Melissa had never heard before – 'is a jewel, one in a million.'

'Do I gather you and she are what is known as an item?'

'Well . . . yes, you could say that.'

'You don't waste much time, do you?'

'I suppose you could say that as well,' he admitted with a chuckle. 'Now, you said something about a favour.'

'Yes. Do you know where the Romanys are camped at present?'

'Sure, not far from Chipping Campden. Why d'you ask?'

'You remember Rachel . . . the woman we saw making lace that day, when they were camped at Upton?'

'I remember. What about her?'

'I want to talk to her again, and I'd like you to come with me.'

'If you like.' He sounded puzzled, but refrained from asking questions, merely asking, 'When?'

'As soon as possible. How about tomorrow morning?'

'Okay. Pick me up at the office about ten.'

'Thanks Bruce. Good night.' Melissa hung up with a sense of relief. It was so much easier dealing with a fellow creature when one was not emotionally involved.

Chapter Twenty-four

The first time they visited the Romany camp, the weather had been fine and mild. Today the sky was overcast with a hint of rain borne on a cold, blustery wind. They located the vans without difficulty, directed by the farmer on whose land they were parked. 'You the police? Not in any trouble, are they?' the man asked. 'I said they could stay and help with the potato picking until they moved on to Stow for the horse fair, but if there's been any trouble—'

'We aren't the police,' Bruce assured him. 'And there's been no trouble that I know of.' Melissa remained silent. Whether or not a report had reached the *Gazette* of an elderly man being set upon two nights before by an anonymous gang she had no idea. If it had, and Bruce was aware of it, he had certainly not made a connection with the Hannah Rose inquiry and she had no intention of enlightening him . . . or the landowner. Without Dudley's evidence, there was no action the police could take at present, although there was always the chance that at some future date a case could be made for attributing his death to his assailants on the grounds that the shock had precipitated the heart attack that killed him. That, however, would require positive identification of the culprits which in the circumstances would be very difficult, if not impossible, to come by. In the meantime, the Romanys presented no threat to anyone.

As before, Bruce parked his red Escort a short distance from the camp and they went the rest of the way on foot. There was no one in sight when they arrived at the clearing where the caravans and a few battered cars, including the one Rachel had used on her second visit to Hawthorn Cottage, were parked. Even the children were missing, but a dog chained to a tree barked as they approached and an elderly woman opened the top section of the door of the nearest caravan and eyed them suspiciously. Like Rachel, she was handsome in the Romany manner, with swarthy skin, aquiline features and coal-black hair. Her attitude was far from friendly as she asked, 'Who are you and what is your business?'

'We've come to see Rachel,' said Melissa with a friendly smile which was not returned. The woman continued to stare for several seconds, her dark eyes darting to and fro between Melissa and Bruce. Then, without looking away, she called over her shoulder and the next moment Rachel appeared beside her. She looked tired and dispirited; the collar of her blouse was awry and several wisps of hair hung loosely round her face. She appeared startled at the sign of the newcomers, but did not speak.

'Good morning, Rachel,' said Melissa. 'This is my friend, Bruce. You remember him, I'm sure. He came with me before and played with the children.'

'I remember.' Rachel's eyes moved briefly to Bruce and back again as she asked, 'What brings you here?'

'I have news for you, about your niece.'

'About Hannah?' The two gipsy women exchanged glances.

'Yes. We thought you would like to know that the person responsible for her death is being interviewed by the police. The man who took her away did not harm her, but he has committed other crimes for which he will certainly be punished.'

Rachel bowed her head and murmured, 'I am glad. Thank you for telling us.' The older woman put an arm round her shoulder and said something in her own tongue. Then, in a deliberate gesture of dismissal, she drew Rachel back into the van and closed the door.

'Is that it?' said Bruce in a low tone.

'It looks like it.' They waited for a short time, but the women did not reappear. Slowly, they walked back to the car.

'Thank you for coming with me,' said Melissa as she fastened her seat belt. She leaned against the head restraint and closed her eyes. 'It's not that I was expecting trouble, but I thought it might get emotional and I've had about all I can take—'

'No need to explain. I quite understand.'

Melissa gave a faint smile. 'I don't think you do,' she said.

Bruce gave her a sideways glance. 'Is there something you haven't told me?'

'Well, yes . . . but I'd rather keep it to myself for now . . . or at any rate, until after the trial. And if ever I do tell you, it will be strictly off the record.'

Ken Harris made no reference to the Hannah Rose case when he arrived at Hawthorn Cottage a little after six that evening. Either he had not heard of the latest developments, or he had decided to let the matter drop rather than risk starting another argument.

To Melissa's surprise, he did not kiss her, but stood waiting while she closed the door behind him and then followed her into the sitting-room and remained standing as if he was visiting the house for the first time.

'Are we going out straight away?' she asked curiously.

'No. I've made our reservation at seven for seven-thirty.'

'Well, don't just stand there. What can I get you to drink?'

'Nothing for the moment, thanks,' he said. 'Will you sit down, Melissa? I've got something to tell you.'

'What is it?' Feeling a little uneasy, she went to her favourite armchair while Ken, as usual, took an upright one facing her.

'I don't know if I've ever told you this,' he began, 'but some years ago, before I was promoted to Chief Inspector, I spent six months with the New York Police Department on an exchange arrangement, shadowing one of their officers and observing their methods. The following year, Hal Hislop – he was my opposite number – came to England and spent the same length of time attached to the Gloucestershire Force.'

Melissa shook her head. 'No, I'm sure you've never mentioned it,' she said. 'Why are you telling me now?'

'We struck up a friendship and we've kept in touch on and off ever since. By coincidence, we both retired within a few months of each other and we both set up as private investigators.'

'And?'

'I had a letter from him a couple of days or so ago. He's asked me to go into partnership with him.'

'In New York?'

'That's right.'

'It's a bit sudden, isn't it?'

'It's not entirely a new idea. We've referred to it once or twice over the years, but until now I don't think either of us thought it would ever become a practical possibility. Now it has. Hal's becoming known as a guy who gets results and his case-load is mushrooming.' Ken got up and walked across to the window, stood for a moment gazing out at the view with his hands in his pockets, then swung round and took up a position in the middle of the room, rocking on his heels and looking down at Melissa. 'He's already taken on a junior assistant to help with routine stuff, but now he needs someone with experience at the coal-face and he reckons I fit the bill.' He gave one of his rare chuckles. 'In more ways than one, eh? Sorry about the pun!'

Melissa had seen Ken Harris in many different rôles, from hard-nosed detective doing his job with single-minded determination to loyal friend and tender, passionate or – especially recently – angrily possessive lover. She had until now believed herself to be familiar with all his moods, but this evening he was revealing a side of himself that was new to her. Never before, even when he was painting a glowing picture of the life they could enjoy together if she would agree to marry him, had he shown such animation. She had always found him inclined to be slow in his movements and ponderous in his manner; this evening there was a spring in his step as he moved about the room, a sparkle in his eyes and a ring of enthusiasm, as he outlined his friend's proposal, in the slightly gruff voice that she had once likened to oily sandpaper.

'You're dead keen on the idea, aren't you?' she said.

'Yes, I am. I thoroughly enjoyed working with Hal . . . and PIs in the States have access to far more interesting cases than in England. I'd need a licence, of course, but Hal reckons he can arrange that.' As suddenly as he had leapt from his chair, he sat down again and leaned forward, taking one of her hands between both his own. 'What do you say, Mel? We could find a house somewhere upstate . . . some parts of it are quite rural, I'm told . . . and you'd be able to see Simon more often . . . you'd like that, wouldn't you?'

Perversely, Melissa felt a stab of irritation at the final words. Something in his tone made the prospect of living closer to her son sound like a sweetener, a bribe of candy offered to a reluctant child. 'We see one another fairly often as it is,' she pointed out. 'He spends a lot of time away from home on business trips anyway . . . as it happens, he's coming to London at the end of the month.'

'Oh . . . well, that's great.' Ken appeared to find her reply disconcerting. He let go of her hand and sat back in his chair. 'Look,' he said in a wheedling tone, 'I realise this must have taken you by surprise, and it wouldn't be fair to expect you to make a decision right away. Let's give it another day or two, shall we?'

'I don't think there's any need for that. You've obviously made up your mind to accept Hal's offer—'

'It's a great opportunity—'

This was the moment she had been dreading for the past seven days. The moment of truth. 'Then go ahead, if you're sure it's what you really want,' she said gently. 'But I shan't be coming with you Ken . . . and I wouldn't marry you, or live with you, even if you were to stay in England.'

The animation in his manner faded. There was a blend of disappointment and resignation in his expression as he said in a quiet, rather flat voice, 'I don't think I ever seriously believed you would.'

'We've had some great times together, Ken. I hope we can stay friends.' *How trite this sounds, like something out of a cheap romance. But what else can one say?*

'Sure we can.'

Bruce telephoned the following morning, shortly after Melissa had finished her breakfast. 'Got something to tell you,' he said. His tone indicated that he was about to impart some particularly momentous news, and her natural curiosity was increased by the slightly self-conscious note underlying a barely suppressed excitement.

'I hope it's good news,' she said. 'I can do with some.'

'The very best.' His voice took on an earnest quality. 'Penny and I are engaged. Isn't it wonderful?' She felt the warmth of his happiness flowing like sunshine along the wire, almost bringing a lump to her throat.

'Well, congratulations!' She was about to add some jocular remark about Penny having her hands full keeping him in order, but held it back. It would have been inappropriate in the face of such sincere, simple joy.

'We told my parents last night, but we wanted you to be among the first of our friends to know. The wedding will be quite soon and we hope you'll be able to come.'

'I'd be delighted.'

'And of course, Ken Harris as well if—'

'If *we're* still an item,' Melissa broke in, with a slightly bitter laugh. 'As it happens, we aren't. He's been offered a job as a PI in the States . . . he asked me to go with him, but I said no.' She could hear her voice cracking and felt a fool.

'I'm sorry,' Bruce said gently. 'That is—'

Something that had been puzzling her suddenly became clear. 'Bruce, the other night, as we were leaving the Lamb and Shearling, you started to say something about giving me advice, and then backed off. It wouldn't have had anything to do with Ken, would it?' When Bruce did not immediately respond, she went on, 'Were you by any chance thinking of warning me against getting too heavily involved?'

'Well, yes, in a way,' Bruce admitted. 'I've had the feeling all along that he wasn't . . . wasn't *special* enough for you . . . I know it would have been a bit of a cheek on my part . . . and anyway I didn't know how to put it—'

'You've just put it beautifully, thank you,' she said. She gave a shaky laugh and felt the sun come out again. 'And it's wonderful news about you and Penny. I'm sure you'll both be very happy . . . and Kirsty will have a super Dad.'

'Bless you. Talk to you again soon.'

Melissa felt her spirits lifting as she put down the phone and went next door. She found Iris in her kitchen, preparing a nut roast for Sunday lunch while Jack could be seen through the window picking runner beans.

'So that makes two weddings,' Iris commented on learning of Bruce's engagement. She gave Melissa a searching look. 'You and Ken going to make it three?'

'No.' Somewhat to her surprise, Melissa managed to tell the story without emotion. Iris's reaction was equally unexpected.

'You've done the right thing,' she said firmly. 'Especially now he's off to play cops and robbers with his American buddy. Wasn't going to push you one way or the other, but—'

'From what you said a few days ago, I thought you were all for my marrying him.'

'Didn't mean it like that. Thought it was time you made up

your mind what you wanted, that's all. Easy to let things drift till it's too late.'

And you weren't the only one to have doubts, thought Melissa, remembering the conversation with Bruce. Aloud, she said, 'I'm going to miss Ken like hell for a while, though. And about the cottage—'

'Forget it. Decided not to sell after all. Might rent it out on short lets for the holidays, but we'll need a base in England if it doesn't work out in France.'

'It'll work out, I'm sure of it.'

'Hope so.' Iris packed her nut roast into a tin and smoothed the surface with a knife. 'You'll stay for lunch? I'll get Jack to do a few more veg.'

'Please.' Melissa hesitated for a moment, then said, 'Iris, about your wedding—'

'What about it?'

'Ken will probably be in New York by then, but even if he isn't—'

'Wouldn't want to come in the circs, I suppose.'

'I'm not sure I'd want him to anyway.'

'Understandable.' Iris covered the tin with aluminium foil, placed it in a bain-marie and bent down to slide it into the oven.

'But neither do I want to be an odd one out.'

'Quite.'

'I was wondering . . . would it be all right if I asked Joe . . . just to keep me company, of course?'

'Of course.' Iris straightened up and closed the oven door. The expression on her face reminded Melissa of Binkie after he had enjoyed a particularly tasty meal. 'I was going to suggest it,' she said.